m

THANK You so much.

THE VIEW BEYOND

UTTERLY LIFE CHANGING

SEQUEL TO THE SWING
BOOK 2

J A CRAWSHAW

XYLEM
Publishing

Published by XYLEM Publishing

Copyright © 2023 by J A Crawshaw

ISBN: 978-1-7394071-0-0 Paperback

ISBN: 978-1-7394071-2-4 Hardback

Editor: Victoria Straw

Cover: Xylem Publishing

❋ Created with Vellum

THE SWING (1ST IN SERIES)

Where True Love Hangs In The Balance

Love across the class divide was never going to be easy.
All Charlotte craves is a simple life, far from the routines of motherhood and the responsibilities of a vast, early inheritance. But, of course, for people of her standing, that was out of the question.
A chance meeting with Peter, a handsome, rugged Yorkshireman, brings a grounded earthiness and deep love that she never thought was possible.
Unlikely kindred spirits, they become inseparable and, as their steamy and passionate love affair evolves, so do the prejudices of the people around them. Will class differences, fickle friends and deception finally force them apart or will Charlotte free herself from her destiny to allow true love to win through?
The swing is her sanctuary, but also the gateway to ultimate freedom.

CONTENTS

1.	Ashes To Ashes	1
2.	Leave Your Past Behind	9
3.	Treason	17
4.	Clarity AND Integrity	27
5.	The Biennale	33
6.	The Intruder	39
7.	Trust	43
8.	Court	47
9.	You're Safe Now	61
10.	White Rose	69
11.	Useless	79
12.	Hermit And The Devil	83
13.	Helpless	91
14.	Forever	99
15.	Resuscitating A Badger!	105
16.	Bad To Worse	115
17.	A Man Of Nature	121
18.	Misadventure	129
19.	Numb	133
20.	A Robin's Song	137
21.	Hold Fast	143
22.	The Village Dance	153
23.	Nuts	161
24.	Nature's Bramble Jelly	165
25.	The Royal We	175
26.	Younger Self	181
27.	Women's Institute	189
28.	Drills	199
29.	Cake And Cheese	207
30.	Home	217
31.	Special Delivery	225
32.	Angel	231
33.	Crackers	239

34. Wedding Bells   247
35. Best In Class   251
36. The Cage   265
37. The Three Musketeers   273
38. Holm   281
39. A Life Worth Living   289
40. Sexiest Woman In Wellingtons   295
41. The Long Walk Home   301
42. The Swing   311
43. Freedom   317
44. A Postcard From Hatty   323
45. Surprise   335
46. The View Beyond   343
    Epilogue   347

    About the Author   349
    Also by J A Crawshaw   351

1

ASHES TO ASHES

'We, therefore, commit her body to the ground, earth to earth, ashes to ashes, dust to dust...'

The vicar's words continued as the stately rosewood coffin descended slowly into the ground by its solid gold handles. Charlotte dabbed tears from her face with her family crest-embroidered handkerchief and imagined the troubled face of her mother looking up beneath the sturdy lid. She shuddered at the thought and tried to banish the image from her mind.

In many ways, she was glad that her suffering had ended. Years of trauma and confusion as the cruel torture of Alzheimer's eventually dominated and ruled her life. Charlotte's bitterness to the disease was evident in the fist-like grip of her hanky. She should have had a longer life, one of peace and joy.

The coffin eventually came to rest at the bottom of the earthy grave. The vicar sprinkled soil into the hole, paid his last respects and then solemnly departed, leaving the mourners to have their own time to say their final goodbyes. Lucy huddled up to Charlotte and gave a reassuring smile.

'She's in a better place now, Mum,' she said, throwing a delicate bunch of flowers she had handpicked from the walled garden.

Charlotte nodded and sobbed and then followed with a tasteful bunch of white roses she had hand-picked too. They were all gone now. No one left of the immediate family except herself and Lucy. Although she had shouldered the heavy weight of family responsibility from an early age, it seemed to be pushing down even heavier now.

Mrs Hathersage handed Charlotte another handkerchief.

'Looks like you might need a fresh one, dear?'

'Thank you. She adored you, you know, Mrs Hathersage. She always said there was no finer housekeeper and regarded you as part of the family.'

'And she adored you too, Miss Charlotte. She said you were her only reason for living.'

'And she lived for the parties!' Charlotte replied, giving a hint of a smile. 'It's been a team effort.'

Mrs Hathersage responded with a gracious smile as her eyes focused on Charlotte's neck.

Charlotte instantly tried to cover her scars with her lace shawl. She was ashamed that she had put Mrs Hathersage through so much torment.

Mrs Hathersage intervened with a hand on Charlotte's shoulder. 'We are all in a better place now.'

Charlotte pursed her lips and nodded. 'I'm so sorry for the harm I caused.'

Mrs Hathersage shook her head. 'I never want to hear you say that again. Do you hear me? It's time for a fresh start. The family is stronger than ever now. What happened in the past has gone now.'

Mrs Hathersage turned to acknowledge Peter, who had taken a respectful yet solid supporting stance just behind the three of them.

'Mother adored you too, Peter,' Charlotte said, reaching out for him. 'Trusting, capable hands, she once said to me. She was right and I'm thankful I have you by my side now.'

Peter huddled them into a group of four. 'We are a team now. A great team. Your mother's torment is over, and so is ours. Let's forget the past. What's done is done. We have all learned a great deal and are stronger because of it. We are unbeatable now, all of us. Nothing can get in our way if we stay positive and confident in our love for each other. Right?'

'Right,' Charlotte said with a stamp of her foot.

'Right,' Mrs Hathersage said with a courageous grin.

They all looked at Lucy.

'Yes, of course,' she said, rolling her eyes, clearly trying her best not to conform yet craving the unity and love.

The other mourners' pristine black suits and respectful dresses had little effect on lightening the mood as they shuffled by, offering their respects and condolences. One by one, they held out a hand or a kiss on the cheek, then seemed to speed up on their departure, eager to move on to the lavish wake which had been prepared back at Loxley. Caterers had been brought in so the whole brigade of house staff could attend.

With the last mourner departed, they began their walk back to the church.

'Just one minute,' Charlotte said, encouraging Mrs Hathersage, Peter and Lucy to carry on without her. She wanted one last moment at the graveside alone.

She peered over the side of the grave and, from her discreet, black clutch bag, produced three cards she'd drawn at

3

first light from her Oracle tarot pack. Over the years, their prophecy had proven to be almost exact, and today was no exception.

The death card had been a regular feature in Charlotte's life for some time. Frightening, not only by the grim reaper's menacing face but the absoluteness of its meaning. Charlotte looked at the card, and an unusual feeling of calm filled her mind. The card had never been for her. Well, not yet, anyway. She had tested it, that's for sure, but her mother's passing confirmed that she was spared, and now hope was the new feeling in her quest for peace and happiness.

Tossing the death card into the grave, she saluted with her hand as it disappeared into the dark void.

She fanned out the remaining two cards.

New Birth. She'd drawn this card before. The picture showed a newborn child held lovingly in his mother's arms.

The words read: *The birth of new life is the greatest gift. Cherish it and nurture your lifelong bond.*

Images of her staring at the pregnancy test before she tied the swing's noose around her neck came flooding back. She had to live with the shame. There was no hiding from the truth, but she felt it was all about her rebirth this time. The new Charlotte. A braver, calmer Charlotte and one who was more in control.

Let Go Of Your Past. This card was a first, and there appeared to be no ambiguity from its title.

There was a picture of an angel moving forward in the heavenly sky, taking one last look backwards. Charlotte didn't read the words. She knew the time was right. She bundled the two cards together, and instead of tossing them into the grave, she hurried back to the car, where she tucked them into the glove box unnoticed.

4

~

Delicate canapés of caviar, smoked salmon, and minute sandwiches with the crusts cut off, adorned one of the many immaculate solid silver platters. In between, exquisitely presented ham on the bone, lobsters with enormous claws, a whole salmon and enough exotic fruit to stave off a navy's scurvy for a decade. Fresh flowers, obviously, and a prominent gold-framed photograph of Mrs Winterbourne herself, enjoying a family gathering with a joyful smile and joie de vivre.

Charlotte chinked her crystal wine goblet with a knife, and everyone immediately paid attention.

'Thank you to each and every one of you for taking the time to pass on your regards to Mother. Most of you will know that she had not been well for many years. She did have a wonderful life, full of love, happiness and adventure.' She momentarily glanced at Mrs Hathersage, Peter, and then Lucy. She crossed her fingers behind her back and then smiled back out to the gathering. She didn't want to tell of the years spent scuttled away in her room, the Alzheimer's playing cruel tricks with her reality or the years of neglect by her father. Instead, she took a few beats to remember the lucid moments they had shared together.

'I know she would have loved to be here, if not only to flit around all of you chattering about life and enjoying her favourite lobster and salmon. She did love a party. I want to take this moment to thank Mrs Cavendish of the Alzheimer's Society for her support and that I will be presenting a sizeable donation to aid further research, and not only that. I will personally finance the design and build of the new hospice facility for many people in less fortunate circumstances.

Mother was, in many ways, the glue that kept this family on the right and proper course, and we will miss her dearly. She has gone to a far better place now, and I'm sure you will all join me in a toast to... Mother.'

As everyone raised their glasses and Charlotte made eye contact with everyone in the room. She was surprised to see a short gentleman huddled in the corner by the Rodin sculpture of Adam. He was the only member of the gathering who didn't raise his glass and kept his head down, as if not wanting to draw any kind of attention. Possibly a new member of staff who barely knew her. But nevertheless, strange and very impolite.

Her attention swiftly diverted to the barrage of well-wishes, including from Mrs Cavendish, who had not had the chance to speak to her at the graveside. Charlotte's diligent and gracious responses were well received, but her attention was broken periodically by the man in the corner, who had barely moved. Just looked into his champagne flute and didn't acknowledge anyone.

Peter whisked another glass of champagne into her hand while showing an interest in the many anecdotes of times gone by.

Charlotte and Peter eventually collapsed onto the chaise longue as the last of the mourners departed, and the catering staff made short of the aftermath. Lucy was nowhere to be seen, and Mrs Hathersage had politely excused herself for a lie-down.

'I'm exhausted,' Charlotte said while putting her legs up onto Peter's lap.

'Me too. I think it went well, though. Lovely to hear so many joyful accounts of your mother.'

6

'Yes. Thank you for being by my side, Peter. I love you being the new man of the house. You really are my rock.'

Peter massaged her feet. 'It's only because you are *the* most beautiful and courageous woman.'

'Peter!' Charlotte replied and blushed.

At that moment, they were both surprised by the presence of the solitary man in his black suit, which was a little short in the sleeve, and Charlotte immediately noticed his brown, scuffed shoes, which didn't match his dated yet pristine black attire.

The man spoke with mismatched confidence. 'Charlotte Winterbourne?'

Charlotte felt disappointed that she had to drag out the front-of-house persona once again for a mourner who hadn't grasped the etiquette of the day and politely left already.

'Yes,' she said, removing her feet from Peter's lap and regaining her dignity.

'I'm sorry to hear of the passing of your late mother. I never knew her personally. Unlike your dear father. I have a letter for you. I wanted to give it to you in person.'

'What is it? Who are you?'

The man presented the handwritten envelope and took a step back.

'My name is...' He paused and, with another step back, stood to attention, with his back straight and his eyeline almost to the chandelier.

'My name is Henry.'

'What is this about, Henry?' Charlotte said, looking at Peter.

Still stood to attention, and his face as serious as a dagger, he cleared his throat.

7

'Our dear, dear father.'

Charlotte looked again at Peter, who was rolling his eyes and taking to his feet to escort Henry to the door.

'I'm Henry... Winterbourne the 4th. Your half-brother and rightful heir.'

2

LEAVE YOUR PAST BEHIND

P eter embraced the chilly morning air by filling his lungs and then over-exaggerating his exhale to warm his hands. A hanging mist gave an eeriness to the extensive private parkland as he negotiated an indiscriminate, narrow path created by the resident fallow deer. He could hear the faint tearing of grass as they ate close to him, but couldn't be seen.

Charlotte and Lucy were still fast asleep in the house. Peter took the opportunity to reflect on the previous day, particularly his new place within the household. He knew adjusting to the opulent house and copious grounds would take time. It was a long way from his previous life of council-estate living and damp, mould-infested flats, but he was comfortable among the trees. Ancient oak, majestic Atlantic blue cedar, abundant sweet chestnut and avenues of lime. He listened as the air started to lift the mist and rustle the surrounding leaves. The trees gave him comfort and reassurance. Assuming the male role within the house was daunting enough, he now had to move aside any working-class prejudice of silver spoons and entitlement and assume his role with confidence and pride.

He'd earned his place, he knew that, but as he picked his way over the exposed roots and tussock grass towards the castellated entrance, he couldn't help feeling an overwhelming sense of misplacement. Like an old, weathered fishing boat among a flotilla of pristine yachts.

He was hungry and, after closing the gigantic oak front door behind him, headed for the kitchen in search of tea and toast, which he would take up to Charlotte and share with her in bed. No house staff were up and about, so he would have space to make it himself without feeling guilty they were running around after him. He placed the teapot, mugs and toast onto a tray and carried them up the overly impressive wooden staircase, which he usually couldn't avoid running his hand over and tracing the ornate carving and woodgrain. Several corridors and steps tested his tray-handling skills, and he eventually opened the heavy bedroom door to find Charlotte wistfully staring into thin air.

'Good morning, gorgeous girl,' he said as he gently positioned the tray on the bed. 'I have tea and toast.'

Charlotte stretched her arms and yawned. 'That's kind of you. I could have asked for it to be brought up, and you could have lied in with me.'

Peter sat on the edge of the bed and stroked her cheek. 'I'm used to doing it myself. What's the point in asking someone else to do it? Anyway, I don't like my butter melted on my toast. I like it cold.'

Charlotte shook her head and gave a little chuckle. 'The staff can handle cold butter on toast!'

After breakfast, they strolled hand in hand around the house, chatting and laughing. It felt natural to peruse the halls and rooms together, somehow cementing their combined authority on the place. Although nothing was said, Peter knew

Charlotte wanted him to feel at home and not only become familiar with the geography but also take ownership and responsibility.

They ignored Charlotte's mother's room and her father's secret office. Although, on passing the wall-mounted candlestick, which was the release for the secret panel, they winked at each other and smiled. Instead, they headed towards the guest rooms and the King's room, which Peter had visited once before. Charlotte retold the story of when King Henry VIII and Princess Margaret, on separate occasions, obviously, had both stayed in the room and that although the impressive four-poster bed was grossly uncomfortable, it would remain untouched in the hope a royal visit may once again be on the cards.

Peter marvelled at the many rooms, which were merely storage for framed paintings of all shapes and sizes, stacked on the floor like books on a grand bookshelf.

'I don't really know why I keep any of these,' she said anxiously. 'Most of them are my father's collection. The ones I like are all out on display around the house, but these old, dusty relics are just not my cup of tea. That's what they say in Yorkshire, isn't it?'

Peter laughed. 'Ay lass, that's right. How much are these worth?'

Charlotte shrugged. 'I have no idea. Some of the Picassos are worth millions, and I can't remember exactly how many there are.'

Peter stroked his chin. 'Do you think it might be a little obscene?'

'What do you mean?'

'Well, expensive paintings, which should be on display for everyone to enjoy, stuck gathering dust in a dark room.'

Charlotte paused and looked at the vast array of artwork. 'There are many other rooms like this too.'

'You're kidding?'

Charlotte's face looked pale, and she began pacing the floor. She raised her voice. 'I don't know what to do with them, Peter. They were fathers. I owed it to him to preserve what he had lovingly collected. I guess you're right. I never thought of it like that.'

They progressed around the house. Periodically looking out across the estate, Charlotte listened intently as Peter highlighted different tree species and their characteristics. 'You have an elm. I hadn't noticed that before,' he said, grinning and pointing to a tall, mature tree in full leaf. 'They're rare. Very rare. One of the truly noble trees.'

'Was that something to do with Dutch elm disease?' Charlotte asked, gazing into his eyes.

'Exactly that. It wiped out nearly all the elms. Just a few left around Brighton and scatterings elsewhere. Must have been a genetic strain which wasn't susceptible.'

'So why is there one here?'

'I don't know. There were probably many elms here. They were everywhere. An iconic English landscape tree, so I guess this one was lucky?'

'Should we do anything to preserve it?'

'It's nature, Charlotte, not a museum piece. We simply let nature make its own decisions and enjoy its beauty. It's worth more than all the paintings in this house, though!'

Charlotte looked out at the tree and then into Peter's eyes. 'Gosh, I never thought of it like that.'

Peter smiled. 'You can't easily replace a rare tree like that, no matter how much money you have.'

Charlotte nodded. 'I don't know how you manage to put

everything into perspective and make sense. You're so grounded.'

'Let's go outside and say hello to the tree. It'll appreciate it.'

~

Charlotte smiled and flung her arms around him. 'I think it will,' she said gleefully.

With both of them wrapping their arms around the mighty tree trunk, they were still only halfway around. They stretched with all their might, but nothing was going to change. The tree was old and a survivor. Genetically and physically strong, and Peter admired that. Charlotte was more interested in how Peter reacted. She loved watching his face as he talked about trees as if he were one of them. She gleaned from his enthusiasm and drank in his energy.

Charlotte looked around at the other nearby trees. 'Is that a yew?' she asked, pointing to a densely canopied tree with a reddish trunk.

'It sure is, and you think the elm is old? This tree is really old.'

She ran up to it and once again flung her arms around it.

'A thousand years!' he said, thoroughly examining it. 'Easily eight hundred to a thousand years and maybe more.'

Charlotte looked up into the array of thick, tangled branches and rich green foliage. 'My father told me it's poisonous.'

Peter nodded, picked off one of the many thousands of ripe red berries, and popped it into his mouth. 'He was right. Deadly poisonous,' he said, over-exaggerating his chewing.

'Well, what the hell are you doing?' She watched him chew

on the berry and then started thumping him with her fist. 'Peter!'

He carried on chewing, smiled, and spit the seed into his hand.

'The foliage is deadly to humans and most mammals. As is the seed. That's the deadliest bit. But not the berry itself.'

He gestured to the seed in his hand.

'You're an idiot. I hate you. Why would you do that?' she said, knocking his hand so that the seed fell to the ground.

She stood with her hands on her hips. 'You're an idiot.'

Peter never took his eyes off her. 'You know I like it when you do that hands on hips thing? Kiss me.'

'You have to be joking. Kiss you? An idiot with a poisonous berry in his chops.'

Peter purposefully walked closer, put his arms around her waist and, while picking her up, pushed her up against the trunk. Their lips met. She loved it when he did that.

'We die together!' he said in his dirtiest, huskiest voice.

His kisses were passionate and attentive. She let him take the lead and was happy to follow.

'If you weren't in recovery, I'd take you right now,' he said in an even huskier voice.

'I'm feeling fine!' Charlotte said enthusiastically.

His kissing became more intense. His tongue played with hers, and his hand ran up her neck and brushed her hair back to reveal her exposed neck.

The feeling of his lips on her skin and the sound of his breath close to her ear made her shiver. She knew, he knew that was her weak spot, and he was exploiting every angle. Nibbling her earlobe and whispering, kissing her neck and then his thumb from his other hand came from nowhere and touched her lips. She kissed it, and then he pushed it provocatively into her mouth. She sucked it. He playfully bit her ear, and then they locked eyes. His thumb still suggestively in her mouth, she felt him push his body against her, and their kissing became frantic.

'I want you,' he said with pure determination in his eyes.

'I want you, Peter. But not here. Someone might see us?'

'There's no one around. I already checked that out.'

'Not in the grounds, Peter. I can't risk one of the house or grounds staff seeing us.'

Peter took a step back. 'Jeez! All these acres of land and still no privacy?'

'Let's go back to the house and start where we left off.'

'You certainly know how to keep a man interested,' he said, chuckling. 'As long as I don't have to wait for someone to plump the cushions and pre-warm the bed!'

'Don't mock the house staff, Peter. They do a fabulous job of making everything perfect for us.'

Peter thought for a moment. 'Spontaneity, Charlotte, that's what life's all about. I want you. I don't want to be treading on eggshells every time I want to make love to you.'

Charlotte sighed. 'I love your spontaneity. Don't ever stop, Peter. That's one thing I love about you.'

Peter took her hand. 'Come on, I understand. I can see that your dignity is important, and it's good that you rein me in now and again. It'll just take me time to adjust to my new home.'

Charlotte felt the tight grip of his hand, and a warm feeling of love made her tingle from head to toe.

'Make the house your home, Peter. Take control and relieve some of the pressure. If you think we need less staff or things could be run better, I want you to sort it out, just deal with it. I trust you.'

'Well, you know I struggle a bit with having everything done for us. There are things we can do for ourselves without having to summon someone to do it. Like making breakfast or running a bath.'

'Make the place yours. I'm happy with your decisions, but don't make life hard on yourself. You've been through just as much as me, and you can have things now you didn't as a child.'

Peter looked at her. 'Careful!' he said, looking stern.

'Sorry, you know what I mean. I'm not taking anything away from your mum or your upbringing, but you don't have to be lumping coal now or even cleaning your own bath.'

Peter shook his head. 'But that's where pride comes from. Scrubbing your own scum from the side of the bath.'

Charlotte shrugged and shook her head. She didn't understand. All she wanted was to make life as comfortable as possible for him now, especially after saving her life.

'I lost all my pride when I was hanging from the swing, Peter. I was selfish to think I could take my own life. I was arrogant to think no one cared. But you did. You knew exactly where to find me and brought me back to life. You don't need to build any more pride.'

'It would be nice to have some privacy, though, that's for sure!'

3

TREASON

'Peter, I want to go away for a week or two, just you and I, take some fresh air and enjoy some quality time together. But first, can we go through the diary?'

'I thought we were meant to be resting!'

'I'm so bored with resting. My scars are healing, and thanks to you, my strength is gaining. Come sit with me and let's find some time that suits us both.'

Peter shivered as he momentarily recalled finding her in the dark, hanging lifeless from the tree. Just the mention of her scars sent painful reminders of the rope around her neck running through his veins.

He finished making coffee and took his place in the window seat beside her.

'It can't be this week. I have meetings with the grounds staff, and I want to oversee the repairs to the driveway,' he said, kissing her forehead.

'Wow. You really didn't waste any time.'

Peter shrugged. 'You said to take some control.'

Charlotte smiled. 'You don't know how nice it is to hear that.'

She took a sip of coffee and pointed into the diary. 'It's not so easy to see when we could fit something in. Sam and Jojo, you remember from school, are staying over just one night. You don't have to be around for that. It's a girlie thing. The Chillington-Smythe-Fitzpatricks are descending on us for two nights next week. They were old friends of Mother's, and they were away in New York and couldn't make it to the funeral. They're nice people, and I couldn't say no.'

Peter smiled politely.

'Also, that week, I've arranged for the art valuer to visit and give some advice on selling some of the old dusty paintings. You see. I do listen to you, and you're right. All those stuffy items gathering dust are of no use to anyone. In fact, I may just loan them to the National Gallery or the Louvre. I'm not sure.'

Peter maintained his smile and sipped his coffee.

Charlotte moved her finger down the page. 'Oh yes! I forgot to mention the Duke and Duchess of Oxford will be coming for afternoon tea on the 19th.'

Peter dropped his coffee mug, and the contents spilt out across the table.

'The Duke and Duchess of Oxford?'

'Yes. It's not the first time we have had royalty here, I told you. Anyway, they will be bringing their son to meet Lucy. It will be pretty informal.'

Peter fetched a cloth and mopped up the mess. 'What do you mean *they will bring their son to meet Lucy*? Like, for a friend or something more serious?'

Charlotte shook her head as she watched him attempt to get coffee off his trousers and dry them in front of the Aga.

'A potential wife, Peter. Lucy is prime real estate when it comes to royalty.'

Peter's jaw nearly dropped to the floor. 'And you say it so... flippantly. As if it's normal?'

'If they request a visit, Peter, you don't say no. Mrs Hathersage is on the ball with the catering and finer details. All we have to do is welcome them into our home and make small talk over champagne and sandwiches.'

Peter didn't move. 'So not unlike our first date?'

Charlotte smiled and raised a brow. 'Only if you go kissing people unexpectedly!'

Peter laughed. 'I'm sure the Duchess will be impressed with a bit of Yorkshire dialect and a snog in the cloakroom!'

'Peter, don't joke. That could be considered treason, and you'll find yourself behind bars. Okay. So when are we going away? The 21st?'

'What about Lucy, the house and, dare I mention it, Henry the 4th?'

'Lucy will stay with her father. Mrs Hathersage will oversee the house. I've decided to auction off all of mother's belongings towards the Alzheimer's charity fund, and I don't want to be around. I'd rather it went without me seeing. With regard to that silly imposter, I want to hear nothing further about the matter. I heard from my solicitor this morning, and he said he's dealing with it.'

'But what about...'

She cut him off before he could finish. 'Peter. It's easy for someone to take the name of my father and try their luck. It was in all the newspapers at the time he died. I'm surprised more haven't come forward and tried it on.'

Peter nodded. 'My lips are sealed,' he said, pretending to zip up his lips with his finger and thumb.

'Good! So Venice it is,' Charlotte said, standing.

'Venice? I've never been. I heard the canals stink? I could take you on a tour of the Manchester ship canal if you fancy somewhere nearer and just as enchanting?'

'Sometimes, Peter, I don't know if you're joking or serious. If it's another northern thing to joke like that, then don't. Honestly! Venice is the perfect place to forget about things. It has an elegance and style, I think even you might appreciate.'

Peter acknowledged her wry smile with a cheeky grin, then proceeded to walk over and spank her on the bottom. 'I'll show you what elegance is, Miss Charlotte.' She squealed with delight, and then he thrust her up against the Chippendale dresser, and they kissed passionately until a bone china cup and saucer toppled and smashed on the floor.

'Naughty girl!' Peter said, still holding her tight.

Charlotte, unusually, didn't flinch at the sound of smashing china.

'And maybe I'll show you a thing or two in Venice? I know the perfect hotel.'

Peter took a step back. 'Look. To be northern and completely serious, I do have work, the week of the 21st, so how about the week after?'

Charlotte rolled her eyes. 'You and your work, Peter. You never have to work again, you know that? Everything is here for you now.'

Peter took his gaze to the floor, paused, and then back to Charlotte. 'I can't just walk away from everything I know. I'm used to working.'

Charlotte smiled. 'Okay. I'll head over there on the 21st and catch up with friends, and you come out and meet me when your work is finished?'

Peter nodded, and Charlotte took a sip of tea. 'That's perfect, just in time for the Biennale art festival. I might even buy something in memory of Mother. She did enjoy the Biennale. A painting maybe, or a sculpture? I'll see what takes my fancy.'

Peter scanned the arrivals hall, and on the right-hand side stood a man in a black suit, a bright white shirt and an immaculate blue tie. His hand held sign said: PETER. Acknowledgement was made with the obligatory raising of hands and eyebrows.

'Peter? Ciao. Benvenuto a Venezia. Per favore, seguimi,' the man said as he led Peter through the glass sliding door and into the car park.

The black limousine cruised along the streets before stopping by a pristine set of white marble steps which led down to the water. Peter peered through the tinted window at a little sign. It said: Canal Grande.

Directly in front of the car was a cafe with a shabby-looking green canopy and a scattering of wireframe tables and chairs. This must be the hotel, thought Peter as he grabbed his jacket. Charlotte said it was near the water.

The driver opened the car door and, instead of taking Peter to the hotel door, proceeded down the steps to the water's edge and to a waiting boat. The driver handed Peter's case to the boatman, and Peter clambered aboard.

The boat's slender and feminine polished wooden hull looked fabulous in the reflection on the water. Peter positioned himself within the cream leather seats at the rear, and the boat purred out into the Grand Canal and glided effortlessly through the water as it gathered pace. He observed how she sat low in the water and how the waves rippled like caramel in the bright sun. Filled with a fantastic feeling of importance as people stopped to watch the boat cruise by, he wanted to shout out loud with happiness. He'd never felt this important before, but held back and kept his calm and poise.

Looking around in awe, his eyes traced the Venetian stonework and then occasionally ducked under a low bridge. St Mark's Square to his left and the frontages of exclusive hotels along the water's edge drew his attention. All decorated with different colours, some with balconies, some with topiary, some with rooftop terraces, but none with its own dock and front door straight onto the water. Apart from the one before him!

Never before had he seen anything like it. The boat stopped, and a man boarded to collect his case. Another offered him a steady hand onto the marble steps and then straight into the hotel lobby. He felt like a film star.

The hotel was grand from the outside, but inside, it was sublime. Prominent stone statues, impressive internal trees, and hedges gave the place an opulent feel. The chandeliers were the biggest he'd ever seen, and a stone spiral staircase rose to the higher floors like something from a fairy-tale castle.

Peter absorbed the decadence and marvelled at the obscene grandeur; as he did so, something caught his eye. He looked up, and there she was, in a cream dress and red heels and smiling like the Cheshire cat. He was transfixed by the curves of her body and how sexy her legs looked in those high, high heels. The beauty of the stonework, flowers and lighting paled into insignificance as Charlotte descended the sweeping staircase and crossed the foyer to greet him. She was beauty itself, and he could feel an overwhelming desire inside.

He looked like a tourist, admiring the display of plants and trees. She knew he'd be trying to figure out how they'd managed to get the trees through the door. Even though he didn't speak a word of Italian, he was asking a member of staff about it. She laughed quietly, and her smile beamed across her face. Without a word, she ran into his arms and held him tightly around his middle. His arms flung right around her and held her tight.

'You are a very beautiful woman,' Peter whispered in her ear.

'Come on, let me show you the room.'

Charlotte skipped across the foyer, pulling Peter by the hand.

She raced ahead of him, her hips wiggling in the figure-hugging dress as she climbed each step. Peter couldn't keep his eyes off her as he let her lead the way. They reached the top together, and as they turned to walk down the hall, Peter gave her a slight tap on the bottom. 'I'm not wearing anything under this dress,' she said with a demure smile. 'Follow me, handsome man.'

She took him to a large wooden double door with an enormous keyhole. From her purse, she produced a mediaeval-looking key. The door opened to reveal a suite with a four-poster bed, classic Venetian furniture, an uneven wooden floor and its very own chandelier. The closed wooden shutters held back the bright day outside, but a chink of light was just enough for him to gauge the splendour of the room. Charlotte walked over to the window and opened the creaking shutters. The brilliant sun came straight in and almost blinded them.

She took in the view as Peter adjusted his eyes for a moment, then came up behind her and peered out.

'It's beautiful, isn't it?'

It was the view of their very own Canaletto. Gondolas weaving their magic through the blue-green water of the Grand Canal before them, decorated with poles and tassels; they bore black-and-white figures and lovers taking in the romantic air.

Peter looked over the water to the dome of the church on the island and the terracotta-tiled roofs and yellow-painted houses. There were trees dotted among the buildings, all set beneath a perfect blue sky as if straight off an artist's palette.

He put his hands on her shoulders as they took it all in.

Charlotte placed one of her hands on his. 'I love it here.'

Peter said nothing but with his other hand, started to unzip her dress at the back. Charlotte squeezed his hand and carried on looking out at the view. The zip reached the hem, and her dress opened. From the front, she appeared to be still wearing the dress and respectable to anyone with an acute eye on the street below. But from the back, she was naked and vulnerable.

She pushed her bottom out.

'Spank me,' she said.

Peter didn't say a word, just ran his hand down her back and over the curves of her bottom and then smack she jerked forward and squealed, then pushed her bottom further towards him, arching her back while still intent on the view. This time, a slightly harder, yet playful blow and another squeal of pleasure.

· · ·

Peter held their position in the window. The hint of danger making it all the more exciting.

His hands caressed her skin and admired the curves of her bottom, back, and hips. He bent her over and ran his hand from her ankle up the inside of her leg almost to the top and pushed her legs slightly apart while caressing her bottom again and again.

He thwacked her again and said, 'That's for being a very sexy girl, standing in front of all those people so they can see you.'

'Yes!' she cried. 'You make me feel sexy.'

Peter grabbed her hair from behind, wrapped it around his hand, and stood directly behind her. Unzipping his fly, there was no doubt of his intention as he positioned his tip ready to enter her, moving it back and forth for a few moments teasing her clit, then pushing himself in very gently. Teasing her by sliding almost out and then in again, he pulled harder on her hair, and she moaned. He felt her trying to pull him in all the way with her hand behind his hip, but he resisted and continued to move in and out with tiny strokes.

'I want you inside me.'

'Naughty girls can't have everything their own way,' he said, pulling her hair so that it was tight against her scalp. With one hand on her waist and the other gripping her hair, he hesitated and then pushed himself in completely.

Charlotte gasped.

'Fuck me,' she said. 'Fuck me hard.'

Peter did just that, his firm body ramming into her from behind, watching her bottom cheeks ripple as he did as she asked.

'Don't stop.' Her voice was high, and her breathing fast. Peter said nothing. He knew he would try to hold off until she orgasmed, and that turned him on even more. His pace quickened; the wooden floorboards squeaked under his feet as he stood on his toes to gain greater purchase. He pulled her hair again, and she cried out, 'Yes, oh yes, fuck me. I'm your naughty, filthy girl.'

He was on the edge, but managed to hold himself back as he gave her everything. He grabbed her hips with both hands and sunk himself deep into her. Then her body stiffened and jerked, her back arched, as she writhed. Her head came up, and she screamed and started shaking. Peter reduced his speed, slowed his rhythm and began to push in slowly but surely. Charlotte's body continued to writhe with every stroke. Peter's eyes locked onto her curved bottom as he watched himself pounding into her. Making her orgasm was his ultimate turn-on, and he wanted to savour the moment as he pushed in one more time and then withdrew completely from her. She gasped, and he released his tension all over her bottom. Charlotte pulled him in close as he kissed her on the neck, as both continued to look out of the window, completely out of breath. Peter smiled and Charlotte smiled too. He put his arms around her, and they felt the sun on their faces before stumbling over to the bed for a cuddle.

Italy was going to be so much fun!

4

CLARITY AND INTEGRITY

Watching him putting on a crisp white shirt was something worth savouring. What was it about broad shoulders and a hairy chest in a pristine shirt? She couldn't put her finger on it but enjoyed her voyeuristic moment intensely. She pondered more as he splashed on aftershave and rolled up his sleeves, revealing his masculine forearms. It was the fact that he looked good without really trying. He just put on his clothes without a care and didn't need to adjust his hair. It just did its dark, curly, effortless thing itself. His stubbly chin and piercing blue eyes were the icing on the cake, and she felt a fabulous warmth when he turned to her and smiled.

'I'm ready. What about you?' Charlotte smiled back. 'I thought I'd go out like this, you know, au naturelle.'

She was alluding to her naked body beneath her dressing gown.

'Perfect, I'm starving!' he said, looking at his watch.

'Honestly. You have a naked woman here in front of you, and all you can think about is your stomach.'

'I've booked a table at Harry's Bar. Hope you don't mind? I

read some good reviews, and the concierge guy said he could probably pull a few strings to get us in.'

Charlotte dropped her gown as she headed for the shower, then looked over her shoulder with a cheeky grin.

'Of course I don't mind. I like you taking the lead. Give me fifteen minutes.'

Forty minutes later, Charlotte declared she would wear a piece of her mother's jewellery she had saved from her personal effects, which she was particularly fond of. She opened a small black velvet box and took out a pair of ruby earrings and a matching choker, which perfectly complemented her little black dress and heels.

Peter helped her fasten the clip. 'You look incredible,' he said.

'Oh! This old thing,' she said, smiling and laughing.

Hand in hand, they negotiated narrow passages, crossed ornate stone bridges and through piazzas with hanging baskets of green, white and red flowers. A busker playing the violin made them stop and enjoy for a moment the classical music within the marble backdrop and azure water. The warm evening air allowed them to linger awhile. Peter dropped a handful of coins into the busker's instrument case, and they continued on their way.

'Harry's Bar. This is it,' Peter said, pointing to a sign above a door.

The doorman showed them to a rowdy bar area crammed with people. It was a noisy, bustling place, with Italians trying to gesticulate their presence over the next.

'Wow, it's busy,' Charlotte said, gripping Peter's hand tightly.

'Don't worry. As I said, they know we are coming.'

Charlotte followed the waiter up the stairs and into the

upper restaurant area. Her face lit up at the sight of white linen tablecloths against the ancient timber work of the table, beams and panelling.

~

'I'm in heaven, Peter. Thanks for booking this. You know I'm going to take some time to get back to normal and gain my confidence socially again. It's strange. Not only do I have physical scars, but mental ones too, but, as always, you make me feel safe.'

'You're a very capable woman, Charlotte. Remember all the speeches, dinner parties and events you've hosted.'

'Well, it all feels like it was all in a past life for some reason. I don't want to spread myself thin anymore. Things didn't go well with the Oxfords. I wasn't ready for such an event, and Lucy hated their son. Too much too soon. I want to concentrate on what's important in life and take time to appreciate them.'

'One thing we haven't really spoken about is the baby.'

'Peter, not now. I don't feel it's the right time.'

'Well, when is it the right time?'

Charlotte focused her eyes on the small crystal vase of flowers in the centre of the table.

'It doesn't seem real to me now. I did a stupid thing, Peter. I didn't mean to harm the baby. I wasn't thinking straight. I didn't even care for myself. You know that. Do I have to go over old ground?'

Peter took her hand in his. 'Of course not. I don't mean to drag up things we need to forget. I just want you to know that I'm okay with everything. Of course, we didn't have time to contemplate having a child or what that meant to us as a couple. I'm sad we could have brought another human into this world, but it is what it is.'

'It's hard for me, Peter. I'm ashamed of what happened and know I've been selfish. Can we draw a line under everything and try to look forward?'

'Of course we can, and I don't want you to feel guilty or ashamed for anything. Do you hear me?'

Charlotte squeezed his hand and agreed. She then noticed Peter looking a little agitated, and his neck flushed with colour.

Peter seemed preoccupied, fumbling in his pocket.

'You're not going to tell me you've forgotten your wallet, are you?'

Peter ignored her and continued looking down, removing his hand from their grip and fiddling.

'Are you all right?'

Peter stood from his chair and wiped a bead of sweat from his brow. He then brought his clenched fist to his mouth and cleared his throat. Twice.

'Is everything okay, Peter? You don't seem yourself?'

At that point, the waiter arrived, placed menus on the table and poured water into the glasses.

Peter took to his seat, his face red and slightly blotchy.

'I know you can be a little odd sometimes. I don't fully understand the Yorkshire thing yet, but you don't have to stand when the waiter arrives, you know?' Charlotte said, looking puzzled.

'Sorry, I was distracted. It's nothing. I mean, bad timing, the menus. Ignore me. I'm blathering.'

'You're being very weird, Peter. Maybe you need some sustenance after your star performance earlier? Take some bread.'

. . .

Peter ignored the food and started fumbling again.

'Peter!' Charlotte's annoyance was noticeable in her tone.

Once again, Peter rose from his chair.

'Peter, what are you doing?'

He stood and, without hesitation, began to speak.

'I can't put this off anymore. I was going to wait, but… but, I can't.'

'Will you sit down and have some bread?'

Peter fumbled again in his pocket and then took to the floor on one knee.

'Peter, what are you doing?'

He raised his head and, with a straight back, looked Charlotte straight in the eye.

Charlotte became speechless. What on earth was he doing? And in such a busy restaurant.

A touch of anxiety hit her as she watched him try to speak. Her heart thumping so hard. She could hear it, and so could everyone else, she thought as the whole place became silent.

Peter took his hand to his mouth again, cleared his throat, and reaffirmed his straight back.

'Charlotte,' he said. 'You are the most beautiful woman I have ever known. Beautiful inside and out. A little worn at the edges, maybe, but that's life's way of telling us how unique and strong we are. But true strength comes within a union. An unbreakable union of mighty strength. A team, a bond, a future.'

Charlotte raised her hands to her face as she felt a flush of heat. 'Oh, Peter!'

'Charlotte?' he asked, producing a dark purple velvet box.

'Yes.'

'Would you do me the very great honour of ending our independent battles of life by becoming my wife?'

Her heart exploded with joy. It could possibly have been the most exciting, thrilling episode of her entire life, and she could feel it in her entire body.

She looked instantly at the ring as he released the lid. She paused for a moment. Looked at the ring again and then at Peter. His eyes full of both anticipation and worry. She could feel that his whole worth was hanging on her reply. Not only that. But her and their future together?

As she continued to look into his eyes, he appeared to turn from a man into a boy. Vulnerable, uncertain and in need of love himself. She could see the naivety in his soul, and his blue eyes drew her deeper in. *I can love him.*

She took her gaze to the perfect little box, held tightly in his trembling hand. A single diamond on a gold band. Certainly not the huge rock she'd seen from her previous marriage, but instead an understated elegance. Perfect in fact. The light caught it with such clarity and integrity. Not a show of ostentation. Instead, she felt it had honesty and a simplicity she respected and loved.

She felt a tear run down her cheek but didn't bother to wipe it away.

'Yes,' she said. 'Yes, I will be your wife.'

5

THE BIENNALE

B rilliant sunlight reflected off the busy water of the Canal Grande, and the day's heat already radiated from the cobbled streets.

'We had cobbled streets outside my home when I was growing up. We used to jump from high point to high point to save twisting our ankles. But this couldn't be any more different to the back alleyways of Yorkshire. What is the Biennale?' Peter asked as he hopped from one cobble to the next.

'That's what I love about you, Peter, and I felt it in our first kiss. Remember our first date?'

'Jeez, how could I ever forget!'

'It was the softest, most tender, yet purposeful kiss I've ever felt. All man, yet with the naivety of a schoolboy. I can still feel it now.'

Peter pushed back his shoulders. 'Well, there's plenty more where that came from.'

Charlotte laughed. 'Not to mention how common you are. What am I going to do with you?'

'Love me?'

Charlotte took his face into her hands. 'I promise to do that until the day we die.'

Peter pointed. 'Look, a gondola, come on.'

Charlotte held him back. 'Peter, it's for tourists.'

'Look, we're not coming to Venice and not taking a gondola; anyway, we are tourists.'

Charlotte relented, shrugged her shoulders, and stepped foot into the boat with her usual elegance.

Peter couldn't stop touching the woodwork and absorbed the ornate vessel and its pilot's unique splendour with his black-and-white striped shirt and quirky tasselled hat.

'Normally, I'd prefer to drive,' he said, pushing back into the seat and wrapping an arm around Charlotte. 'So what exactly is the Biennale?'

Charlotte laughed. 'At this rate, we'll never get there, but I'm loving it. Can we set a date?'

'What for?'

'The wedding. Had you forgotten?'

Peter winked. 'How about next spring? Loxley is at its best then, with bluebells and the optimism of the trees bursting into leaf. It'll be warmer then too.'

'I think that's a perfect idea. It will give us time to organise everything. I'll have a spring bouquet and, of course, Lucy will be a bridesmaid.'

'Let's hope she doesn't poison the cake!'

'Peter. That's not fair.'

'Sorry. Do you think she'll be happy for us?'

Charlotte pondered for a moment. 'I hope so. She's been with us on our journey, and at the end of the day, it was you and her together, who made this all possible.'

Peter acknowledged with a tender kiss. 'That's true. I

would never have saved you if she hadn't called me that night. I love you so very much.'

'I love you too, Peter. I'm so very happy.'

'Maybe I'll drive us away for the honeymoon in the car?'

'The DB5?' Charlotte replied, to much surprise.

'I think I'm ready. You did say it was mine?'

'Absolutely. It's just, you know, your mum. You said you could never have such a car?'

Peter gave her another kiss. 'Time moves on, Charlotte. We've said it before: it's no good dwelling on the past. It was a gift from you, and I'm grateful. Imagine the spring sunshine and the roof down as we drive off into the sunset?'

'The great escape. I'll wear my red heels.'

Peter grinned from ear to ear. 'God, you're sexy.'

Huge frescos and oil paintings filled the gallery walls. Sculptures of every conceivable size in marble, wood and steel stole centre stage, and Peter could not believe his eyes.

'So this is the Biennale?'

'Honestly, Peter, you've seen nothing yet. I'd like to see some of the modern art exhibits, and there's a pavilion of Plensa sculptures which are high on my list. I am on the lookout for something to remind me of mother, remember? A painting maybe, or some glassware perhaps?'

'Are there any Lowrys?'

'Lowrys?'

'You know, "Matchstick Men and Matchstick Cats and Dogs",' Peter replied, singing the song.

'Do you mean L. S. Lowry?'

Peter shook his head. 'Not sure, but I do like the expression of life in his pictures.'

'You sound like a proper critic. Come on, let's go and find the Plensas. Lots of female form in smooth alabaster.'

'How about we go back to the room, and I'll critique your female form?'

'Tonight, Peter. Tonight. You've instilled a naughty streak in me, and I have an idea. Call it a little fantasy of mine.'

'Sounds exciting. What is it?'

Charlotte stroked her exposed thigh while showing off her diamond in the sun.

'A stranger. I want you to be a silent intruder in our room, and you can do whatever you want.'

Peter took a cursory glance at the gondolier.

'Bloody hell. It is true what they say about convent girls. I'll be whoever you want me to be.'

Charlotte tried to look as if butter wouldn't melt and, with a coy glance, moved her hand onto his thigh.

'I have no idea what you mean!'

'To be honest, I'm not sure I get all this art. What I mean is, I love the textural stuff, sculptures, wood, marble and the like, but some of the modern art just feels like it's trying too hard. Does that make sense?'

Charlotte topped up Peter's glass with sparkling water. 'Yes, complete sense. I knew you'd love art.'

'But I just said I don't.'

'Exactly. You won't like everything. You have to feel it in your body, in your soul. If it doesn't reach out to you, then move on to something that does.'

'But some look like a five-year-old did them. Those Picassos. I reckon I could do better.'

'But you didn't, and he did. Have you ever tried to reproduce a Picasso? We did at college, just for fun, and it's impossible. It's unique. Whether you like it or not, it's brilliant.'

Peter scrunched his lips. 'I guess so. You're really quite clever, aren't you?'

'Just relax and enjoy what you see. You're forever telling me to relax and take things a step at a time. Just find what appeals to you.'

'I've already found that,' he said, looking at her. Then took her hand and examined the diamond as if he were a gemologist.

'You chose well, Peter.'

'What do you mean?'

'It's understated chic. Good quality, I can tell. And exquisitely presented. It shows a lot about your taste.'

Peter nodded and said nothing.

The late afternoon light began to cast longer shadows, and after shared pizza, sparkling water and a glass or two of Brunello di Montalcino, Charlotte turned her attention to the evening's plans.

'Okay. Are you still up for my little fantasy? It just seems like the ideal place and time.'

'As long as it doesn't involve ropes.'

'Peter!'

'Sorry. Forget I said that. What's the plan?'

'I'm going to head back to the hotel and *get ready*. You give me forty-five minutes and come up to the room. You must be silent. I don't want to know it's you. Okay?'

Peter started to laugh.

'Are you up for this, or not?'

'But you will know it's me.'

'Peter, it's a game. I wouldn't want a real stranger to come in.'

'Right, okay, I get it. A silent stranger? Like the Milk Tray man, but with more than chocolate on his mind.'

'Exactly! It will be worth it. I have new underwear, and you can do what you want with me. Just don't ask or enquire whether I like it. Okay?'

'Jeez, you have this all mapped out. Have you done this before?'

'No! I most certainly haven't. I never thought about it until I met you.'

'Okay. Forty-five minutes and I'm coming to get you. I'll order a beer.'

Charlotte took from her seat, walked a few paces, and then turned.

'Bye!' she said with a wiggle in her hips.

'Bye,' he said while tracking her every move with his eyes.

6

THE INTRUDER

C harlotte's heart raced. She showered and pampered her skin, blow-dried her hair and gave it extra waves, which she knew Peter loved. Lace underwear with stockings would also send him wild, and she wanted him at his best.

Just one candle flickering in the corner to give some idea of where she was, and that was it. She had five minutes to go and kept resisting the urge to touch herself. The thought of him forcing his way in and taking her was starting to be unbearable.

Three minutes to go, a sudden pang of insecurity and vulnerability kicked in as she waited alone. Would he think she was weird? She hoped he got the whole role-play thing?

One minute to go, she heard the door latch and then the door quietly clicked shut. There was silence. She looked at the bedroom door for any hint that he was there and waited. Suddenly a dark figure appeared, his silhouette created by the faint, flickering candlelight from behind. Then the light went out, and it was almost entirely dark apart from a hint of moonlight behind the window shutters. The shadowy figure had vanished into the room. She was nervous and excited; she didn't know for sure who it was or where he was. After a few agonising seconds, she smelled his woody aftershave and relaxed. The next thing she saw was a naked silhouette coming towards the bed. She had never felt so vulnerable and sexy. What was it about him which had driven her to set this up?

A hand came and started stroking her hair and caressing her cheek. Then a single finger touched her mouth as if to say: *shh*. Her brain, high on adrenaline from just the anticipation. The figure came onto the bed, and she could sense his presence hovering over her. She imagined his muscles and hairy chest. He ran his hand down her neck and along the necklace and kissed her on the lips just once. It was a kiss with full intention and one she had felt before from him. She started to crumble.

Taking her hand to his, he immediately took it and, together with her other hand slowly but assertively pushed them down onto the bed, either side of her head. She was trapped.

He moved his body down, and she felt the hairs on his chest against her skin and then a kiss on her left nipple and one on the right. Her back was arching. Her skin was alive to the slightest hint of a touch as he dominated above her. A hand ran down her leg and paused as she felt him examine her stocking top. Then he parted her legs without warning. She could feel his breath on her. He wasn't touching her, and she was nearly exploding. She could feel the occasional prickle from his stubble as he surveyed every part of her body, and she felt more and more exposed, available and vulnerable to him. A hand went under her knee, lifting it and started to turn her over. She obliged and ended up on all fours, his hands caressing her back and bottom. She could feel him close behind her and then both hands on her hips, and he pushed deep inside her with pure unadulterated gratuitousness. No messing, no probing, no not quite hitting the mark. Just in straight in and deep.

She squealed and could feel him so, so deep.

'I want to be your filthy whore,' she said and gasped. Filthy whore! She wondered where the hell that had come from. She'd never said anything like that to anyone before. But wow, it felt good, and he was treating her like one, spanking the cheeks of her bottom and fucking her like he owned her. He still hadn't spoken a word. She felt her hair gather at the back of her neck and then tighten as he wrapped it around his hand and pulled it. She felt like she was tethered to him as he continued thrusting. She moaned with delight as her body and mind gave in to his leadership.

It was building. She could feel it. Everything was right, *just don't stop.*

'Fuck me hard. I'm such a naughty girl,' she blurted out and, instead of cringing, gave the green light for every emotion to come flying out. He pulled her hair a little tighter and slowed his rhythm to a purposeful tupping. A warmth filled her soul, molten lava bubbling up from deep within and searching for a place to erupt. Then it did. It felt like she had been wound like a rubber band and finally released. He was beautiful.

He kept on tupping. His hands were now on her hips and speeding up slightly. She felt he was rock solid, and then another flurry of ecstasy came from nowhere, different from the first but equal in magnitude. Her mind was above the clouds. His rhythm never faltered. His arm somehow came around her waist, and his finger started rubbing her clit while he was still thrusting from behind.

Oh, oh, oh my... I'm going to come again. She felt her entire body giving way and going from super eruption to category one earthquake. Her body was jerking. She screamed. With one last shot of his drug, he pushed in hard, and his whole body started bucking. They orgasmed together, and it lasted and lasted. He ran his fingernails down her back as he jerked one more time like an aftershock, and Charlotte moaned with complete delight. Then she collapsed and started to cry.

He dropped beside her. 'Did I hurt you?' he asked.

Charlotte looked at him. Floods of tears ran down her cheeks.

'Ask me if I'm okay?'

'You said not to ask you? Are you okay?'

Charlotte struggled to get her words out.

'Peter...' She put her hand to his face. 'Peter. I love you so very much.'

In a rush of relief, Peter smiled and then shed a tear.

'And I am in love with you too. You are everything.' Peter held out his arms and cuddled her tight into his chest. They cried together, sobbing, then the odd laugh and then more floods of tears. He squeezed her tight, and she felt safe, then pulled the blanket over them, and they drifted off to sleep in each other's arms.

7

TRUST

B ooks from floor to ceiling, books on shelves, books on tables and books stacked on more books created a seemingly chaotic yet academic feel to the vast library. A moveable wooden ladder enabled access to the upper levels, a monumental chandelier took centre stage, and Charlotte's desk was positioned in the bay window, which overlooked the verdant croquet lawn and backdrop of a mature deodar cedar and pleached hornbeam hedge.

It wasn't real. It couldn't be real! She was determined to fight it. No one had ever mentioned a brother. Her father was a secretive man sometimes, yes, but there was never any hint of him fathering a son.

She stood in the window, felt the cold air around her feet, and re-read the document before her.

'Hong Kong is plausible,' she said to her solicitor, who was sat on a book-shrouded seat. 'He made frequent visits there when I was a child. Business trips, he would call them.'

The solicitor reclined back.

'There were many business deals struck in Hong Kong

between 1965 and the early 1980s. He would sometimes stay for weeks, and although he mainly resided at the Excelsior Hotel, he travelled around too. The claim is that he fathered a son, Henry the 4th, but chose, for obvious reasons, to keep it secret. He wouldn't want word of an affair getting back to your mother.'

'Too fucking right, he wouldn't!' Charlotte said, throwing the paperwork onto the desk. 'So what evidence does he have?'

'Well, I'm aware of a birth certificate and an amendment to the will.'

'What do you mean, an amendment to the will?'

'I'm not entirely sure at this point, but I'm doing my best to find out.'

'I'm sure you will. My father trusted you, and I trust you to make this watertight.'

The solicitor cleared his throat. 'It will be in the hands of the court. If he can't prove who he is, which we think is the case, then it's business as usual. The court has already requested DNA testing, and we are lucky enough to have your father's records on file.'

Charlotte scowled. 'Why would he have given his DNA?'

The solicitor fidgeted and then stood. 'He trusted no one, Charlotte. When you were born, he merely double-checked. You know what he was like.'

Charlotte shook her head. 'So the bastard didn't even trust I was his own flesh and blood?'

'He was a risk-taker but cautious in matters of the heart,' he said, continuing to fidget on his feet.

'I guess the positive is that we have hard and fast proof against likely imposters in this instance.'

The solicitor headed for the door.

'So what is the worst-case scenario?'

'If they deem him to be the lawful heir, then he could claim the entire estate.'

'And what happens to me?'

The solicitor paused. 'I wouldn't worry at this stage. The court will be diligent, and as of yet, there is no DNA evidence.'

'Everything is at stake here. I want you to do everything you can to resolve this.'

'I can assure you I'm doing everything I can and as I said, I'm doubtful he will produce any compelling evidence.'

Charlotte showed him to the door, where Peter was waiting impatiently.

'You were my father's solicitor for a long time. If you can't resolve this matter, then no one can.'

Peter opened the door, shook his hand, and then closed the door behind him.

'Do you know you can trust him?'

Charlotte stood firm. 'Absolutely. I've known him a long, long time, Peter, and my father trusted him implicitly. He's a good man.'

Peter held her tight. 'That's good.'

Charlotte pushed her elbows against him. 'Tell me we won't lose Loxley?'

Peter's eyes fell to the floor, and Charlotte could see his Adam's apple prominent in his throat. 'Peter!'

'Of course we won't. You heard what he said. Anyway, whatever happens, we have each other. We've been through worse than this. Don't worry, it will be okay.'

Charlotte looked deep into his eyes. 'I've dreaded this moment all my life, Peter. Someone taking everything from me.'

'It won't come to that. The court will be strict, and the

solicitor has your back. Stop worrying. You're your father's daughter, remember?'

'Thank you, Peter. I don't know what I'd do if I couldn't talk to you like this.'

'We'll be fine. We won't end up in the gutter.'

8

COURT

Killer heels, grey pinstriped trouser suit, red lipstick, hair up and a stride which meant business was Charlotte's front line against that unscrupulous man. Her brave face was defiant following the many months of worry and anxiety which had deepened since her first interaction with him.

Peter held her hand on the car's back seat as they approached the court.

She stared at the bald patch on the back of her solicitor's head, who was sitting in front. Her mind cast back to when she was younger. He always had grey hair. As long as she could remember, he always looked distinguished.

When she was growing up, he was at the house so much that she almost treated him as an uncle. Her father even confided in her when she was around twelve.

'He knows everything. Every investment, every property, every penny. When I die, he's your man.'

And indeed, he was right. He'd managed the transfer of the will and kept the entire estate running when she needed him. Bald patches were trustworthy and competent. A full head of

J A CRAWSHAW

hair on an older man was always something to be wary of. She always knew that.

She looked at Peter. His thick hair was the exception. Although he was starting to thin slightly, she loved the grey beginning to creep in too. That was sexy, especially in his stubble.

The car left them at the door and, in line, the three of them ascended the Portland stone steps into the grand court building.

There he was. The first person Charlotte set eyes on. Slouching uncomfortably on a flimsy plastic chair and in the same ill-fitting suit he'd worn to the funeral.

'Let's sit over here.' Charlotte pointed to a series of chairs by a window, out of sight of anyone else.

'So what's our position here?' she said to the solicitor.

'Everything, of course, hinges on proof. A birth certificate has been produced, but we believe it to be fake. There is a DNA analysis, but I have no knowledge of the results. As far as we know, there isn't anything else.'

Charlotte butted in. 'How do you mean "as far as we know"? That doesn't sound watertight to me?'

Peter interjected. 'I thought possession was nine-tenths of the law, anyway?'

'That is true. You are the estate's current owner,' he said, looking at Charlotte. 'We are in a very strong position going into this and, like I say, without compelling evidence, he has very little to go on. I wouldn't worry.'

Charlotte leaned forward in her chair.

'I'm nervous. You sound so calm and collected, which reassures me somewhat, but I could still lose everything. I will appeal to his better nature and ask him to climb down.'

Charlotte sighed and looked at Peter, who spoke assertively.

'It sounds like we have a plan. Let's go in and hold our heads high. We just have to be honest and believe. What have you said to Lucy?'

'She's with friends for a few days. I didn't want to scare her. No need, really.'

'Good. Okay, well, remember, we are a team, and truth will win through. That's what your father said, and we still hold strong to that. Here, have some water.'

Peter handed bottles of water to them and then stood in anticipation of entering the courtroom.

'It's time,' he said, fastening the button on his suit and looking around to see if they had been watched.

At that moment, the doors opened, and everyone took their places. Charlotte scowled over at Henry, who was chatting with his solicitor and occasionally glancing over.

'All rise,' the usher said and then the judge appeared from a panelled door behind his ceremonial seat and brought everyone to order.

'It is not often I have presided over such a case. All evidence will be given under oath, and this court takes matters of this nature extremely seriously. First, to the witness bench, I call Ms Charlotte Winterbourne.'

Charlotte spoke clearly and concisely.

'My solicitor will present our main case, but I'd like to say that, in memory of my father, the late Henry Winterbourne: he was a generous man and an honest man. As a family, we knew nothing of an extra marital affair or another sibling. If there was a true brother, son, my father would have had the courage to say so, and there would have been provision made within the will. This was not the case. I hope that the gentleman will see sense and withdraw his case at the earliest opportunity so that we can carry on with our lives in peace.'

Charlotte's solicitor took to the bench and highlighted various documents that had already been supplied to the court some weeks ago. The will, a breakdown of movements and costs associated with travelling and working in Hong Kong, and other items proved Charlotte to be the rightful heir. Charlotte watched his bald patch throughout and rested comfortably in his knowledge and historical record.

Next to the bench was Henry. He looked awkward in his overtight, half-mast suit.

'I want to say what a shock it must be to suddenly find you have a brother you never knew existed. I understand that. I wish no one here any harm. I just feel I should claim what is rightfully mine as the first born and only son of Mr Winterbourne. Sorry... father.'

Charlotte shook her head but tried to resist losing any dignity.

She leaned over and whispered to the solicitor. 'There isn't such a thing as a rightful heir just because he claims he was born first, and a man, is there? The will was the will. What is he going on about?'

He replied with a smile and a nod, then focused back on the proceedings.

'I also want to say that he was a good, honest man, and although he wasn't around all of the time, I felt he loved me. He even told me that, one day, I would be a successful man.'

Charlotte bit her lip but couldn't contain her outburst. 'Fuck off,' she blurted.

'Silence, please,' the judge said.

Peter squeezed Charlotte's hand in an attempt to calm her.

Henry continued. 'My mother took me away at an early age. She was an interpreter, and we moved around a lot for her work. We always had nice houses. It was only much later I found out that my father was supporting us, although I didn't see him.'

'So when your father wasn't around, where did you think he was?' the judge asked as he looked Henry straight in the eye.

'My mother said he was an international businessman. I thought he was travelling and doing business. I thought nothing of it.'

'Did you miss him?'

Henry put his face into his hands. 'Dearly. As a young boy, I remember him playing football with me and taking me fishing.'

Peter looked at Charlotte and shook his head.

'Next, we have your birth certificate. Can you provide evidence under oath that this is your birth certificate?'

'Certainly, your Honour. I found it among my late mother's papers. Sadly, she is no longer with us. I always felt different. I looked and sounded English because of my father and mother's almost perfect language. My mother always said I would one day travel to England and see where she studied, so we always spoke English.'

'With an Essex accent!' Peter shouted.

'Order,' the judge said.

'Charlotte.'

'Yes.'

'What record do you have regarding your brother?' the judge said, directing his attention to her.

'None whatsoever. My father never said anything about any siblings. I grew up all my life knowing I was an only child. When my father died, it was an unexpected shock. Taking on the responsibility of the estate at such a young age was hard, but I always knew it was expected.'

'Did you ever travel to Hong Kong with your father?'

'No, your Honour. Never. I know my mother travelled with him a few times when I was younger, but she grew tired of travel and, of course, her condition made it difficult.'

'Thank you. When your father passed away, and you went through his personal affairs, you found no evidence of a sibling or even the financial commitment your father had to a lady in Hong Kong?'

'My solicitor dealt with all of those matters,' she said, glaring at him.

'We knew there had been regular payments to a female in Hong Kong, and they were recorded as being for employment purposes only,' the solicitor said with confidence.

'I see in the paperwork before me, there is DNA evidence,' the judge said, peering over his spectacles.

'Yes, your Honour. I have supplied a sample at the request of the court, and the results are before you,' Henry replied with a smile.

The judge perused the document as Peter squeezed Charlotte's hand.

'99.98%.'

'Yes, your Honour. My swab was tested against stored DNA from my father.'

'And how was his DNA made available to you?'

'It was requested by the court, your Honour, and supplied by Ms Winterbourne's solicitor.'

Charlotte dabbed her cheek with her handkerchief. She couldn't believe what she was hearing.

'I also see you have presented a letter of wishes attached to the original will?'

'Yes, your Honour.'

There was a gasp from within the courtroom.

'What the hell is a letter of wishes?' she said, glaring at her solicitor. 'Did you know about this?'

'Silence. Please,' the judge said, letting Henry continue.

'It is a legally binding attachment to the will, your Honour. Only when I tried to find my father all these years later did I find evidence of it, or I would have claimed sooner.'

Charlotte's heart was thudding like a sinking depth charge about to explode.

'And can you present it to the court?'

'Certainly, your Honour. The will sets out various properties and items to relatives of my father and, of course, the main estate and finances to my sister.'

Charlotte retched as she continued to listen.

'It was only when I requested a full copy of the document that I found an accompanying letter of wishes. Albeit a separate document, it clearly states that the will should be overwritten if I were ever to be located or declare myself, as I am doing today. My father states: I, Sir Henry Charles Bartholomew Winterbourne, declare that my son, Henry junior, born in Hong Kong, February 21st 1967 to Ms Rai Chi will be the rightful heir to my estate if he is found to be alive following my death. Should Henry Winterbourne 4th declare himself to be my legitimate son, then my express wishes are for him to take the estate in my name and preserve the male bloodline to future generations. I also wish that any future male offspring be subsequently named Henry in my honour.'

The court was silent. Charlotte looked at Peter, who was shaking his head.

'The final section states that as rightful heir, I am trusted with fair and compensatory allocation of funds and resources to my sister, Charlotte Winterbourne, in which to relieve her of the burden and responsibility of the estate and allow for the comfortable, secure and stress-free lifestyle she deserves. In addition, that the Sir Henry Winterbourne wing at her old school, St Cuthbert's, be renamed the *Charlotte Winterbourne Wing* in her honour.'

Everyone was stunned.

Charlotte took to her feet. 'You are an imposter and a liar. Surely the court can see this is a fabrication. I do not accept this. I do not accept this!'

The judge intervened. 'Ms Winterbourne. Please. Take your seat. I understand this is uncomfortable evidence to hear, but please be respectful of the court.'

Charlotte reluctantly took her seat and spoke assertively to her solicitor. 'Were you aware of this? Why wasn't I informed of this letter of wishes? I thought I could trust you.'

'We will discuss this at the break,' he forcefully replied.

'Does anyone have anything more to present to the court?'

The room remained silent until the uncomfortable air was broken once again by Henry.

'My dear father did say to me on more than one occasion that his entire fortune would one day be mine and the truth would win through.'

Charlotte banged her fist upon the table and stood.

'I knew my father better than anyone here, and he was a decent man. A man of honour and standing. He wouldn't have had such a sordid affair and promised things which were out of the question. I don't believe a word of this, and I ask for more time to gather evidence to the contrary?'

She looked at her solicitor for backup, and he nodded while taking copious notes.

The judge quietened the commotion.

'We have to take cases like this very seriously indeed. People's livelihoods are at stake, and if we unearth any criminal activity, we will take the appropriate action. If all the evidence is before me, then I will adjourn and return with my final decision in one hour from now. Court dismissed.'

Charlotte flung herself into Peter's arms. 'This cannot be happening, Peter. It seems all one-sided, and you can see that he's lying.'

'They will have checked everything. If the birth certificate is fake, it will be pivotal in the outcome. A letter of wishes is easily produced with a bit of thought, but it doesn't mean anything. We just have to hope their investigations have been thorough.'

Charlotte held a glimmer of hope in her eyes as she searched within Peter's for the same.

He continued, 'Records and such are easily checkable these days. I think we're going to be okay. As your father said, the truth will win through. Let's hope he was a man of his word.'

Out of the courtroom, Charlotte scowled as Henry walked past. He didn't have the courage to even look at them. Instead he skulked with his head down and proceeded to the bathroom.

Peter edged on his seat. 'Shall I go in there and have a word in his ear? Maybe if I put the frighteners on him, he might see the light of day?'

'He doesn't even look anything like my father. He's like a thin weasel. His stature is all wrong. Father carried himself with pride and confidence. He was never a skulker.'

'I could easily *lean* on him,' Peter said, almost on both feet and ready to go.

'No, Peter. As you said, the truth will win through, and we don't want to jeopardise anything by you being arrested. Leave it.'

The solicitor appeared with three cups of tea and huddled them together.

Charlotte didn't hesitate. 'What the hell is the letter of wishes? Did you know about this?'

The solicitor took a sip of tea. 'I do remember something accompanying the original will. It's a long time ago, and we must have felt it irrelevant at the time to disclose it as you were the only apparent heir. The two items must have been separated within our filing system, and it has been the best part of thirty years.'

'With all due respect, Mr Scrivener, this smacks of incompetence. I expressly asked that you make this case watertight, and it's everything but.'

'The court will have undertaken diligent checks, and I'm still confident the birth certificate and letter of wishes will be fake.'

Charlotte paused and took a sip of tea. 'I'm not so sure. The wording in the letter sounded just like my father.'

Peter took her arm. 'What are you talking about?'

'Those were the words of my father. So self-centred and arrogant. Wanting the male bloodline to dominate and giving me the insult of a re-named school wing. It's what I would have expected from him. It's simply all about himself. He didn't have the courage to tell anyone about an illegitimate son. Instead, he waits until his death to declare the sordid truth. I hated him as a child, and I hate him now. I thought he was a strong man, but he was a coward and a liar.'

Peter took her face in his hands. 'I can't believe what I'm hearing. You can't concede now. We know this man is an imposter. Don't give in to what he says.'

Charlotte held on to Peter's hands and looked into his eyes.

'My mother mentioned something about my father just before she died. I thought it was just her dementia.'

'What did she say?'

'It was nothing specific. Just that my father had been a cheat and that she knew he had lied to her, although she never declared it to him. She mentioned some lady in Hong Kong. She knew Peter, she knew!'

Peter released his hands from her face. 'I don't believe a word he is saying. It's all too convenient, and how come it took this long to come to light? I'm not conceding now, and neither are you.'

'I just have to hope that Henry is a benevolent man.'

'Enough of that, Charlotte. Keep a positive mind.'

At that point, Henry returned and this time with a weaselly smirk.

Peter took to his feet and blocked his path. The stand-off attracted the attention of the whole building. Eye to eye, Peter held his shoulders broad and had fists ready for action. Charlotte watched them vying for position and cringed at the sight of Henry in half-mast trousers and greasy hair, still maintaining his smirk.

'Leave it, Peter,' she said, tugging on his arm. 'Leave it.'

Peter reluctantly retreated, and Henry continued around the corner and out of sight.

'No one smirks like that at you or me. The last time I witnessed a smirk like that, I punched the school bully for disrespecting my mother. He was a loser, too, and I won't stand for it.'

Charlotte encouraged him to sit. 'Just calm down, Peter. There are press here, and they'll be watching our every move. We are not in the school playground now. Anyway, where is Mr Scrivener?'

'I saw him making calls and taking lots of notes. I think he's on the case.'

'Hold me, please, Peter. Hold me and tell me everything is going to be all right.'

'All rise,' the usher said, and everyone stood while the judge appeared from his concealed room and took his throne-like seat.

'I have reached my conclusions based on the evidence before me. My team has checked the evidence and is satisfied that the decision is based on sound and binding legal judgements.'

Charlotte gasped, and Peter moved onto the edge of his seat.

'The entire Winterbourne estate is included within the decision and comprises the following: Loxley estate, all buildings, grounds, woodlands, peripheral land ownership under rental agreements and all contents. Undisclosed figure.

All art works and sculptures totalling £155 million. The London house and all contents, including works by Picasso and Rubens, £81 million.

The Alpenblick Hotel, Austria, and all associated assets. Undisclosed figure.

Investment portfolios and property, £178 million.

Private accounts within the Winterbourne Trust, £291 million.

All vehicles and machinery excluding a vintage Aston Martin DB5 gifted to Mr Peter Heath.'

The court burst into gasps and mutterings to the point the judge had to use his gavel to summon silence once again.

Peter squeezed Charlotte's hand and closed his eyes.

Charlotte dabbed her cheek with the family crest-embossed handkerchief, and the solicitor sat rigid and calm.

'I hereby declare that the rightful and legal heir to the entire Winterbourne estate is... Mr Henry Winterbourne 4th.'

Charlotte couldn't believe her ears. Everything before her was as if she was watching a silent movie. A horror movie. She looked around the room to see Henry jumping up and down and hugging his solicitor. People in the gallery were shaking their heads and waving their arms in the air. The courtroom was in complete pandemonium. All Charlotte could do was watch. She searched for her solicitor, who was shaking his head.

'We will be appealing. You can rest assured,' he said.

'I trust you will,' she said with the overwhelming taste of bitterness in her mouth.

'We will examine the evidence and put a robust appeal in as soon as possible.'

Henry Winterbourne 4th took to the bench to give his reply.

Charlotte tried to control her rapid breath and crossed her fingers tightly. Peter was up on his feet, shouting and jeering and shaking his fist. Charlotte sat silently. She was the only one sitting and couldn't move. The hustle and bustle of the room created confusion in her mind.

Then, the judge hit his gavel again onto the bench, and everyone gradually took to their seats.

'Mr Winterbourne,' the judge said, introducing him to speak.

'Thank you, Judge. In the words of my fabulous father, the truth will win through, and today is a monumental day for justice.'

'Can't contain the Essex accent now, though,' Peter shouted.

The judge intervened. 'One more time, Sir, and I will remove you from this court and charge you with contempt.'

Peter reluctantly regained his seat, and Charlotte put her hand on his knee.

Mr Winterbourne continued, 'I want to thank everyone for their support. As custodian of the Winterbourne estate, I want to reassure everyone that it will be business as usual. At the beginning of this hearing, I was minded to be benevolent regarding my dearest half-sister. But I find myself torn between compassion and reality. Living in the lap of luxury all your life can't have been easy, while others lived in abject poverty. Watching people beneath you struggling to survive while you revelled in opulence and greed. I take on our father's wishes to relieve you of any burden, and I, therefore, give you... nothing.'

Charlotte wept uncontrollably, and Peter put his head into his hands. The court once again erupted.

'I will be lenient, though, allowing one full week to vacate the estate. Thank you.'

9

YOU'RE SAFE NOW

Charlotte rampaged through the house, knocking over ornaments and tearing paintings from the wall. 'I am not leaving, Peter. I am not leaving. This is my home. It's everything I've ever known. You can't just walk into someone's life after forty years and sling them out onto the street.'

Peter watched her run across the hall and out into the garden. Rooks noisily abandoned their roosts in the nearby trees as Charlotte screamed at the top of her voice.

'This is my home. Please, please, someone listen to me,' she shouted.

She ran into the walled garden and pulled the heads off flowers, kicked over pots and trampled on the array of garden produce and herbs.

She collapsed in a sorrowful heap against the wall and let the full, unrelenting sun hit her face. Her crying echoed within the walled garden and mixed with the raucous cawing of the rooks.

How could this have happened? All her worst nightmares had come true. Why hadn't her father had the courage to tell her about her brother? She could see that her father was trying to relieve her of the heavy burden the estate and fortune bestowed upon her, but why did he leave it to Henry's discretion? None of it made sense, but she knew they were his words deep down. As a child, she constantly craved his attention and sought approval. The rejection often taking her to the brink, and now, nothing short of the ultimate of ultimate rejections. His name and legacy were the only things important to him. She should have fought him then, created her own life free from his chauvinistic and egotistical world. If only she'd known.

Her thoughts continued to bombard her mind as she tried to look directly into the sun. Maybe burning her eyes out would be less painful than the reality before her? The sound of Peter's voice distracted her.

'Are you all right?' he said, kneeling beside her.

'No. Not at all. I feel betrayed. I feel totally and utterly humiliated and betrayed.'

'You still have your beauty,' he said, smiling.

His calm and reassuring voice made her look at him. He was amazing. Solid, grounded, dependable. Everything her father wasn't.

'What would I do without you, Peter? Despite everything we've been through, you have been at my side. I've treated you badly in the past, and you saw through that. I mistrusted you in the early days, and you showed me you cared. And now I have nothing, and you tell me I'm beautiful. It is you who is beautiful.'

Peter laughed. 'I'm just a working-class idiot who fell in love with an amazing woman. I see huge strength in you. I feel your love, too, and that helps me be strong.'

'You are my strength, Peter, but I can't understand why you love me.'

'Don't doubt yourself. You no longer have to seek approval from anyone, not me and especially your father. You've seen his true colours now. You are a very capable woman and one who deserves to be loved, simply because you have shown love yourself. With our hearts combined, we are an unstoppable team. We can do anything. I don't care if you're wealthy or not. In fact, I prefer it if you're not.'

'Now you *are* being an idiot.'

'Look. It means we can discover who we really are. Find our inner strength and build on that together. I promise you that everything will be okay. I will make it work for both of us, but I need you on side.'

Charlotte flung her arms around him. 'You are my rock, Peter. Please tell me I will be safe.'

'We can do this, Charlie. We have to look beyond the here and now and see what lies beyond. Let's show the world that we are here to stay and that nothing can phase us.'

Charlotte could do nothing but stare into his eyes. She didn't know how he could make such sense and be so optimistic in these dire circumstances.

At that point, Lucy came in through the gate. 'There you are,' she said, sobbing.

They huddled in a group. 'I've been sitting in my room in a daze. It's impossible to imagine this isn't our home anymore. It's made me wary of everyone like I won't be able to trust anyone again.'

Peter put his arm around her. 'There are unscrupulous people out there for sure, and it's good to have your guard up, but don't let it spoil your view of the majority of good people in this world.

Furthermore, if you let the bad people get to you, then they have won. Just like your mother, you are a capable young woman who knows the difference between good and bad. Tune in on the good people, surround yourself with them, and you'll be fine.'

Lucy dried her eyes on her sleeve. 'Thanks, Peter. I know you're right. I'm so sorry for all the hurt I caused when you came into our life. I hope none of this is my fault.'

Peter hugged her tight. 'You've done nothing wrong, Lucy. You have no bearing on what has happened. Your mother and I love you, and whatever you decide to do in life and wherever you decide to go, we will always be there for you. Isn't that right?' he said, turning his head to Charlotte.

'Of course,' Charlotte said. 'Peter is right. Have you decided if you're coming with us?'

Lucy paused. 'I've decided to move in with Daddy and see how it goes. I have a room there anyway, and it's in London, so I'm close to most of my friends.'

Peter nodded, and Charlotte smiled a reluctant smile. 'It's your choice, my darling. Is your father okay with that?'

'He's fine. I'm not so keen on his current girlfriend, but she doesn't live there. Anyway, I can always push her down the stairs.'

Peter rolled his eyes. 'Don't joke, Lucy.'

'Sorry. I'm older and wiser now. I wouldn't do that.'

Charlotte put her arms around both Lucy and Peter. 'What a mess. I blame myself entirely. I should have—'

Peter cut her short. 'Enough! It is what it is, and we live to fight another day. Lucy, you are welcome to stay with us at any time, and from now on, we will stop blaming ourselves or each other. Anyway, I can hear vehicles on the drive. It must be time.'

Two blacked-out Jeeps parked alongside the white storage

facility van. Charlotte eyed up the almost military-looking vehicles. They looked menacing, with oversized front grilles, beefed-up wheels, tyres, and blacked-out windows. The white van still had its back open, and the last few of her personal items were being loaded.

Lucy peered into the back. 'What are you taking?'

Charlotte took a deep breath. 'Just a few personal things I couldn't bear to leave behind. Paperwork, photographs and books mainly, and some of your things from when you were a baby. I'll put them in storage until we establish a new home.'

'I hope it will be nice there.'

Charlotte pursed her lips and shrugged. 'What about your things?'

'Daddy said he would be here any minute.'

Charlotte's face dropped. 'Fantastic! Why don't we invite everyone so we can have an absolutely humiliating send-off?'

Lucy flung her arms around Charlotte. 'He will just pick me up, and my things will be collected next week. It's been arranged.'

Charlotte shed a tear, and Lucy did too. 'I'm sorry it's come to this. Come visit us as soon as possible, won't you?'

'Of course I will, Mama. You could always come and live at Daddy's too. I think he'd have you back. He often speaks of it.'

Charlotte shivered. 'Make sure you take your jewellery and everything which is yours.'

'I will.'

Henry stepped out of one of the Jeeps, followed by two heavyweights with shaved heads and less-than-friendly faces.

'Not taking anything you shouldn't?' he said, raising a disbelieving eyebrow and casting a look into the van.

Charlotte said nothing, allowing Peter to intervene. The last thing she wanted was to speak with him.

Mrs Hathersage appeared as Henry and his men skulked away to peruse the exterior of the house with their hands in pockets and their eyes covered by gangster-like shades.

'My dear. I don't know what to say,' Mrs Hathersage said with a tear in her eye.

'Dear, dear Mrs Hathersage. I don't know what to say either. I hope he's good to you. I feel ashamed I never allowed you to retire early. I guess I needed you around too much.'

'I'm made of strong stuff, Miss Charlotte. I will stay here until I claim my pension. Then, as you know, I would like to be near my sister by the sea. I hold strong with that vision.'

They held each other tight, and Mrs Hathersage continued, 'I want to thank you for everything. I couldn't have been happier here, and it's been a joy seeing you grow into a fabulous lady and a true friend.'

Charlotte didn't hold back her tears. 'You are family, Mrs Hathersage. I will pay you back, I promise. I will work out a way to get you out of his clutches as soon as I possibly can.'

'I'll be okay. Just get yourself sorted in Yorkshire and let that fabulous man take care of you. You deserve each other. He's a good one. Don't let him go!'

'I know. I'm scared of what is to come, but without Peter, I don't know what I would do.'

'But there's a house, isn't there?'

'Yes. A contact of Peter's. I don't know what it's like. Peter just said it was adorable and rustic.'

'Then, it will be perfect,' she said, placing her hand on Charlotte's cheek. 'Take care, my love, take care.'

They parted but maintained contact with each other with both hands and then Charlotte whispered. 'Don't tell him about the secret passage. I'd like to keep at least one secret from him.'

Mrs Hathersage winked, squeezed Charlotte's hands, and, with an accompanying smile, disappeared up the stairs into the house.

Charlotte immediately looked over to see a silver Mercedes pull up, and down went the electric window. The smiling face of her ex was not what she wanted to see at her moment of weakness. She grit her teeth so hard her ears and eyes clamped shut too. She tightened her fist and tried to calm her rapid breathing.

A tight squeeze and a kiss on the cheek made her open her eyes. 'Love you, Mama,' Lucy said, then clambered into the car and, with a wave, she was gone.

Peter finished loading Charlotte's more personal items into the car and gestured to the passenger door.

'I can't do it, Peter!' Her rapid breathing took control of her body and her mind, and she started shaking. Her head at first, then quickly spread to her chest, back and arms. Her legs, in contrast, started to run. She ran away from the car and up the steps into the house. 'I can't do it, Peter. I can't do it!'

She closed the large solid oak door and backed away, tripping over her feet and trembling.

'This is my house,' she said to herself.

With her back and arms tight up against the wall, she felt herself spinning out of control. The walls began closing in on her. She was trapped, and she wanted to be. Unable to leave, she could stay forever. Locked in the hall, she needed nothing else other than to be in the house she loved.

The darkness became heavy as the walls closed in further, and the ceiling descended speedily towards her.

'This is my house, and this is where I belong,' she said, now crouching like a timid animal about to be slaughtered.

Suddenly, the stark, bright light of day came flooding in as the doors flung open. Charlotte just about made out the silhou-ettes of two giant people coming towards her. They picked her up by both arms until her feet were entirely off the floor.

'Put her down,' Peter said firmly. 'I said, put her down.'

Her eyes adjusted to the light and saw Peter in the doorway.

Henry's heavies lowered her feet to the ground, and Peter took her by the hand.

'It's going to be okay. It's going to be okay,' he said, leading her calmly to the car. The thud of the door, the only tangible thing she remembered until her daze was interrupted by inter-mittent, dazzling light hitting her face as they raced beneath the parkland trees and then out through the gate and beyond.

Peter placed his hand on her knee. 'You're safe now.'

10

WHITE ROSE

'The white rose of Yorkshire,' Peter said as he pointed to the large granite stone which held the bold white rose plaque depicting the border. He noted Charlotte's despondent face in the reflection of the window as she silently looked out into the wet, barren landscape. The car roof was securely closed, and the windscreen wipers were on red alert. The heather moors appeared bleak and inhospitable. The larger roads turned into narrower ones and, in turn, single tracks bordered by high and sometimes crumbling dry stone walls.

'Beautiful, isn't it?' Peter said, relishing being back on his home turf.

Charlotte took a moment to reply. 'It's barren, unwelcoming and scary. I wouldn't want to get lost out there. Reminds me of the Alps but with no snow, no charm, no cute wooden chalets with open fires and gluhwein, just sheep and rain. And stones.'

'That's the Yorkshire charm,' he said, trying to lift the spirit. 'You know that the dry-stone walls were all formed when the land was cleared of rocks to make the fields? They were here already, just scattered everywhere.'

Charlotte said nothing, just huddled her coat over her knees.

'It's been a shock. There's no doubt about it. Until the solicitor has found a way around this mess, we have to take each day at a time. The harsh reality is that we simply can't afford to live anywhere else. House rentals are cheaper up here. London is out of the question unless you want to live in a tenement with rats.'

'I don't understand, Peter. I don't understand not having any money. It's just always been there. In fact, I've never had to think about it. How could that evil man do this to us?'

'The appeal will be heard soon. We have to remain hopeful that new information turns up. Meanwhile, we're in survival mode. I've been here before. It's uncomfortable, but it's doable. I'm liaising with the solicitor now and want to rule out any wrongdoing, so put your faith in me. I won't let you down.'

Charlotte's face crumpled with disbelief. 'I don't think I can do this, Peter. I don't think I want to do this. Everything I had was in the estate. I have no personal savings or even a bank account. It was all wrapped up together. I can't believe I've been so foolish to not even give myself a backup plan.'

'Come on, Charlie. You're stronger than this. You didn't have a need to. Don't blame yourself.'

'Do we have anything?'

'I have a small amount of savings, this car, obviously. It was a good job you gifted it to me when you did. And you have your jewellery and whatever was in the van.'

'I'll never sell my jewellery, Peter. Don't ask me to do that.'

'We have enough to pay the rental deposit, and we should be okay for food etc. for a month or two, but that's it. I can find work here, I have contacts, and you'll have to get a job too.'

'I've never worked in my life, Peter. I can't see myself doing it now or ever. This is so dreadfully awful.'

Peter placed his hand on her knee. 'We'll get through this. We have shelter and transport, and I thought we agreed we were the best team?'

'Well, that's before I realised we have nothing.'

'Don't say that.'

'It's true.'

'After everything we've been through? I thought we had a pact?'

Charlotte squeezed his hand. 'I don't want you to think I'm ungrateful.'

Peter raised his eyebrows.

'I don't. I've learned so much from you, and yes, of course, I'm grateful for being alive. It's just... I have no skills to offer anyone. This whole thing has made me realise how useless I am.'

'You're a very capable woman.'

'Well, who's going to employ me? I've never worked a day in my life. I have no skills. I don't know anyone up here. I'm a liability.'

'Stop that. You're being ridiculous. Of course you have skills. You can read and write, you're extremely organised, and you have an artistic flair.'

· 'Artistic flair? I'm not an artist.'

'I'm thinking about interior design. Look at what you did with Loxley.'

Charlotte started to cry.

'Damn my father. Just when I thought I was rid of him and

everything was on an even keel, he springs this horrific surprise. I hate him, and I hope he's listening.'

'He's dead, Charlotte. He screwed some other lady, and you have a half-brother. Shit happens. It's hard to say, but we just have to deal with the now and not dwell on the past.'

'God, you're so matter-of-fact.'

'Someone has to be,' he said, raising his eyebrows. 'Anyway, I think we're here. Yes. This is it. Holm Cottage.'

The cottage looked old. Shrouded by overhanging trees, a black-and-white, half-timbered construction with a weathered oak porch, rambling and neglected roses over the front door, and a crooked moss-covered roof with missing tiles.

The sign hung from one screw in the corner.

'Holm Cottage? It doesn't resemble anything like a home to me,' she said, looking at the miserable state of the house.

Charlotte opened the car door and immediately stepped in a slurry of cow dung and mud. Her face curdled as her brilliant white trainers disappeared up to her ankles.

'I don't like it, Peter. I don't want to stay here.'

Peter walked around the car, lifted her over his shoulder and carried her to the front door.

'Come on, give it a chance. Let's look inside.'

The door creaked open, and the smell of damp instantly hit them.

'It's been empty for a while,' he said with a smile.

'It's creepy and cold,' Charlotte said, poking her nose into the sitting room and observing a moth-eaten sofa, torn curtains dangling from a broken pole and a 1930s dressing table covered in thick dust.

'The kitchen looks good. There's a wood stove and a range, and look... a dead pigeon. I wonder how that got in,' he said, holding the mummified bird by its leg.

Charlotte sighed.

'Oh, Peter. It's dreadful. It's infested with dead animals! And goodness knows what else.'

Charlotte stood rigid to the spot while Peter located some dry wood from a store in the garden and brought the wood stove to life. It coughed and spluttered at first, and after a plume of smoke filled the room, it eventually took hold and began to provide a little warmth and optimism.

'We'll soon have this place feeling like home,' he said, disappearing down the very dark and cobwebby cellar. 'Why don't you take a peek upstairs and check out the bedrooms?'

Charlotte inhaled the smoke. 'I'm not staying here. It's a health hazard. I hate it. Please don't make me stay here.'

'The owner said there was a boiler down here for the central heating. Let me know what you find upstairs.'

He seemed oblivious to her request, and she felt empty.

'Go on. Have a look upstairs.'

Charlotte reluctantly ascended the sparse, exposed wooden stairs and checked out the bathroom. The bare wooden floor was cold and rough. She'd left her trainers by the door, and her socks offered little protection. A very old roll-top bath appeared to have been re-enamelled, and a brown stain descended from the taps down and around the plug hole. She shuddered and then lifted the lid on the toilet. Retching uncontrollably, she observed the same brown staining within the bowl, and as she closed the seat, it came off in her hand.

'Peter. We are not staying here. It's disgusting, it's a health hazard, and I can't believe you've brought me to such a foul place. Peter!'

He didn't hear. He was in the cellar trying to bring the antique boiler to life, with little success.

. . .

Charlotte rushed downstairs. 'Peter,' she shouted. 'Did you hear me?'

'I'm in the cellar.'

Charlotte, not daring to put her hands on anything, came close to the top of the stairs. A cobweb grabbed her face, and she flapped her hands around, trying to remove it.

'Peter. I want to leave right now. I hate it here.'

Suddenly he appeared, holding a hammer.

'I think that did the trick. Just needed a little practical encouragement. How was it upstairs?'

'I want to leave, Peter. It's disgusting, vile and a health hazard. The toilet and bath are horrific, with god knows what. And the place feels haunted. Please take me home.'

Peter laughed. 'This is home.'

Charlotte started to break down, her arms shaking and an overwhelming feeling of despair making her skin crawl. She knew she would vomit if she coughed one more time with the stench of damp. 'It's not a laughing matter, Peter. I'm serious, and I'm scared.'

Peter put his arm around her.

'I know it's tough. But you have to trust me. The brown staining will be the high mineral water. It's limestone county here. All it needs is some Ajax and some elbow grease. With some heat, we can sort out the damp.'

'How come you are so bloody optimistic? It's a hellhole!'

'We have little choice, Charlotte. The truth is, it's shelter. We're starting from scratch here. I know it's not a palatial country estate, but with a little bit of vision, and some solid grafting, this place can be our home.'

'I need to feel safe, and I don't. It's creepy here, and I'm definitely not sleeping in that old bed. Someone probably died in there.'

'Don't worry, I took the liberty of ordering a new one. It arrives tomorrow. We'll have to go into the village and get bedding, though.'

'I noticed the rain was coming through the edge of the window too, and the woodwork was rotting, with things crawling out of it.'

'Is there a plague of locusts in the wardrobe and anthrax in the spare bedroom too?'

Charlotte hit him repeatedly with her fists.

'Peter. I'm not in the mood for your jokes, and I can't see that some new bedding will make this feel any more like home.'

'I love you,' he said, kissing her on the cheek. 'Trust me, I'll make everything okay.'

Charlotte smiled a hint of a smile. Not a full one, but a hint nevertheless, and Peter saw it.

'Let's head into the village and get some supplies and bedding. I spotted a hardware shop and a fish and chip shop, so that's tea sorted.'

'You mean dinner?'

'Oh, you might stay then? And you have a lot to learn,' he said, laughing. 'Dinner up here is at dinner time. Remember at school, dinner time wasn't in the evening?'

'We had Sisters lunch. It was a convent and supper in the evening. Dinner was at home with family in the warm and safe drawing room.'

'Well, either way, the fish and chips are the best you'll ever have in Yorkshire. Fresh fish from Whitby and proper chips cooked in dripping.'

'So, there's no sushi then?' She asked, pushing her tongue into her cheek.

Peter looked at her.

'That's better. We can do this. Come on, let's explore the village.'

~

'That toilet has come up a treat. I told you a bit of effort would do the trick. How's your fish and chips?'

Charlotte licked her fingers. 'Lovely, actually. You were right, they are the best fish and chips, and you say it's tradition here to eat it with your fingers?'

'Absolutely, or a little wooden fork. They have them on the counter, so if you're on the run or just fancy eating them in the park, you can.'

'Things get stranger and stranger here. You'll be telling me next that instead of racing horses, they race pigeons.'

She pointed to the dead bird, still residing in the kitchen sink. Peter choked on his fish.

'Well... funny you should say that!'

'We'll sleep down here tonight by the fire. The blankets we bought earlier should be good for one night, and hopefully the new bed will be here tomorrow.'

'I hope so.'

'There's something I've been meaning to tell you.'

'What now? Don't frighten me even more, Peter.'

'I didn't know when the time was right. I contacted Chris. Remember my old mate in London? Well, he has a friend in the serious crime squad.'

'What? And you've reported this place for gross indecency?'

'No... Ever since your brother—'

She cut him off. 'Half-brother!'

'Sorry, half-brother... came marching in, I couldn't help but think about what you said about him neither looking nor behaving like you or your father. I know he has a mother, and her genes may be highly prevalent, but he seemed scrawny and unhealthy. You agreed. None of your family was poor-looking from the portraits I saw. The interesting thing, though, was his accent kept slipping. You can't cover up that Essex twang forever, and I'm pretty sure he didn't get that in Hong Kong.'

Charlotte listened intently. 'Of course I noticed. I thought it was just his quirky way.'

'There's more. During the handover, I overheard him on the phone with someone, and I didn't get all of it, but he said something like: *They didn't get a whiff, and if they don't, this will be the greatest coup of all time.* Then he turned his back, and I wasn't able to hear anymore.'

'What does this mean?'

'Well, I'm not entirely sure. Something doesn't sit right with me. The accent, the fact that he wasn't benevolent to you, and the heavy mob in tow. It all seems... odd.'

'Do you think we should go to the police?'

'Well, Chris's mate says we would have to prove a crime has been committed. I think we should see what happens at the appeal. If Mr Scrivener doesn't pull anything out of the hat, which we hope he sincerely does, I think we should. In the meantime, he suggested we send him a photograph of Henry for them to run through their system.'

'What good will that do?'

'They can see if he shows up on any of their records. It's worth a try.'

'I do hope Mr Scrivener manages to turn things around, but what additional evidence is there?' She paused. 'And there's something in the wording of the letter of wishes which makes me believe it was written by my father. His ego was larger than him. It was always all about him! I don't think anyone else would have written like that.'

'Don't you want to get everything back?' Peter said, raising his voice.

'Of course I do. You think I want to be here, living in these conditions?'

'Okay. Well, don't rule anything out at this stage, and I'll do a little more digging.'

Charlotte nodded. 'Okay, do whatever you think is right.'

11

USELESS

Peter stacked wood on the stove and then clambered back underneath the blankets. Charlotte cuddled tight against him and pushed her cold nose against his neck.

'I thought about what you said yesterday, but I can't see a way forward, Peter. I feel empty, like we've been raped of everything we had, and now we have nothing.'

She started to shake and put her cold feet onto his.

'We're in a desert. A lonely, bleak desert with no idea how to get out. This house is creepy. I didn't sleep a wink, with all the moaning and groaning from the cellar and then the noises outside. And the damp is bad. I can feel it on my chest already. We're going to be ill. Thank God Lucy can stay with her father. Her chest would not cope at all. I feel like we might as well just die here, like forgotten squatters, sleeping rough on the floor and turning to drugs because there's no way out. How could we be so naïve to think we were safe from gangsters like him? I should have seen it coming, and I should have trusted no one. You let your guard down, and then, bam, you've lost everything. I feel afraid, Peter. I'm scared. What do we have to live for?'

Peter squeezed her tight. 'Everything. That's what we have to live for. Our dignity, our pride and our future together. With all due respect, you need to get a grip, Charlotte, and show some steel here.'

'Steel? Show some steel? It's okay for you. You came from nothing. You can rough it on the floor with the spiders and the bugs, but I'm better than that.'

She began to sob.

'You are no better than me, let me tell you. When you've roughed it like I have, not knowing when you'll eat again and without someone else's warm body to comfort you, you'll soon see how important the simple things in life are.'

Charlotte continued to sob. 'I see. Now I understand exactly how you feel about me.'

Peter took her wrist in his grip. 'You know damn well how I feel about you. But someone has to say it as it is. The time has come for you to realise life is not a bed of roses. It's tough for most people. We have a roof over our heads here because I know people who are prepared to give us a chance. Some people are on the streets right now. We have everything to fight for. You have to pick yourself up, stop feeling sorry for yourself and don't be such a princess.'

'How dare you speak to me like that? I should have known better than getting involved with a man like you.'

'What do you mean, a man like me?'

'From the gutter. I knew you would bring me down to your level.'

Peter took a couple of deep breaths and maintained a grip on her arm. 'You don't mean that. You're angry, and you're scared. I can see that. I'm sorry. I over reacted. I'm stressed about this too. Just take a minute and realise that you are a very capable woman. You've had setbacks before.'

'Yes! And I didn't handle them well.'

'I think you've learned a great deal about yourself. Resilience, strength of character, determination. You have all those things; you just haven't told yourself. Look, it's at times like this, you dig deep into your soul. Forget about how you've been conditioned and find the true Charlie. You always wanted to be free of all the responsibility, well you are now. The only person you are responsible for now is yourself.'

'What about Lucy?'

'She's a woman in her own right now. She's dealing with her own self. Dig deep and find your true spirit, Charlotte. I know it's in there. I know you can do this. I have faith in you.'

Charlotte began to relent. 'You always seem to know what to do.'

'We're in this together. You don't have to fight me. I'm not the enemy. The bottom line is... I love you, and as far as I'm concerned, we are a team. There is a way out. No one says it will be easy, but there is light at the end of the tunnel. You just have to open your eyes and believe in yourself.'

Charlotte huddled herself into his arms. 'I can't see it, Peter. It's easy for you to say, but I can't see it. You're stronger than I am. All this talk about having to get a job and surviving in this god forsaken hovel is scaring me.'

He squeezed her tight to his body. 'Well, often when there seems little hope, that's the best starting point. You know you don't want to die. You tested that theory. So the only way is up. It might be a ladder you can't see the top of, but the climb starts on the bottom rung, and you take it a step at a time.'

'I don't know. You make it sound so simple.'

'That's because it is. What's complicated about putting one

foot in front of the other? You have to put your anger aside and think positively. Anyway, as I said, I already have the wheels in motion to try to establish the truth. It may lead nowhere, but there is hope. In terms of getting a job, it's a harsh reality. We need money coming in, and we both have to do that.'

'But what can I do, Peter? I'm useless.'

'There'll be something. It doesn't matter how small or insignificant a job. We just have to pay the bills.'

12

HERMIT AND THE DEVIL

Charlotte wandered aimlessly around the house. Peter was in the garden, and she took the time to contemplate everything he had said, but her mind conflicted with her heart. She trusted him and knew what he was saying was practical and probably true, but she felt helpless and overwhelmed by the sudden pressures to survive.

The new bed had been delivered, albeit a couple of days late, but Charlotte saw it was a lovely gesture from Peter and ventured slowly up the wooden stairs. A wood splinter gouged its way into the sole of her foot. The pain shot straight to her head, and then blood dripped onto the floor. She sat on the step in disbelief and pulled at the protruding splinter. It was as if everything she did had to be painful.

'Are you all right?' Peter shouted from the kitchen as she heard him deposit a load of logs for the stove.

'Yes. I'm fine,' she replied.

She remembered what he had said about feeling sorry for herself. He was right. She was wallowing in self pity. Somehow it made him feel even less in control, making it easy to blame everyone else.

She let the blood clot, found some socks among her boxes and boxes of clothes and shoes, and stood watching Peter through the window, chopping logs in the undercover yard area. His back and shoulders were strong, and he looked capable with the axe. She smiled and let her eye wander across the garden and out across the fields. It was dismal out there, inhospitable and wild. Alien territory and somewhere she was happy not to explore. The mass of holly and ash trees which overhung the house was foreboding. It was almost dark at the front of the house, even when the sun was shining, and the trees adjacent to the house formed what seemed like an impenetrable forest. She couldn't see where the landscape ended. She was used to the parameters of the estate and felt uneasy that something may never end.

Taking the new bed linen, she began making up the bed. She'd gone for classic white cotton with an embroidered flower in blue. She smiled as it started to resemble a proper bed. Somewhere comfortable and safe.

Downstairs, she made coffee and shouted to Peter.

He came in, deposited more logs and sat on the chair with his legs wide open and sweating like a true lumberjack.

'I contacted Mrs Hathersage, and she said she will try to take a photo of him.'

'How on earth will she do that?'

'Some excuse, that she wants all the staff to be able to recognise him and that some of the grounds staff might not meet him in person. A reference to their new leader if you like. Does that sound plausible?'

'Not really! But if anyone can do it, Mrs Hathersage can.'

'She's amazing. I feel guilty that she and the staff will have to work for that tyrant. I should have given her early retirement, and she would be clear of all this.'

'Well, she's in on it now and our best insider. She said she would stick it out for the time being and then hopefully leave and move in with her sister if she's fit enough. The sister, I mean. By the way, I've managed to get some survey work with a local consultant. I start next week.'

'Well done, Peter, you're incredibly resourceful.'

'Dare I ask how your job hunting is going?'

Charlotte's eyes skulked along the floor. 'I'm counting on Mrs Hathersage rumbling the imposter and going back to Loxley. I'm sorry. I did have an appointment this afternoon at the careers office, but I'll hang fire.'

'You most certainly won't. At this moment, we have no shred of evidence, and Loxley should not be in your thoughts. Come on, Charlotte, we've been through this.'

Charlotte's glum face made him frown. 'I'm not coping very well. My chest doesn't like the damp. I don't know anyone around here, and this house... Well, this house just doesn't feel like home.'

'Don't miss your appointment. We need the money coming in. Pull yourself together. I have complete faith in you.'

'I can't go there, Peter. I have nothing to offer anyone. I've never been in a careers office. They'll want to know answers I can't give them.'

'Like what?'

'Like what have you been doing the last forty years, and how's your computer literacy? I'm not going, and that's final.'

Peter brought his face close to hers and spoke softly, 'Look. I'm doing my damnedest to make this life for us as good as it possibly can be, and not only that, I will endeavour to get back what is rightfully yours. But in the meantime, I need you to find that steel we talked about, realise what a capable woman you are, stop being so defeatist and get yourself up to the office and start bringing in some money so we can at least eat.'

～

The walk up the lane into the village was steep, to begin with, then levelled out through the beech copse, then followed by a rolling descent passed the Norman church and then finally the junction to either the village or the next valley.

Charlotte's nerves eased slightly as she listened to the church bells. The campanologists often practised in the week, and today was no exception as the bells rang out a resonating medley. Charlotte could see the vicar by the gate, obvious by his black suit and white dog collar. His grey hair, in contrast, made him look distinguished.

'Hello,' Charlotte said.

'Hello,' he replied. 'I haven't seen you before. Are you staying locally?'

'Yes, we've just moved into Holm Cottage,' she said, pointing back along the tree-lined lane.

'Ah, yes. I know. That's a beautiful little cottage and one with a long history.'

'Really?'

'Holm is old English for Holly. It's reported that there was a dwelling on that spot going back millennia. Well before this church was built, certainly, and a hermit lived there. A hermit with special powers.'

'Go on.'

'They say that the hermit confronted the Devil, and the Devil threw a boulder as big as the earth down onto the dwelling and that the hermit, in her belief for good and kindness, defended herself with a stout holly branch she grabbed from the closest tree and smashed the boulder into a billion pieces, and in doing so, banished the Devil forever. That's why there are stones everywhere.'

'Gosh! Yes, I noticed there are a lot of stones. Who was she?'

'No one really knows. She bore the brunt of the rock with her bare hands and carried the scars forever. They do say that whoever enters and stays in the house will be free from evil and find eternal happiness.'

Charlotte lowered her head. 'I doubt that will be me. The place is virtually falling apart and a health hazard.'

The vicar nodded and put his hands together to pray for her.

'What are you doing here?' she said, looking at a huge board with a thermometer drawn on it.

'It's our save the roof thermometer. We are in desperate need of fixing the leaking roof, so we are fundraising. I'm grateful to announce that the Mountjoys have donated the first thousand pounds, and I'm colouring the thermometer in red to show it.'

Charlotte watched the vicar paint a big red splodge in the bowl at the bottom of the chart.

'Who are the Mountjoys?' Charlotte asked.

The vicar gestured with his eyes to the stately manor house up on the hill. 'They're wealthy. I guess a thousand pounds is small beer for them, but the parish is extremely grateful. Lady Mountjoy supports the Sunday school too, when she can. God bless her.'

'I'd like to meet her sometime.'

'We've a long way to go, and any help is greatly appreciated,' he said once again, bringing his hands together in front of him.

'I have only a few pounds if that helps?'

'We value every penny...' The vicar waited for her to introduce herself.

'Oh, yes, I'm Charlotte. Pleased to meet you.'

'May God be with you, Charlotte. May God be with you.'

Charlotte turned up into the village and noted every house was made of stone and every house had something unique about it. One had the old stone milk table outside, where the milk churns would have stood ready for collection. One had a huge timber cheese press in the garden, and one had wheelbarrows planted with geraniums and many more, with wicker and willow sculptures, baskets of flowers or other simple, rustic items made from local materials. The village had history and a lived-in look, she thought.

The careers advice centre was in a part of the library and civic centre, and as Charlotte walked through the door, she narrowly avoided bumping into a very old lady with a handful of books heading for the exit. She was almost bent double. Her back, bent and twisted, and a hump was visible within her blue knitted cardigan. Charlotte held the door open for her and took a closer look at her face. Her nose was gnarly with warts, her chin hairy with grey and black sporadic tufts, her teeth brown and crooked with some missing, but her eyes were bright. Observant and keen, like an owl, and they were black, jet black. She huddled awkwardly to the door while maintaining direct eye contact with Charlotte.

'Hello, do you need help with those books?' Charlotte asked.

The lady didn't answer, but as she continued through the door and out onto the pavement, her eyes never left Charlotte's.

88

'You must be Charlotte,' a voice from inside broke Charlotte's deadlock with the old woman.

She turned. 'Yes, hello.'

'I'm Mrs Cox, but you can call me Sara.' They shook hands, and Charlotte looked back at the door to see the old lady had gone.

'Please take a seat. So, you're new in the village? Where have you moved from?'

'I moved up with my partner, Peter, from Oxfordshire. He's a Yorkshireman originally, so he's had his way,' she said jovially.

'He'll be a good man, I'm sure of that, but don't tell anyone about our secret.'

'What secret?'

'Our village. Despite the weather, one or two hoity-toity residents and the hard graft that keeps us going, we are a community, and although some might wear their smiles close to the ground, we are all pretty friendly.'

'I'm beginning to notice.'

Sara shuffled through some papers and then asked Charlotte for details to get her on the system.

'So, what kind of work are you looking for?'

Charlotte squirmed in her seat.

'To be honest, Sara. I'm not entirely sure. I didn't work when I was bringing up my daughter, so I'm not so up to date with many new skills.' She didn't want to be completely honest.

'Hmm, okay. What sort of work have you done before?'

The harsh reality that she'd never done a day's work shocked even herself. She'd never been confronted on the issue before and felt somewhat ashamed.

'I've done a bit of charity work and some public speaking, I know my way around an art gallery, and I'm a dab hand at organising dinner parties.'

Sara's surprised face buried itself with the paperwork. 'Hmm, I'm wondering exactly where those skills might be best deployed in a remote Yorkshire sheep-farming village.'

Charlotte laughed. More out of embarrassment than anything else.

'I have opportunities in a supermarket in Harrogate, but that might be too far for you. I have a part-time vacancy waiting tables at Marco Braithwaite's new Italian. There's a mobile sheep shearer's position locally.'

Charlotte smiled politely. 'Is there anything admin related? As I said, I'm quite organised, and I'm good on the telephone.'

'I do believe Mr Frogatt, the veterinary, is looking for help in the office. How are you with animals?'

'I love animals.'

'Okay. I'll get some information to him and see what he says. Are you available for interviews?'

'Yes, of course, but please tell him I'm a little out of practice, and if they use computers, I might need some coaching.'

The vicar was nowhere to be seen on her walk back to the house, but the dappled rays of sun through the beech copse canopy highlighted the top of ant hills dotted within the bare ground beneath.

The sun made the stone roof of the house steam as the heavy rain evaporated into the blue sky.

13

HELPLESS

The wolf howled incessantly. It was close. So close she could hear it scratching at the door in a relentless attempt to gain access to the house. Another door repeatedly slammed, then a moment of respite, before... bang... bang... it started again. Charlotte pulled the duvet up close around her neck and watched the shadows moving aggressively outside the window.

'Are you okay?' Peter asked, cuddling her up with his arm. 'You're fidgeting.'

She didn't move, although her mind reacted to everything around her. 'You didn't tell me there were wolves in Yorkshire? Are they big?'

Peter said nothing.

'Can it get in through the door that keeps opening? Will it just eat the food in the kitchen? I left bread and olives out.' She paused. 'Or will it come up here?'

Peter said nothing.

'I'm scared, Peter. And I'm cold. Will you go and check that we're safe?'

Peter groaned and spooned up to her. 'It's the wind.'

'It's a wolf, Peter. I can hear it scratching.'

'Trees on the roof, probably,' he groaned. 'And wind over the wood stove chimney.'

Charlotte remained rigid, but her eyes maintained direct contact with the shadows as they cast disturbing shadows in the moonlight.

'Will you go and check, though?'

'It's the wind, Charlie. If a wolf devours the bread and olives and then decides to come for us, I'll grab it by the throat and break its neck.'

'Peter! You don't have to be so brutal.'

Peter chuckled. 'Would you rather me tickle it under the chin and befriend it?'

'Why do you always turn everything into a joke? I'm actually scared.'

Peter moved his hand to her breast and nuzzled her ear. 'I'm good with wolves,' he said, licking her lobe and growling.

Charlotte removed his hand and huffed. 'Not now, Peter. I don't like it here. I can't stay another night. I don't feel safe, and you're doing nothing to change my mind.'

A cold water droplet hit Peter with a splat on his cheek. 'Goddamn it!' he shouted as he sat directly up and wiped off the droplet. 'That's the one thing I can't abide. I had enough of that in the London flat.'

'So you're with me now, then?'

Peter shook his head. 'I'll get up on the roof and fix it. I'm not letting that fester.'

'Can we just move somewhere different?'

Charlotte huddled by the back door as she watched Peter apply a drop of oil to the gate hinges and latch. 'That should stop the wolves scoffing our olives,' he said with a smile.

He then positioned the ladder over his shoulder and gesticulated, nodding to a bucket on the ground. Charlotte picked it up and examined its contents.

A reel of thick string. A trowel and the bottom, thick with mortar. It was heavy, and she struggled to follow him to the front of the house.

As she turned the corner, Peter had already erected the ladder and was stacking stone tiles against the wall.

'Right! I'm going up,' he said confidently, scanning the apex. 'Just stand on the bottom rung as I climb, and then once I'm on the roof, I'll pull up the bucket.'

Charlotte stared at him. 'Can I just ask one thing?'

Peter tightened his jeans belt and tested the ladder by shaking it and stamping his foot on the rung.

'Why are we doing this? Can't we move somewhere dry and warm? I don't like the thought of you high up on the roof.'

Peter put both his hands on her shoulders and looked her in the eye. 'We're not going to be defeated, Charlie. We are here, and we're going to make this home. I know it's tough for you, but I'm asking you again to pull yourself together. I need you on my side here. If I fall, call an ambulance. If I stay up there, I'll pass the bucket back down, and you load up the first tile. Okay?'

'Promise me, you won't fall off.'

'That's not the plan. It should be easy to fix. It's just the moss I'm concerned about. Might be slippery.'

'Why is everything so much hard work?'

Peter gripped her shoulders once again. 'Once it's done, it's done. With the roof fixed, we can make it drier and warmer.

You never know, you might even feel like you've achieved something.'

'I doubt that,' she said, scowling into the bucket.

Peter scaled the ladder, and Charlotte stood firm on the bottom rung. She watched nervously as he traversed the moss and then grabbed hold of the ridge.

Suddenly, the bucket began to ascend. She watched it get stuck on the guttering and then skid along, before it continued onto the roof to various grunts and groans from Peter.

'Now the tile,' he shouted as the bucket came back into view.

'Can I leave the ladder?'

'Of course. Just load a tile and lift it as high as you can to give it a head start.'

Charlotte gritted her teeth and mustered all her strength to load the tile into the bucket. It was solid stone and thick. She had never contemplated the size or weight of a roof tile. But bizarrely, she found herself being interested. She held the bucket as high as she could, and as the bucket left her hands, she examined the rest of the roof and how intricately the tiles were positioned. Overlapping each other and staggered.

'You okay?' Peter shouted.

'Erm... I'm having a little moment!'

'Well, don't go fainting or disappearing for coffee.'

'I'm finding myself admiring a roof. I think I'm having a turn.'

What a strange feeling. She'd never contemplated what was involved in a roof. They were just roofs. Nothing exciting about a roof, but somehow, the two of them physically handling the stone and working as a team filled her with a sense of pride and downright bewilderment. This wasn't something she would mention to the girls, that's for sure.

'Let me know when you need the next tile,' she shouted.

Peter was perched just below the ridge. She watched his hair blowing in the wind and then felt a wave of something very strange as he smiled a huge smile.

Down came the bucket, and she spared no time grappling with the next tile and holding it up with enthusiasm, ready for him to take the load.

She thought those roses could do with a good prune back as her eyes wandered to the front aspect of the house and the sun, just beginning to highlight the front porch. She noticed a bunch of teasel heads and holly within the pile of leaves by the front door. On closer inspection, it appeared to be an old Christmas wreath. Some previous inhabitant had obviously displayed the wreath upon the door, and then it had been dislodged and forgotten about in the leaf litter and debris. She propped it up against the window and set about shaking out the doormat.

'Are you on the ladder?'

'No! Give me a second.'

Charlotte dashed to take her position on the bottom rung and watched Peter slide down the roof and then turn to find the top rung with his foot.

He arrived at the bottom and, without any warning, kissed her passionately on the lips. It left her stunned. Frozen to the spot in a heady daze of... well... a heady daze.

He hoicked up his jeans and loaded the ladder again onto his shoulder.

'Let's have a cuppa and then go explore down the fields,' he said with a spring in his step.

Charlotte followed, bucket in hand and wondering if they had any secateurs.

~

Charlotte sat on the back step while Peter rooted around in the ramshackle wooden shed. She warmed her hands on the tea mug and looked out across the garden and into the view. The house was almost surrounded by dense, dark-green holly trees. Tall ash, which towered over other smaller trees and bushes with catkins. Her eye was drawn down into the garden. Beneath an oak and a beech tree, a little dilapidated gate hung precariously on what resembled a thick boot lace instead of a hinge. A narrow path within the long grass wend its way out of sight into what appeared to be a valley below.

Peter placed some rusty secateurs in her hand. 'Best I can do. Drop of oil, might make a difference. Shall we go and explore down there?' He pointed along the narrow path. 'A wolf track, by the look of it.'

Charlotte looked at him. 'You're joking? Is that where it lives?'

Peter laughed. 'Fox, probably, or even deer, something uses this route. Come on, let's find out.'

Charlotte hesitated. 'I'm not so sure I want to. It looks private. There's no official path or sign to anywhere?'

Peter sat beside her. 'When did that ever put you off? What happened to Charlie, the intrepid explorer? You used to jump weirs and climb trees. A rebel, you once called yourself, I seem to remember.'

Charlotte's eyes drifted to the floor, and she pondered a moment. 'I don't know, Peter. I guess that was all my home turf. I'd grown up there. This is new, alien. I don't know what lies beyond, and I'm scared to find out. Maybe I've lost a bit of my rebellious streak following... you know, my accident.' Peter put his arm around her. 'Some might say that was the ultimate rebellion. Anyway, I can still see it in you. It's one of the things I love about you. It's in there. Your steel. I can see it shining deep in there.'

'Well, you have more faith in me than I have in myself.'

'You're an amazing woman. Don't put yourself down. I'm telling you, you're incredible.'

14

FOREVER

The smell of her man and the sun beginning to warm the room were perfect conditions for a cuddle. Charlotte spooned herself tight up against Peter's naked body. His arm around her had given protection all night, and Charlotte revelled in his masculine strength. She pushed her bottom into his groin in the hope he may wake. The stormy conditions from the previous day had now relented, and she felt easier in the house. No more banging doors, dripping water or wolves. Not that night, at least.

She felt him twitch, and he pushed back gently. His other arm came around her, so she was completely wrapped within him.

A wave of excitement filled her, as his hand touched her breast. His other hand moved down her thigh, and she could feel his practical hands on her soft skin and, in her mind, a filthy combination of her vulnerability and his masculine intention. She pushed her bottom up against him again and felt him beginning to stiffen.

His hand moved from her thigh across her waist, which

always made her tingle. He kissed her neck and whispered, 'I want you.'

He somehow instinctively knew exactly which buttons to press, and she could feel herself getting ready for him. His hand moved down her thigh and tugged gently for her to lift her knee, and as she did, his erection seamlessly moved into position. She touched him and rubbed it against herself. Knowing he would love it but secretly relishing the thought herself, she orchestrated his tip, so it nudged her clit, and moved her hips as he repeated the nudging.

His arm, which was doing the protecting, moved in across her chest and began toying with her nipple. The combination of nipple and clit together was ecstatic for her. His breath on her neck and his attention to detail filled her with a rising tide of pleasure and emotion. She already knew the result but held it at bay as the intensity built. The wave of a deep desire for him and the pangs of sheer pleasure sent her head spinning, her feelings were deep, and without compromise, and then, just when she thought it couldn't get any better, he kissed her neck again and whispered,

'You are the most beautiful woman.'

The molten lava which had been building and building reached its peak. He pushed himself inside her, not hesitating, just blatant and deep. One hand stroking across the top of her nipple and the other now fully in charge of the button below. She could feel him inside her, his body, hands and kisses doing all the work, and she let it all happen, knowing she was about to erupt.

'You feel amazing,' he said as he quickened his pace. 'You feel amazing' was the release. 'You feel amazing' was the golden ticket, and she listened to it deep within her heart as the heat rose across her shoulders, up her neck and into her brain. An explosion of desire, trust, love, and submission to his carnal desire made her scream, and the passion inside her consumed every thought, every feeling and every emotion. Then, to top it all, the feeling of him thrusting and writhing in sheer pleasure inside her gave a flourish which she had never felt before. Like liquid chocolate running through her veins.

Charlotte craved to be in his arms forever; warm, safe, desired and loved.

'I love you, Charlie. Will you be mine forever?' he asked, releasing her from his grip and reaching over to the window. She watched him put his finger on the glass and draw a love heart in the condensation, which then let a small ray of sunlight onto Charlotte's face.

'I will be yours forever. You have my word.'

～

Charlotte's phone buzzed.

'I have news,' she said as her face went pale.

'I have news too, but go on,' Peter said.

'Well, I might be getting an interview.'

'Wow, I'm impressed. I said you could do it. What's the job?'

'Assisting at the veterinary office. Answering the phone, making bookings, that kind of thing.'

'You're amazing, you know that. I'm so proud of you. It took guts to follow that through.'

'Well, I haven't got the job yet, so we'll see. What's your news?'

. . .

'Well. Mrs Hathersage came up trumps, but the photo came back as unknown within the police system. It just means he hasn't shown up on their system before. There is some other news.'

'What is it?'

'A source in Hong Kong suggests that a child could have been born by that name, but it's unclear what happened because there are no further records. Chris' mate says that the police will only be interested if we can provide proof there has been a crime committed. The only way we can do that is to find out exactly who this man is.'

'So, he is an imposter?'

'Don't get your hopes up. We can't be sure.' Peter looked her straight in the eye. 'It does mean that I'm heading to Hong Kong next week to meet the contact and see if we can find the birth and/or death records. It's our only chance.'

'Hong Kong? No, Peter. I need you here. You're supposed to be starting work. I don't want you to leave me.'

'Look, we have one chance of getting to the bottom of this and putting you back where you belong. I'll only be gone one week. I sold my mother's jewellery, so the next month's rent, food and heating are all covered, and my flights, too, so even if you don't get your job, we'll be okay. We have to take the risk.'

'I'm coming with you.'

'You have to be here for the appeal.'

'Appeal. After hearing that, how can we appeal if we don't know if there has been any criminal activity? I don't like it, Peter. You're messing with people we know nothing about. Can we just let the police deal with it?'

'As I said, our man on the inside says their hands are tied without hard evidence. The best thing to do is stall for time, and hopefully, I return with fruitful news.'

'One week?'

'One week, I promise.'

Peter sighed. 'You have to be strong. I'm feeling confident that we can get everything back for you. There has to be a chink in this man's armour, and I'm determined to find it. I know it's not easy for you here. Just have survival in your mind. It's short term, and as hard as it might be, try to see the light at the end of the tunnel. Maybe ask Lucy to come and stay. Or what about Sam or Jojo?'

'They have offered me a room, but Jojo's ill mother is staying with her, and Sam is away travelling.'

'What about Mira?'

'I dropped her a line to tell her the news, but I haven't heard from her.'

'Well, at the end of the day, it's better to keep the house warm and lived in if we are going to banish the damp.'

'The place is a hellhole, Peter. I'm not happy. No sooner have we arrived, and you're jetting off and leaving me.'

Peter kissed her on the forehead. 'I have complete faith in you, Charlie. I know we can get through this together.'

Peter decided to travel light. He loaded the rucksack into the car and double-checked his passport.

'Just two more minutes,' Charlotte shouted as Peter waited impatiently.

Her procrastination was almost intentional. She didn't want him to go to Hong Kong; the house was still creepy, and she was dreading her interview at the vet's.

'Come on, I'll miss my flight, and if you want a lift to the village, we need to leave now.'

'Okay, okay. A girl has to look presentable for her first interview ever.'

Charlotte appeared at the door in a pencil skirt, white blouse, and her hair tied up.

'Sexy secretary is definitely one we're going to explore on my return,' he said, eying her up and down.

'You're such a naughty boy,' she said, adjusting her hair and feeling more confident at his comment.

Moments later, as they passed the church, doubt began to infiltrate her feelings.

'I'm not capable of being a real secretary, though. What if I don't get the job?'

'You will. As I said, I have every faith in you; just be yourself and ham up your secretarial skills somewhat,' he said with a wink.

'Oh, Peter. I don't think I can go through with this. I'm scared.'

Peter stopped the car. 'You are an incredible woman. This is new for you, but I know how resilient you are, how reliable you are and what a great communicator you are. That's what they'll be looking for. Whatever skills you don't have, we can learn those when I get back. You can do this. Okay?'

Charlotte nodded. 'Okay, thanks, Peter. I feel good when you're here. Let me know when you arrive, and phone me when you're settled.'

'I will,' he said, starting the car. 'I'm with you every step of the way. I know it will be tough in the house on your own, but hang on in there, and hopefully, I'll be back with good news.'

Charlotte watched the car disappear along the high street, waving and blowing kisses. Then, with sadness and trepidation in her heart, she turned and headed up the road.

15

RESUSCITATING A BADGER!

If it were possible to wear a groove in a solid York stone floor, then Charlotte gave it her best effort. She hadn't heard from Peter, and she hadn't heard from the vet. It had only been an hour since her interview, but it was an hour too long.

It seemed strange not having Peter around, and although she could still smell him on her, and his socks and shoes were still dumped on the floor, there was an emptiness in the house. Her anxiety was building. Not only was she pacing, but she was also fiddling with her hair, wrapping it around her finger into knots and letting the pain take away some of the lonely agonies. Charlotte broke off from her pacing to clean the cupboards. Cleaning cupboards was something she did when she was really agitated. As a girl, she would clean her room or re-organise it. It busied her mind. She rubbed and scrubbed, made coffee and then paced some more. The wait was agonising. She knew she wouldn't hear from Peter until much later, but it didn't stop her from checking her phone every few minutes.

It was only when she decided to go full-hearted on cleaning out the cupboard under the sink that she heard her phone.

'Charlotte?'

'Yes.'

'It's Mr Frogatt here. I just wanted to say thank you for attending the interview this morning. It was a pleasure meeting you. To be honest, we thought your CV was a little light in places, and a working knowledge of spreadsheets is essential. We would also prefer to go with someone who is settled in the village; someone who was, perhaps, buying a house, rather than renting. It gives us the hope that there would be some longevity.'

'Oh, I see. Well, we are only just in the village, and we haven't had a chance to see anything we'd like to buy,' she said, being economical with the truth.

'Yes, I understand that. I also forgot to ask whether you had any first-hand experience dealing with sick animals?'

Charlotte's heart sank, and her pulse began to race. 'Erm... no, not really. I love to think I'm compassionate to animals, but I've never resuscitated a badger or castrated a dog.'

What the hell was she saying? She was rambling with hideous consequences, and she knew she had to stop before things became even more embarrassing.

'Well, that doesn't happen too often for me either, and I've been doing this job for forty years,' he replied.

An uncomfortable silence followed, and Charlotte paced the floor, not knowing what to say. She thought it pompous to mention her past involvement and funding of her beloved animal shelter, so she kept quiet. He was enquiring about hands-on experience, anyway. That was different.

The silence continued, and Charlotte felt another comment

about animal genitalia was sure to slip out if it went on any longer.

Thankfully, Mr Frogatt broke the deadlock. 'So, when would you like to start?'

Charlotte wasn't sure if Mr Frogatt had suddenly found a ridiculous sense of humour.

'Sorry... what was that?'

'We would like to offer you the job. On a trial basis, of course, but we were hoping you could start on Monday?'

Her mouth was open so much it was almost impossible to reply.

'Monday. Yes, of course. Monday it is.'

'Marvellous. Shall we say 9am sharp?'

'Thank you. I'll see you then.'

A text to Peter was the first thing that came into her mind, but before she did, she jumped up and down, clapped her hands and pulled off a few disco diva dance floor moves that John Travolta would be proud of.

'Peter, hope you arrive safely? I have good news. The vets have agreed to take me on. It's a trial, but hopefully it will lead to a full-time job. Are you proud of me?'

She didn't expect an instant reply. The flight was long, and she knew he would be glad she had defied all odds and made him proud.

Over the weekend, Charlotte looked at the house with new vigour. She did clean out the cupboard under the sink and the entire bathroom. She busied her lonely mind but also wanted the place to feel a little like home. Maybe it was her new purpose in the village, but in the back of her head, she hoped it wouldn't be for long. Either way, she wasn't going to live in a hovel.

With pride, she walked into the village. The church thermometer had increased its red marker by one millimetre and hoped her meagre few pounds had helped to make a difference.

Scented candles, bleach, scouring pads and rubber gloves filled her bag, and Bob from the hardware shop couldn't have been more helpful and even suggested keeping an eye out for local events on the parish noticeboard and maybe joining the Women's Institute as his wife found it a great way to make friends.

Charlotte wasn't rushing to make many friends if their residency in the village was short-lived. She wouldn't want the distress of another emotional goodbye.

Charlotte received a text she wasn't expecting to receive.

Charlotte, Mira here. So sorry to hear your news. What a scoundrel. I heard he hasn't left you a penny. If there's anything I can do, just call. Or if you want to meet up for coffee sometime? All is well with me. Dashing around as usual. Speak soon. x

What planet was she on? *Meet up for coffee?* It was as if Mira's blinkers never enabled her to see reality. She was beginning to see how fickle she was, and it hurt.

Charlotte replied.

Thank you for your kind words. I'm fine. Surviving. Nothing you can do. I'm awaiting the appeal, but it keeps being put back. Mr Scrivener's retirement hasn't helped, but I won't bore you with the detail. We're also looking into other means, I can't say much, but Peter's being amazing, so all my fingers are crossed. x

Charlotte kicked a stone along the road. It somehow enabled her to feel more grounded. On passing the church, she thought about how everyone is different and some people you just grow away from. Mira was definitely in that category. She knew she didn't mean what she said. Maybe it was her way of saying her life was stable and I was doing fine. It was easy to get angry and take it personally, but, surprisingly, Charlotte reacted completely differently. Instead of feeling angry and rejected, she felt sorry for Mira and hoped she was really okay and doing well.

She continued. *Thanks for your kind offer. It's remarkable how resourceful one can be when needs must. Glad to hear all is well with you. Stay safe Cxx*

She left it at that. Nothing more to be said, and she was grateful. She was getting wiser in her old age.

Peter was right, after all. Mira had been a leech and a selfish one at that. On hand for all the glory moments and cash handouts, but only token gestures of *If there's anything I can do* now, the reality was not so benevolent.

Charlotte set to work in the house, sprucing up neglected corners, cleaning out more cupboards and shelves and making it feel more liveable. In her mind, she knew she wanted to come home from her new job and be able to relax. She still hadn't heard from Peter but decided not to hound him and let him find his feet out there.

She eventually fell asleep with her phone in her hand, and the next thing she knew, it was 7.32am and time for work. Thank goodness she had woken. She'd neglected to set an alarm and Mr Frogatt had said 9am sharp.

No news from Peter was concerning. Maybe he was exhausted after his flight? Maybe he had been kidnapped? Maybe the plane had crashed? She checked the news, and there was no mention of either. She tried to stay calm and focus on getting ready for work, but her mind was in turmoil.

'Peter darling, hope you had a good journey? Please let me

know you're okay? Wish me luck on my first day! Lots of love Cxxx.'

She decided that the same skirt as the interview, a different blouse and short-heeled shoes were perfect. Fortunately, it was dry, so the lane was free from rivers of liquid cow poo, but the shoes were not made for the ruts and stones or the long walk. It was too late to turn back. She was already late. Anyway, note to self, boots tomorrow, she thought as she hobbled her way past the church.

Exhausted, she finally arrived and flung herself in the door, gasping for breath. The clock on the wall said 9.13am.

'I'm so sorry I'm late. I underestimated the walk.'

'Come in, Charlotte. It's fine, but as a team, we do like to make a good start to the day.'

'Of course,' she said, adjusting her shoes which had worn blisters. 'It won't happen again.' She couldn't bear anyone being late and considered it to be the height of rudeness.

Mr Frogatt smiled. 'Please, let me introduce you to my assistant, Amanda. She's been with us just over a year and is about to take her final exams.'

'Charlotte, pleased to meet you,' she said, shaking her hand.

'And you. Did you have to walk far?' Amanda said, showing compassion at her feet.

'Just beyond the church. It's not so far. I just chose the wrong shoes. Maybe I need a bike or something? I'm such an idiot.'

'It's always difficult on your first day to know what to wear, right?'

Charlotte nodded and mopped her brow with a tissue.

Mr Frogatt cleared his throat. 'This is your desk. Make yourself at home. Basically, enquiries and sometimes emergencies will come in on the phone. You'll be required to take the call and note down the relevant information. Relay it to Amanda or me, and when we've dealt with it, we'll let you know and log the job as closed. It's important to keep the appointments book organised and up to date, and we take it in turns to make a brew, so don't be afraid to put the kettle on. Any questions?'

Charlotte listened intently, and still flustered, turned to observe the tea-making area, when her bag swung around and knocked the telephone clean off the desk and onto the floor. Charlotte panicked, scrabbled around, picking up the various components, and tried to organise the desk as it was.

'I'm a bag of nerves. I'm so sorry.'

Amanda came to help, and Charlotte noticed her maternity dress and a very large bump.

'No, please, I'm fine. Don't want you bending over in your condition.'

Amanda smiled and held back.

'Where do the people come in with the hamsters and cats, etc.?'

Mr Frogatt intervened. 'We are predominantly an agricultural practice. We do allow emergency pet referrals, but we deal with our clients on-site, dogs, cats, pigs, sheep, cows, that kind of thing.'

'Oh, I see, so if anyone comes in, I have to turn them away?'

'No, we never do that. Sometimes there is a genuine emergency, and there's a room at the back, should we need it. Let me know, and we'll assess accordingly.'

No sooner had Charlotte reorganised the desk, the phone rang, and Amanda and Mr Frogatt watched Charlotte, hoping she would be able to deal with her first call and not make any judgement about her abilities so far.

She made copious notes, and there was a lot of 'Okay... yes... really... can you explain more as she spoke politely.' Mr Frogatt and Amanda looked at each other anxiously.

'Okay. So, Mrs Brunswick at Swaledale farm has a high peak sheep which she says is having trouble delivering triplets.' She looked over at Mr Frogatt, who already had his coat on and then at Amanda's huge bump.

'So sorry, I hope you don't...' Amanda interjected before she made an even bigger fool of herself. 'It's twins, but don't worry.'

Mr Frogatt grabbed his bag. 'So, let's get this straight. Mrs Brunswick, Swaledale Farm, high peak sheep?'

'Yes,' Charlotte said confidently.

Mr Frogatt smiled. 'I think it might be Mrs Brunswick at High Peak Farm with a Swaledale sheep, perhaps? She's a long-standing client.'

Charlotte closed her eyes and shook her head. 'I've never heard of a Swaledale sheep. I'm so sorry. I can't believe I'm so nervous?'

'Not to worry. First-day pressures and all that,' he said with compassion. 'I can deal with this on my own. I'll leave you and Amanda and call for assistance should I need it.'

Charlotte's first day really did go with a bump. She'd also managed to insult Mrs Frogatt, who popped in to introduce herself. Because she made Charlotte and Amanda a coffee, she thought she was the cleaner and asked her if the fridge could be cleaned. She ignorantly gave Mr Sharples short shrift when she slammed the phone on him. Little did she know about his deep breathing speech impediment. There were so many idiosyncrasies to know and learn, and Charlotte felt more and more out of her depth as the day wore on.

Exhausted by the end of the day, the walk back to the cottage in her crippling heels was the last straw. She still hadn't heard from Peter, and she began to worry. She sent another text and constantly checked for a reply while running a hot bath and pouring a glass of wine to calm her nerves.

No reply.

She felt something was wrong, and her tiredness made her feel tearful, anxious and alone.

She decided to call Chris. Peter had left his number, just in case there was an emergency. Chris reassured her it was early days and that he was probably keeping a low profile until he could establish where he needed to be and the information needed. Charlotte took some comfort from his confident and reassuring tone and took to her bed early, ready for her second day at work.

She slept little. A couple of desperate texts were sent to Peter, but there was still no reply. She tossed and turned and eventually nodded off around 4.30am and was up at 7.30am for work. She looked at the dreadful mess in the mirror. Her pale face and red eyes appearing ghostly. She contemplated calling in and telling them she wasn't fit for the job.

Washing her face and brushing her teeth gave her time to contemplate. She was useless. Due to her nerves, she didn't earn the respect of the Frogatts or Amanda yesterday. Who was she kidding that she could hold down a full-time job?

There was one infuriating thing she couldn't ignore. She knew she couldn't let Mr Frogatt down, though. Her conscience wouldn't let her. Despite all her shortcomings, he had been fabulous. Calm, understanding and even jovial.

The application of thick foundation and lipstick made her

feel slightly better. She checked her phone, and there was nothing. Her heart was thudding, and she knew something wasn't right.

The same skirt as yesterday, a simple non-confrontational blouse and suede boots seemed appropriate. She applied plasters to her blisters and closed the door behind her. She couldn't remember the walk up to the village. Her mind was in a daze. Her first day was embarrassing and not hearing from Peter gave her an anxious twitch in her cheek.

She checked her phone for the time, and there it was. A notification. Without hesitation, she opened the text.

Charlie. I made it. The flight was delayed, and my sim in my phone didn't work here. I had to find somewhere to stay and then obtain a sim which wasn't easy as there was a complication with my bank card. Anyway, all good now, and I'm on the scent x Don't want to say too much. I know you know what I mean. Hope your first day went well. They won't be able to do without you. Pxxx

Deep foundation, smudged lipstick, and mascara running down both cheeks was just the impression she wanted to show as she walked in for her second day. But at least she was on time.

Thankfully, Mr Frogatt hadn't arrived, and Amanda let her in and supplied her with a box of tissues and the promise of a cuppa.

16

BAD TO WORSE

There must be a term for things which go wrong and look like your fault, but aren't, just because they haven't been fixed or for some reason have never happened before, yet just happen on your watch? Charlotte thought as she sat on the back step of the practice with the afternoon sun on her face.

Surely someone in the world knew what she meant? It seemed everything she laid her hand to ended in some kind of disaster. How did no one notice the loose wire at the back of the kettle? How long had it been loose? And why, of all the times to come loose, did it come loose that day and set fire to the spilt cleaning fluid on the counter when she was making tea?

Fortunately, Mr Frogatt and Amanda were out on a callout to free a swan entangled in fishing wire on the river. The sparks were scary at first, but when the adjacent cloth burst into flames, that's when things became really scary and out of control. Charlotte was amazed at how fast a fire could take hold of a kitchen counter and how acrid the smoke was. Fortunately, there was a fire extinguisher to hand, and without it, she feared the whole building would have gone up in flames.

Instead, just a foul mess of scorched worktop, a half-melted plastic kettle and a lingering smell akin to a chemical factory.

On Amanda and Mr Froggatt's return, Amanda took a turn due to smoke inhalation, and Mr Frogatt lost the plot for a moment, saying things like, *Can I not leave you alone for just one minute?* And *Jeez, we asked for help here, not the other way around.*

In her defence, Charlotte did not find that encouraging, and any chance of explaining about the loose wire was futile. To see a normally calm man turn crimson and start shouting was unfortunate. She felt guilty, of course, but when Mr Frogatt accidentally tripped over the discarded fire extinguisher, things started to look ugly.

In his rant, he landed awkwardly by the filing cabinet on his wrist and lay there in agony while Amanda was shouting for water and requesting an ambulance.

Charlotte lay on the bed, fully dressed, looking up at the brown-stained ceiling. Why had she even contemplated getting a job? She knew she was a liability. Yes, unfortunate circumstances had taken place, but they were also her fault. Those things were probably obvious to a trained eye. Someone with office experience and a diligent work ethic would have spotted the wire and acted on it. She was incapable of making a cup of tea without causing mayhem. She wondered how she ever ran an entire estate? The difference was this was a job. Running an estate was just life. She realised the whole trial thing made her nervous, and things were obviously out of her control.

Suddenly, it was the morning, she hadn't changed from her work clothes, washed or eaten. At least the events of the day had enabled her to forget, temporarily, about Peter. Although, she was taking the fact that no news was good news.

She changed her clothes, took a sip of water and headed up the road. She knew what her fate was. Her trial was far from ideal, and she had to face the inevitable like an adult. Of course she wanted to remain at the house and not face the music, but she also wanted to help clean up and check that both Mr Frogatt and Amanda were fine, as well as collect her things and leave with a modicum of dignity.

The vicar was colouring in another minuscule red layer on the towering thermometer and held his hands together for Charlotte as she passed. Somehow, it felt like he knew.

On turning the corner to the practice, the door was open.

'Charlotte?'

'Mrs Frogatt. So sorry about everything. I laid awake all night feeling so terribly guilty. How is Mr Frogatt? And Amanda?'

Mrs Frogatt was wearing yellow rubber gloves and was emptying bin bags into a skip by the back door.

'They're keeping Amanda in hospital. She's almost full term, and they don't want to take any chances.'

Charlotte felt a mighty sense of responsibility and regret. She could be responsible for her miscarriage, and not only that, the collapse of the veterinary practice and the Frogatt's livelihood.

'Oh no! I do hope she will be okay and there's no harm to the twins?' she said, shaking.

Mrs Frogatt threw a pair of gloves at Charlotte.

'You'd better help me get all this cleaned up.'

Charlotte nodded, put on the gloves and entered the building. The stench of melted plastic was almost unbearable. The kitchen worktop was scorched black, and so was the wall. Charlotte felt sick. Not just from smoke-induced nausea but the devastation she had caused to so many lovely people. It was her fault and she felt the full weight of responsibility.

'What about Mr Frogatt? Is he okay?'

'That old bugger needs a kick up the arse,' Mrs Frogatt replied while bagging up the molten kettle and lead. 'I told him weeks ago this kettle needed replacing. I had a tingle. Well, a shock, really, when I plugged it in last week. I said I thought it needed looking at.'

Charlotte paused. 'So, you knew it was faulty?'

'No. I didn't. I don't come to the office regularly. My health isn't what it used to be, and I've almost fully retired. I come in now and again to help, especially with Amanda being pregnant. That's why we advertised your position.'

Charlotte took the remains of the electric lead. 'But you had a shock?'

'Yes. He said he would look at it,' Mrs Frogatt said, looking Charlotte in the eye.

She put the molten lead back into the bag, perched on one of the chairs and began to weep. 'It was such an awful day. I wanted to show I was helping. That I was of use to you. You're such lovely people, and all I wanted to do, was—'

Mrs Frogatt intervened. 'It's not your fault, Charlotte. It was unfortunate. Sometimes, these things happen. We live to fight another day and I'm sure that Amanda will be okay. The fire could have started at any time. I feel bad that it happened to you and not to me that day I mentioned it.'

Charlotte's emotions flooded out with her tears. She couldn't contain her pent-up anxiety and worry she'd held in all night.

'I'm so sorry,' Charlotte said as Mrs Frogatt came over and put her arms around her. Charlotte wiped her eyes and reciprocated with both arms, and the two of them hugged. Not the hug of strangers, but the hug of two people who meant it.

A hug that said a thousand words.

'Thank you. I'll make it up to you,' Charlotte said, squeezing Mrs Frogatt.

'I think Mr Frogatt may have to rethink your position, though. The decision will be with him, not me, and he won't be happy about his broken wrist.'

Charlotte nodded. 'I understand entirely.'

17

A MAN OF NATURE

'Charlotte, we have an emergency out at Outerthwaite Farm. The call came in just before you arrived. A sick horse and pregnant, by all accounts.'

'Okay, do you want me to phone ahead to let them know you're on your way? Where's Amanda?'

'Well! That's just the thing. She went into labour early this morning. It's you and me now.'

'But you've broken your wrist.'

Mr Frogatt looked anxiously at the clock above the door.

'I need you to drive me there. We don't have a second to lose.'

The gears of the Land Rover were awkward, to say the least. Charlotte pulled and pushed at the lever, crunching and grinding the gears, and then the vehicle gathered pace once again along the muddy access to the farm where there was barely the width of the Land Rover between the dry-stone walls on either side. Charlotte gritted her teeth and persevered towards the farm as the windscreen wipers tried to differentiate between rain and mud. Suddenly a dishevelled black-and-white sheepdog dashed out in front and barked incessantly.

Charlotte wrenched up the handbrake, opened the door, applied the hood of her raincoat as she zipped it up, and then dashed around the vehicle to open the door for Mr Frogatt.

'Ow do.' The farmer surprised Charlotte as he appeared from the dark stone farmhouse. It almost looked abandoned, with unrepaired broken windows, missing tiles on the roof and rusting machinery in the yard.

'Hello,' she said, wiping raindrops from her eyes.

Mr Frogatt handed Charlotte his veterinary bag and then engaged in the awkward greeting that could only accompany two proud men who would normally grip hands like wrestlers.

A glare into each other's eyes for no more than one second, then a nod of acceptance on both parts seemed to do the trick, and the broken wrist and full arm cast brushed off as a minor inconvenience.

'She's in the field,' the farmer said as he hastily hobbled to the wooden five-bar gate. 'I think she's pregnant.'

Charlotte waited by the Land Rover.

Mr Frogatt looked back. 'Come on, Charlotte, and bring my other bag. It's on the back seat.'

Charlotte sprang into action and immediately stepped into a cow pat. Her expensive suede ankle boots, with a wedge heel, were not up to farm life's rigours. She cringed as she grabbed the bag and then stood rigid on the spot. Cow faeces covered her feet, rain dripped into her eyes, and the smell of the farmyard made her well up inside. What the hell was she doing? she thought as she looked down at her steaming feet.

'Come on, Charlotte, bring the bag,' Mr Frogatt shouted again.

Charlotte slammed the door and gritted her teeth. 'I'm coming.'

The horse lay on its side, close to the edge of the field next to the wood. The rain dripped off the overhanging trees onto the horse, and Mr Frogatt instructed the farmer to get some blankets and water.

Charlotte precariously picked her way through the tussocky grass and horse manure, twisting her ankles while still gritting her teeth. She instantly recalled her friend Emma, who kept horses, and how she never smiled. No wonder!

'Hurry with the bag,' Mr Frogatt said, raising his voice politely.

Charlotte was still some distance away. She threw the bag on the floor and stamped her foot. Wiped the rain from her eyes and sat down on the sodden grass. She looked at her destroyed boots and then proceeded to remove them, throwing them one by one into the field. She stood, gave herself a shake and, without any audible reference, spoke firmly to herself.

'Pull yourself together, Charlie,' she said, before filling her lungs with country air and starting a march over to the scene. 'You owe him.'

She approached Mr Frogatt, who was already intently listening to his stethoscope at various places on the horse's torso. Her bare feet cold and sodden, she handed over the bag.

'Is he coming with those blankets?' He said, folding the stethoscope away in his pocket.

Charlotte scoured the field. 'I can't see him.'

She could see Mr Frogatt was agitated and frustrated as he sighed out loud and fidgeted.

'Is he coming?' he said again, scouring the field himself.

Charlotte diligently searched but to no avail. 'He's not there,' she said.

'Okay, I want you to listen to me carefully and do everything I say.'

Charlotte nodded.

'Look in the bag and take out the syringe. There's a little glass bottle in there, too. Give it a shake, turn it upside down and push the needle in. Fill the syringe and make sure you're drawing liquid, not air. You got that?'

Charlotte's heart began to pound. She looked at the mighty horse at her feet. It was shaking and, occasionally, its leg twitched, but its ears were low, and its head heavy against Mr Frogatt's leg. Suddenly the horse became agitated, and the shaking was much worse. It raised its head and started convulsing.

'Concentrate on the syringe,' he said with authority.

Charlotte stepped back as the horse became even more uncomfortable and then tried to get up on its feet. Its legs kicked out as it tried without success to rise. Its head pushed forward and then vomited violently before collapsing again into a heap.

'Where is he? I can't do this with one hand.'

Charlotte glanced along the tree line towards the gate. 'I still can't see him.'

'Okay. Take the syringe, turn it upside down, flick it so that any air rises and eject some liquid.'

'Sure,' she said, feeling the importance of the exercise.

'Now, push the needle in here.' He pointed to the horse's neck. 'And give it everything. It will be tough to start.'

Charlotte did exactly that. It felt strange piercing the skin of an animal, and she closed her eyes to somehow make it easier for both her and the horse. She trusted Mr Frogatt, injected everything as he said, and he looked at her as she withdrew the needle.

'Now get the big green glove out of the bag.'

'What?'

'You can do this,' he said, looking at his arm and then stroking the horse's neck. He then turned to Charlotte, who was now holding the long latex glove at her fingertips and looking anxious. He carried on reassuring the horse.

'Put the glove on, Charlotte.'

She looked straight into his eyes while raising her eyebrows.

'Oh no. I mean, Mr Frogatt, with all due respect. I've never—'

He cut her off before she could finish.

'I'll talk you through it, Charlotte. You'll be fine. We can't wait for the farmer. What the hell has happened to him?'

Charlotte shrugged again and then inserted her hand into the glove and squirmed.

'You're just inserting this ultrasound probe so that I can see if she's pregnant. Lift the tail and go in carefully. I'll tell you when to stop and when to rotate your hand so I get a clear view.'

'How far do I go?'

'Probably most of your arm, but, as I said, I'll tell you when to stop.'

Charlotte gulped. 'I don't think I can do it. It doesn't seem natural.'

'We need to be quick, Charlotte. We need to know whether we are saving one horse or two.'

Charlotte gulped again. She handed the monitor to Mr Frogatt and could barely open her eyes as she lifted the tail and followed his instructions.

'Oh no. I can't believe I'm doing this,' she said, thrusting her arm all the way in and now, with her eyes clamped shut and head turned away, she wished she'd taken employment at the Italian restaurant. 'Am I there yet?' she cried out.

As before, the horse became agitated and kicked out and raised its head. 'Stay with it, Charlotte. You're doing a great job. Just turn your hand to the left.'

She did exactly what she was told until Mr Frogatt signalled for her to stop.

'Hold still now. Mmm... right a bit. No that's left. Yes, that's it. Mmm...'

They looked at each other in complete silence. Even the horse pricked up an ear.

'It's there. The foetus is there, and it's alive. Yes, I'm sure.'

Charlotte smiled. 'Really?'

'Yes.'

Charlotte slowly began the withdrawal, and the mare became restless again, kicking and lifting her head and forcing it forward. Charlotte became free, threw all the equipment and glove on the floor and rolled back into the grass as the horse vomited again.

A blanket suddenly appeared over the horse, and the farmer placed a tin bucket of water on the ground. 'Struggled to find a bucket without a hole,' he said, kneeling.

Mr Frogatt calmly instructed him to place more blankets over the animal while pointing frustratingly at his arm in the sling.

The farmer did just that, leaving the horse's head exposed. 'How'd you do your arm?' he said.

Mr Frogatt looked at him. 'A horse. Damn thing kicked me. Forty years, I've been in this business and have never been kicked so hard. Then, the other day, I fell on it again. Think I'm losing my touch,' he said, looking at Charlotte.

The farmer huffed. 'Sixty-five years, and I don't think

there's a place I haven't been kicked.' He observed the contents of the horse's stomach. 'She vomited again, I see.'

Mr Frogatt nodded. 'She's pregnant.'

'Thought so. She's been to the stud, so knew it was possible. Unusual for her to be sick, though.'

'Mmm,' Mr Frogatt said, stroking his chin with his good hand. 'Anything unusual happened? She always in this field?'

The farmer scrunched his lips. 'She's usually in the lower field with the others, but I had her in here two or three weeks as I didn't want her mixing with the stallion. He's her brother.'

'So, she's been on her own in this field? You fed her anything new?'

The farmer shook his head. 'Nope.'

'I don't understand what is causing the vomiting. Are you sure you haven't been feeding her differently?'

The farmer shook his head once more.

'Give her some water, just small amounts. She'll be dehydrated.'

The farmer did as he was instructed, and Charlotte offered her arms for a good rinse of water, too, and then stood back.

The rain began to ease, and the vet stroked the horse in silence, and the farmer fed drops of water.

Charlotte put her hands on her hips. 'You say the horses are not usually in this field?'

'Yes. It's always been used for machinery, hay bales and timber, but I cleared all that out to give a new grazing field,' the farmer said while persevering with the water.

'There are yew trees along the woodland edge. There are ash, birch and field maple, but yew as well. I can see them overhanging the fence.'

The farmer shook his head and shrugged.

'You're a genius. You're a goddamn genius,' Mr Frogatt

announced. 'Look. Red berries and green foliage. Yew, if I'm not mistaken,' he said, pointing at the vomit.

Charlotte straightened her back and grinned.

'The vomiting might not be a bad thing. If she digested the yew, it would almost certainly kill her. The fact she's getting it all up might just save her. Keep going with the water. She'll let you know when she's had enough, or she'll vomit again. In that case, keep drip-feeding with water and keep her warm. I recommend some fresh hay or dry food later if she's ready and fence off the woodland edge until you can get her moved indoors.'

'Thank you, veterinary,' the farmer said, showing his appreciation with a slap on the back.

Mr Frogatt and Charlotte proceeded to the Land Rover, carrying the equipment as best between them. They passed Charlotte's boots. Mr Frogatt looked at her.

'They're beyond repair. I'll get the farmer to burn them,' she said shaking her head.

Mr Frogatt laughed. 'How about I get you a pair of regulation wellingtons?'

Charlotte laughed too. 'Do they do them in pink?' They both laughed together.

'How do you know so much about trees?'

Charlotte paused.

'Well. It's a long story. Let's just say, I owe everything to one man. A man of nature.'

18

MISADVENTURE

A week passed, and Peter's phone appeared to be out of action. She'd not heard anything from him. Her positive thinking was beginning to wane, and even Chris couldn't shine any light on what was happening. It had been a busy week, but there wasn't a moment she didn't think about him.

Something wasn't right. No communication was odd. Charlotte knew it was a covert operation, but not even a text was worrying. She wandered aimlessly around the house, clutching her coffee mug for comfort. The smell of coffee barely masked the fusty air.

She checked her phone and looked back at the last messages she had received, then typed again. 'How are you Peter? Please let me know you are okay?' her text said, hoping for an instant reply.

A stout knock at the door broke her thoughts. Who could that be on a Saturday morning? Resting her mug on the windowsill, she descended the stairs and unbolted the door.

'Ms Charlotte Winterbourne?' the commanding voice asked.

'Yes?'

'Can we come in?' The other man said as he removed his unmistakable black peaked hat.

In a moment of insecurity, she scanned their immaculate uniforms, white shirts and numbered lapels.

'What is this regarding?'

'We have news regarding your fiancé.'

Charlotte's heart momentarily stopped beating. 'Peter! What is it?'

'Can we come in?' the first officer asked, having removed his hat too.

Charlotte showed them into the kitchen. 'Coffee?' she offered, but they both declined.

They introduced themselves and showed their warrant cards, which made Charlotte judder. No matter what the circumstances, it was never a pleasure to get a visit from the police.

'You might want to take a seat,' the first officer said.

Charlotte remained standing and leaned against the sink.

'We are very sorry to inform you that your fiancé, Mr Peter Heath, has been found dead in Hong Kong. You knew he was there?'

Charlotte wasn't sure if she'd heard correctly.

'That's impossible! That can't be the case. What exactly are you saying?'

The second officer presented her with a letter. 'A random shark attack while swimming off the coast. There had been warnings of sharks in that area.'

'That can't be right? I remember him saying he wasn't fond of swimming, having once slipped into the canal as a boy.'

'Maybe the letter will explain more,' he replied.

She picked up the letter and turned it over. It had a serious look to it. She looked at the police officers and then back at the letter.

Dear Ms Winterbourne,

I write to inform you that with great sadness, we have recorded the tragic death of Mr Peter Heath on the sixth day of this month.

We are not able to fully identify the remains, as the sea water and associated damage to the flesh has made this impossible, and we are missing some vital remains, which would quantify all reasonable doubt about the cause of death. But a Caucasian adult male and paperwork belonging to Mr Peter Heath were discovered together at the scene. We believe a shark attack is the primary cause, but until we investigate further, we are recording Peter's death as misadventure. Please contact me directly to arrange shipment of the remains, or alternatively, an appropriate cremation can be carried out with or without your presence.

I await your soonest response.

Mr Chang

Charlotte drew a deep breath. 'Why would he have his papers with him?'

'He was found washed up on a beach. There was a bag, I think.'

'It doesn't make sense. My Peter can't be dead. He just can't…'

19

NUMB

Everything was lost.

The dream taken. All hope, all meaning, all purpose, all light, all justice, all energy gone. A void of never-ending darkness prevailing.

One's life stretched out along a cold and lonely corridor. Youth and childhood to the left with various doors leading off into the past, and then, with a turn of the head, to the right, the route ahead. Dark, bitter, enclosed and infinitely long. As far as the eye can see and then further into nothingness. A still and calm nothingness. Her brain filled with a billion thoughts and, at the same time, empty and numb. No light, no movement, no texture, no glimmer, no sense, no reason, no end.

Just nothing.

Best to just sit and let the numbness take over her whole body. Fighting was useless, reasoning futile and hope the most destructive of all. Best to let it eat her. Best to let it devour her. Best to let it destroy her until she had nothing left to offer.

Time had no meaning. No touch, no hearing, no smell, no

life. The hands tick forward and then back in the blink of an eye. Tick tock, tick tock, not moving, just stuck in time.

Best to just let go into the void.

It must have been a day or maybe three? Her eyes never moved from the kitchen wall. Her world was silent and calm. A knock at the door made her eyes shift momentarily, but she remained welded to the simple wooden kitchen chair. The letter on the table, the wood stove cold and then, another knock.

Charlotte heard voices but couldn't react. She could do nothing but stare at the wall. Suddenly the back door opened. It was never locked. They let themselves in.

'Charlotte, are you all right?'

She couldn't move. Her body drained of any response.

'Charlotte, it's Mrs Frogatt. We've been worried sick about you.'

Mrs Frogatt gestured to Mr Frogatt to try to get a reaction. She put her hand on her shoulder while he crouched down in front of her. She didn't flinch. Her eyes glazed over and lifeless.

'Charlotte, we're here for you. Whatever it is, we are not here to cast assumptions,' he said, hoping for a reply.

'She's had a shock. A big shock. What's that on the table?'

Mr Frogatt took the letter and read it to himself, then silently handed it over.

'She's going to need time, and she's going to need food.'

Mrs Frogatt rummaged in the cupboards and produced a tin of chicken soup.

'Put the heating on,' she said. 'I'll make some soup and call the doctor.'

'I'm going to call in every day with food. The doctor has prescribed something to ease the pain, and Mr Frogatt says take your time. Is there anyone you want me to call?'

Charlotte made eye contact. She could feel the kindness in Mrs Frogatt was unconditional as if she were her mother. She looked at her face. A woman who had been at the coalface of life. She could tell, just from her eyes, she had not had an easy life and was still eager to give. Charlotte had never seen this so close up before. Certainly not from her own mother. Why was she bothered enough to help? Charlotte would have just given up. But the Frogatts had brought a warmth to her. Gave her a helping hand in the darkness and prevented her from falling down the inevitable rabbit hole.

'I'll let my daughter know. She lives with her father, and I'll call my friend, Mira. Other than that, I really have no one.'

'What about Peter's family?' Mrs Frogatt asked.

Charlotte shook her head.

Mrs Frogatt put on her coat. 'I must leave now. I have to be at the office. Mr Frogatt says he's looking forward to having you back at work and thinks you might benefit from some fresh air and a change of scenery.'

She opened the front door.

'Mrs Frogatt?'

'Yes?'

'Thank you.'

Mrs Frogatt smiled and nodded, then closed the door behind her.

20

A ROBIN'S SONG

Being alone was suddenly a reality. Charlotte took each day as it came, and each day seemed just like the last. She had discovered the true meaning of heartbreak. The crippling pain of utter and complete emptiness was unbearable. A pain so powerful yet hidden deep within. Not able to take a tablet or bandage the wound. Not able to see or touch it, not even able to explain it.

Her scars from the swing and knife cuts on her arm, inflicted when she was younger, had all healed. You could pick them out if you tried, but they had all but disappeared. She couldn't see an end to her current agony, though. People told her time would heal, but how could it?

She'd proved herself to be a dreadful mother. Lucy had high expectations and had been used to life in the upper echelons of society. Not that Charlotte hadn't. It was just that she had always fought against it. Naturally, in search of a life with more meaning and depth. And that was the problem. She'd invested everything in a man who could deliver that and show her the true value of simple living and true love. Holm Cottage was far from perfect, and the truth was, she was struggling to see a way forward with it, but in a way, it had character and a soul. Not something she'd ever felt at Loxley, the London house, or even the Alpenblick with its frozen lake and alpine mountain backdrop.

Peter was so confident about everything. He solved problems easily, and even just joking about them often worked. He had been brought up in a world where you didn't sit around feeling sorry for yourself and blaming others. His was a world of true grit, determination, resolve and humour. Why cry about a dead bird in the kitchen when you can laugh about it? she thought.

What did she have to feel sorry about? The man she loved had died trying to find the truth for her. In her vein. In her honour. It was the most courageous thing anyone could do for someone. But she still hated him. She wasn't from his world. He told her to find her steel, but she had no concept of what that meant. Why was it so easy for him to find his steel when all she could feel was hopelessness and cowardice? Why did he have to go off in search of something that killed him? Why did he leave her so vulnerable and weak? Why wasn't he still around to solve her problems and protect her from the real world?

The more she thought, the more she resented him, and the more she resented him, the sorrier for herself she became.

She barely ate with the pain. In between bouts of uncontrollable crying, she would find herself standing in the corner of a room, just staring. Once or twice, she sat up in the churchyard, hoping she wouldn't see the vicar. The solitude, among other dead people, seemed to have an appeal, although thoughts of taking her own life reared its ugly head once again.

It was the prominent yew tree that grabbed her attention. Ripe with fat red berries and within easy reach.

She popped one in her mouth. It tasted bitter. Not bitter like a banana skin, but bitter like wood varnish, a toxic bitterness, which she felt down her throat as she stripped the seed of its flesh and swallowed it.

Was the seed the bitterest bitter could be she wondered. Peter had said it was almost instant death.

A robin appeared from nowhere. It swooped in and perched on the top of an ancient-looking grave. One whose engraved writing had almost entirely eroded away. The robin's breast was as bright as the yew berries, and its song louder than any church bells. It bobbed up and down and attracted her attention. How could a small bird give out such a loud song? It was beyond nature. The energy within the bird was so magnificent and joyful. It never took its beady eye off Charlotte.

She placed her teeth around the seed, ready to crunch down on to it. She toyed with it in her mouth and kept bringing it back to the same place between her front incisors. The robin's song became louder and louder. It flapped its wings and seemed to dance as it leapt in the air, fluttered and then continued to bob up and down.

Charlotte held the seed in place and applied pressure to it. What better place to do it than in a graveyard? It was easy. It was the easy way out. No more heartache, no more conflict, and no more worry. Then the robin flew over and landed on her knee. Its seemingly greenish eye fixed on hers. She noticed the colour within its feathers. Not brown, but reds, yellows, black and orange, even gold set against its beautiful red breast, which was proudly on display. Charlotte spat out the seed, which scared the bird. It flew away into the undergrowth.

Charlotte spat again to rid her mouth of the taste and the foul thought of cowardice and defeat. She searched for him, but then her eye was distracted by a human form moving among the graves.

A figure moving slowly, hunched over and only occasionally visible in the gaps between the headstones. Charlotte spat the bitterness out again and hurried to head off the person at the gate. Had they been watching her all the time? She felt uneasy about who it was but felt compelled to find out.

She noticed the figure approaching the gate and hastened her stride. On reaching the path, Charlotte could make out it was an old lady with a crippled back, almost doubled over and shuffling. Despite this, Charlotte struggled to keep up. The lady reached the gate, and as Charlotte approached, she turned her head and looked directly at Charlotte. It was the same old lady she had seen at the library when she had her interview. Her nose, large and knobbly like an old potato, and her chin hairy and prominent. Charlotte noticed her hands were deformed, with scars and crooked fingers. Her eyes fixed on Charlotte's. This time, they were green. Emerald green and shining bright, like the eyes of a young girl. The light of day bringing them to life.

Charlotte couldn't move. She felt hypnotised. Those eyes had depth, they had knowledge, and they had energy. Charlotte suddenly felt her heart start beating very fast. A little unnerving yet exhilarating at the same time. The old lady continued to stare knowingly and Charlotte, who was now hot, felt her fingers and toes tingle with life.

'Hello, Charlotte.'

The voice of the vicar made her turn back to the church.

'Hello, Vicar,' she said, trembling.

She then looked back at the gate and saw no one was there. 'Did you just see the old lady? Who is she?'

The vicar brought his hands in front of him. 'I saw no one. Are you all right?'

Charlotte looked at the vicar and then the gate and then back at the vicar.

'I think so? I feel... different.'

'God has a wonderful way of helping us when we need him the most,' the vicar said, still offering his hands to the sky.

'What about the old hermit you told me about? Could she still be alive?'

'My child. She was in history before the history books were written. Just a fable, just a fable.'

21

HOLD FAST

'It's good to have you back, Charlotte.'

'Thank you, Mr Frogatt. I wasn't sure I was going to make it. I've been... you know, weak and disorientated.'

'I understand. It's good to get out of the house and apply your brain to something other than... you know.'

'I know. I couldn't have coped without you and Mrs Frogatt. How is she, and how's your wrist?'

'She's okay. Seems to have lost some of her energy recently, and as for me, this old blighter is really taking its time to heal,' he said, holding up his bandaged wrist. 'Anyway, it looks like you've just been promoted.'

'What do you mean?'

'Well, Amanda's on maternity leave, I have... this, and you're the new horse whisperer in town.'

'Mr Frogatt, I don't think putting my arm inside a horse's rectum represents any kind of knowledge or aptitude towards animal wizardry. Anyway, I nearly burnt the whole place down.'

'Well, you proved your worth, and I'm grateful,

notwithstanding the horse. Apparently, both are doing fine. We'll visit again next week and see how the two of them are getting on.'

'She gave birth, then?'

'A healthy foal, thanks to you. If you're up for it today, we'll visit a lame dog. He's old, so we'll see what we can do. The owner's a nice guy; I've known the dog since he was a pup. You're on driving duty again. Oh, and there's some new footwear by the back door too.'

Charlotte smiled, picked up the vet's bag, turned the corner to the door, and there they were. Bright pink wellingtons with a blue ribbon embossed on the side. She shook her head and smiled again.

'It's good to have you back,' he said, putting on his coat.

'It's good to be back. I might need time to get back to normal. In fact, I wonder if I ever will, but I'm grateful for the second chance.'

Mr Frogatt held up his bandaged hand. 'What's normal?'

The Land Rover sped along the lanes. A little jerky at first, while Charlotte settled into her new footwear. On reaching the house, she rolled her sleeves up, tied her hair back into a half-hearted bun and opened the vehicle door for Mr Frogatt.

'If you have any miracle cures for dog's legs, let me know sooner than later!' he said jovially.

Mr Buckley welcomed them in. 'Hello, Oggy. Thanks for coming at such short notice.'

Charlotte couldn't contain a little giggle as she heard Mr Frogatt's name.

'And who is this new member of the team?' Mr Buckley asked, smiling a huge smile and offering his hand to Charlotte.

She reciprocated with a handshake. 'I'm Charlotte. Very nice to meet you...?'

'Jim. People around here call me Jim. Are you in town for long?' he asked, looking her up and down.

'That depends on whether I like it,' Charlotte said, withdrawing her hand abruptly.

'So. Old Froggy hasn't told you his name, then?'

Mr Frogatt interjected. 'If you don't mind, Jim, we'll keep this purely professional if that's okay?'

Jim gave a nod of approval, and Mr Frogatt looked at Charlotte, who raised both eyebrows inquisitively.

'Okay, okay. My name is Ogden. Of course, I blame my parents. It means *from the oak valley* in old English.'

'I think that's a beautiful name. Ogden. It's grounded and unique, just like you.'

'Shall we get on?' Mr Frogatt insisted as his face blushed. 'And it's Mr Frogatt from now on, please, Charlotte.'

Bullet, the old English sheepdog, lay on his blanket in front of the fire.

'He's either been in a fight or else trapped it somewhere. There's a wound near his paw. I tried fixing it, but he's not walking on it now. He's fifteen years old, so not as fit as he used to be,' Jim said, welling up.

Charlotte knelt down beside him.

'Hello, Bullet,' she said, stroking his forehead. 'What are we going to do with you?'

'Can we get him up and walking, so I can take a closer look?' Mr Frogatt said while perching on a chair.

Jim picked Bullet up and encouraged him to walk. He was listless and slow, his head down and dribbling. Charlotte noted his watering eye and that he seemed to have very little energy.

Mr Frogatt examined the leg.

'It doesn't look good. It looks like cancer. Probably in the joint too, and maybe more?'

Jim shook his head. 'What are you saying?'

'I'm not a hundred per cent, we could take him in and do tests, but it doesn't look good. I could amputate his leg, but the stress of the operation and the aesthetic... I don't think he'd make it.'

Jim wiped a tear from his cheek, Charlotte stroked Bullet's head, and Mr Frogatt sat back in the chair and stroked his chin.

Charlotte broke the silence. 'Is there anything we can do?'

Mr Frogatt kept his eyes focused on the dog, curled up on his blanket.

'We can put him out of his misery?'

Jim wiped another tear, and Charlotte handed him a tissue and a comforting arm around his shoulders.

'I've known you a long time, Oggy. I trust your judgement.'

'It's not easy losing someone you love, but, sometimes, you just have to make the right decision and deal with it,' Charlotte said, handing Jim another tissue.

'I know that. Do what you need to do. I don't want him hurting.'

Jim comforted Bullet while Charlotte fetched the bag and helped Mr Frogatt prepare for the injection. 'You going to do it again, Charlotte?'

'This one's not for me, if that's okay? I don't think I'm ready to... you know,' she said, biting her lip.

Mr Frogatt acknowledged with a cautious nod, and while Charlotte held the dog, Mr Frogatt administered the dose with his trembling left hand. 'It's done.'

Charlotte couldn't speak. It was heartbreaking to see. Mr Frogatt packed away what he could. 'You have anyone to comfort you tonight?'

'No. You know I've been on my own for a while. Bullet was

my only companion since Judy left. I don't know what I'll do without him.'

'You're welcome to stay at ours if you want?' Mr Frogatt offered.

'I'll be fine, thank you. I'll just take my time to get used to the silence.'

The drive back was a quiet one. A sombre air filled the Land Rover while it rattled and squeaked its way back along the narrow country lanes.

'I don't know how you do it.'

'What?'

'You know. Putting an animal to sleep. Death is such a tragic thing. Made me think about how important life is, but also how cruel it can be,' Charlotte said, releasing her hair.

'Life is cruel. We both know that, but if we don't let it bring us down, we can grow stronger, and the next time, we can fight it easier.'

'But, like Bullet. Don't you think sometimes it's not worth going on anymore?'

'It is for an old dog who's in pain at the end of his life. You're not thinking of doing anything stupid, are you?'

'I've learned my lesson with that one, Oggy. But I tell you something...'

'Mr Frogatt, please. Anyway, what were you saying?'

'I promised myself I wouldn't have those dark thoughts again, but what good has it done me? I've lost everything too. I have no one to love me anymore.'

'Look, Charlotte. You're still a young woman, and you have a lot to offer. I don't know where you're from or what you've done before, but I can see a compassionate heart and gutsy determination in you. Your time will come. Learn to love your-self first, and when you like yourself, others will feel the same.

It's like Mrs Frogatt. I didn't meet her until I was fifty-two. She'd been married before and lost her husband, and look at us now. I couldn't live without her. Only when I stopped feeling sorry for myself did I enable her to come into my life and love me. She's my greatest treasure.'

'Wow, you really do love her.'

'There's someone for everyone out there. But the truth is, we all have to die. It's inevitable. It's just the hardest thing to come to terms with. Time is a great healer, and if we are fortunate to have a life, we should make the most of it.' Mr Frogatt chuckled. 'I think it was John Lennon who said, life is what happens when you're busy making other plans. You have to embrace life and make it what you want. Go out and get it.'

'I like that,' Charlotte said as she applied the parking brake and turned off the lights.

'Anyway, why don't you come up to us for dinner one evening?'

'Yes, I'd love that.'

'Let's say Saturday, 7pm?'

'It's a date.'

Mrs Frogatt had laid the most beautiful table. White cotton tablecloth with embroidered sweet peas at each corner, Her best bone china crockery and antique silver cutlery. Charlotte examined everything, running her hand over the embroidered flowers and picking up a knife and fork and examining the handles.

'You've made such an effort, Mrs Frogatt. I'm learning to cherish everything now. There was a time when I wouldn't have noticed the silverware or the delicate flowers on the tablecloth.'

'You're welcome, Charlotte. It's not so often we get visitors,' she said, using the back of the chair to steady herself before slumping into the seat.

'Are you okay?' Charlotte said, seeing that she looked a little weak and her face was pale.

'I'm fine. Just fending off a cold.'

'I'm very grateful for everything you've done for me. You and Mr Frogatt have hearts of gold.'

'Ogden hasn't always had it so easy. He lost his first wife. Did he tell you?'

'No. He mentioned about you.'

'He wouldn't tell you, but he lost her in quite tragic circumstances. She took her own life. He came home from work and found her hanging from the ceiling rose.'

Charlotte immediately felt weak and took to the nearest chair while holding her neck.

'My goodness. How dreadful.'

'Let's have some dinner, and you can tell me about your daughter. Oggy, dinner's on the table,' she shouted up the stairs.

'It's vegetable tagine with couscous and homemade flatbread. Hope you like vegetarian food?' Mrs Frogatt asked, spooning the feast onto Charlotte's plate.

'I'm loving the thought more and more each day,' she said, helping serve Mr Frogatt.

Charlotte explained that when she spoke to Lucy, she had announced she was moving to the US with her father. He had a job opportunity, and she couldn't see herself living in a 'damp and dark shepherd's cottage', as she put it.

Mrs Frogatt ladled more tagine. 'The US? How do you feel about that?'

'I miss her dearly, but she has a life to live. She'll visit me if she wants to. In a way, I want her to be free. I was so constrained as a girl, and she is so much brighter than me.'

'They will find their own way.'

'Yes. Do you have any children?'

Mrs Frogatt left the table and returned with a raspberry pavlova and whipped cream. 'No. We couldn't. I mean, I couldn't.'

Charlotte nodded and chose not to push it any further. 'I don't think I've eaten this much food ever,' Charlotte said, cleaning her plate.

'Talking of food, have you decided what you're bringing to the dinner dance next Saturday?'

Charlotte looked stunned. 'I didn't know there was a dance. Anyway, I won't be attending.'

'We think you should. Might be good to get out and maybe meet other people in the village? We're not having you at home, alone on village dance night. Anyway, I'm inviting you as my partner. Oggy won't be dancing. He's using his arm as an excuse this year. I know he only goes to please me, and he'll be there, but if you're there, we can at least enjoy the music and have a reason to get dressed up.'

Charlotte responded as delicately as possible. 'I don't want to gatecrash your dance. I just don't think I'm ready. I'm not sure I'd like to see all those happy couples dancing together.'

'Charlotte. I have my ear pretty close to the ground, and I can tell you that most of them aren't actually that happy! Look, seriously. You'd be helping me out. I can ditch invalid Harry over there,' she said, laughing, 'and let our hair down. We deserve it.'

Charlotte looked over at Mr Frogatt with his poor arm in his sling. 'I'm really not sure.'

Mrs Frogatt put her hand on Charlotte's. 'Only if you're ready. No pressure. But I'd love for you to help me out more than anything.'

Charlotte pondered for a moment. 'Is it a formal dress code?'

'It's whatever you feel like wearing. Anything goes.'

22

THE VILLAGE DANCE

Alexander McQueen, Givenchy, and even a couple of Vivienne Westwood numbers were pondered upon and rejected as Charlotte searched for the perfect outfit for the dance. She hadn't even started unpacking the numerous boxes of outfits in the spare bedroom. She knew which shoes. Of course, the Louboutins, every time. Not the sexy red sole, but a more sophisticated cream high heel. She didn't want to appear too over the top. Then again, the Salvatore Ferragamo, with an understated heel, might be more fitting. The choice was endless, and Charlotte agonised over the most suitable ensemble.

She looked up into the air. 'Which ones would you like me to wear?' she asked Peter. 'I hope you don't mind me attending the dance?'

Removing each item from the wardrobe and hanging it on the curtain pole, so she could examine the potential, the rain outside caught her eye, and the droplets turned from slow trickles into fast torrents, and the sky appeared grey and miserable. The weather was something she hadn't considered, and neither the Louboutins nor the Ferragamos were going to get her there unscathed without a taxi right to the door itself.

What to wear? What to wear? She paced the floor, ransacked a couple of boxes, and then paced the floor again. She didn't want to upstage Mrs Frogatt or look like some kind of village tart. She was grateful for the invitation and felt the time was right to breathe again.

She paced the floor and went to the back door to get a better look at the weather. In the process, she kicked over her new wellington boots.

Maybe Mrs Frogatt herself had the answer? She immediately called.

'Mrs Frogatt. I wondered if Mr Frogatt might be up for lending the Land Rover for an urgent non-business issue?'

'I'm sure he would be fine with that, Charlotte. Is it important?'

Charlotte replied instantly. 'Yes. It's a matter of life.'

'Oh, dear! What is it now? You mean life or death?'

Charlotte replied with a grin in her voice. 'No. Just life.'

Mrs Frogatt paused. 'Well, I'm sure you wouldn't ask unless it was important. He's here now. Shall I ask him?'

Moments later, she returned to the phone. 'He said yes, but don't disappear with it or crash it. Other than that, it's yours for the day.'

'Brilliant.'

The rain poured relentlessly. The windscreen wipers nearly danced off the vehicle, they were going so fast. She backed up as close to the front door as possible. Then she proceeded to create as much space as possible in the rear by folding down seats and removing anything personal of Mr Frogatt's.

She started with the boxes. Squeezing them in, pushing them into any available space. Then the dresses out of the wardrobe and the ones hanging on the curtain rail. Each and every one, crammed into the footwells and front seat. Last but by no means least, the shoes. Boxes and boxes of them. She didn't even lift the lids to look inside. The decision was made, and she was not going to waiver.

More shoes went on the roof rack, which she secured with a ratchet strap she found in the shed. Thankfully, there were no low bridges. She closed the boot and set off to the main town.

Five charity shops in total benefitted from the designer giveaway, and all appeared grateful, despite their surprised faces. The whole lot had gone. It didn't even feel strange handing them over.

Driving home, Charlotte felt clean. Like a weight had been lifted from her shoulders. Her head was clearer, and a feeling of great motivation filled her thoughts. Peter would have told her to buck her ideas up and get a grip of herself, and she wouldn't let him down.

On entering the village, she detoured slightly to the library, picked up a DIY book for beginners, then went to the bakery for a cake, and then headed home to reload Mr Frogatt's items and return the Land Rover to its original state.

All but Charlotte's most essential clothes were left, and they all fitted perfectly into the wardrobe, although some shoes didn't quite make it to the charity load. Those, Charlotte packed carefully into the spare bedroom.

She celebrated her cathartic clear-out with a coffee and perched herself on the edge of the window seat, where she could look out across the fields. Acres and acres of unspoilt view. Well, if the rain decided to clear, and the windows were not steamed up. The quiet moment gave her a chance to reflect on what she'd just done. It was like throwing out all her past. Discarding all the unnecessary waste and clutter which, really, in the grand scheme of things, was pretty worthless. She laughed at the thought of someone going home with an Alexander McQueen dress for the price of a coffee, and it felt good inside.

There was one remaining dress left hanging on the curtain pole. Full length in light blue and covered in delicate white daisies, with their glorious yellow centres, smiling joyfully. With a large pair of scissors in hand, she set to work chopping off the bottom and introducing a new fun look to the garment. She carefully sewed a hem and replaced a missing button on the back. She made the decision to embrace the dance and try to move on. Mixed feelings filled her head. Loyalty to Peter, he was still her fiancé, after all. But also, a hint of something new. Like Peter had given her something much more than she could ever have wished for. His energy to survive and, in a way, his ability to find the positive in any situation. He'd brought her here, and she was beginning to see things differently.

The rain had cleared as Charlotte left the house, but the ground was soaking, and fast-flowing rivulets ran down the road, carrying leaves, moss and the odd village dance flyer, now sodden and somewhat redundant.

Charlotte abandoned the idea of a taxi and instead braved the lane on foot while balancing the cake in one hand. She hadn't had time to make anything and guessed everyone liked cake. On reaching the village hall, Mr and Mrs Frogatt were, by chance, just arriving too.

'Charlotte, I'm so glad you decided to come. Ogden says, as

long as he can hold a beer and rest his legs, I can do all the dancing I want. Come on, let's see who else is here.'

Charlotte followed her in, and immediately they were swamped by greetings and much cheek-kissing.

'Charlotte, this is Margaret.'

'Hello.'

'Nice to meet you, Charlotte. Oh, a cake, how lovely.'

'These two are Georgina and Chloe, both from the WI. I must have a word with you about joining.'

Georgina held out her hand. 'Love the dress.'

Charlotte shook hands. 'Thank you.' And then Chloe did the honours too.

'And the boots! Love them. Inspired.'

Everyone looked down at Charlotte's feet. 'Thank you,' she said as she did a pirouette. 'I couldn't decide, and it was awfully wet today.' She gleefully displayed the pink wellington boots with the blue bow, which matched the dress perfectly.

Charlotte looked up into the sky. 'I'm doing this for you. My lovely, lovely man,' she whispered.

Before she knew it, Charlotte was being whisked around the floor by Mrs Frogatt and then a myriad of husbands, granddads and the ladies from the WI. It wasn't long before she ditched the wellingtons and just barefooted it without a care.

'Thank you,' Charlotte said to Mrs Frogatt while they did a dosey doe with each other. 'I really needed this. I haven't had this much fun in a long time. I really appreciate your help today, too.'

Mrs Frogatt came in close. 'What did you use the Land Rover for?'

Charlotte giggled. 'I got rid of the past, Mrs Frogatt. You helped me do that.'

Mrs Frogatt shrugged. 'I have no idea what you're talking about. I just hope it means you're here to stay.'

The song came to an end, and Charlotte stood alone for a second or two. A voice she recognised came up close behind her. 'It would be a great pleasure to have the next dance, if I may?'

Charlotte turned quickly on the spot.

'Jim! Lovely to see you again. I'm so sorry about Bullet.'

'Life doesn't last forever. It's sad when you lose someone you love. But we have to put our best smile on and try to heal the wounds. I could have brought you some shoes if you'd said you were desperate.' He said looking at her feet.

Charlotte smiled. 'I'm fine, thank you, and never a true word spoken, Jim. We have to look up, realise what we have and be thankful. Although we never forget.'

Jim took her hand, and they started a slow waltz. 'That's good to hear. It's no good getting bogged down with unnecessary sadness. You're a good dancer. Where did you learn to waltz?' he asked.

'Thank you. At school, with Sister Josephine. She, being the man, obviously. It's complicated. A convent, you know?'

'You're a beautiful woman,' he replied.

Charlotte stopped in her tracks and looked at him.

'I mean it. I also liked your compassion for Bullet just before he left us.'

Charlotte carried on looking at him.

'Sorry. I... I shouldn't have said that. I'm embarrassing myself.'

'No, Jim. It's a lovely thing to say. You haven't embarrassed yourself at all. Thank you.' An awkward silence lay between them, neither of them knowing what to say next. Then Jim intervened. 'Look, how about we get a drink, maybe take them out onto the veranda?'

Charlotte nodded. 'Great, I'm parched. Just a tonic water or lemonade for me.'

Charlotte followed Jim outside. 'Cheers,' he said, as they chinked glasses.

'So, do you think you might get another dog?' Charlotte asked.

Jim's eyes were fixed on the floor. 'I really don't know. It's too early to say. I'm not sure I can replace Bullet so easily.'

'I totally understand. Sorry. I didn't mean to —'

Jim stopped her. 'No need to apologise,' he said, placing his glass on a nearby table. He took his hand and placed it on Charlotte's cheek. 'Thanks again for being so kind.' Then, before she could answer, he came in close and kissed her on the lips.

'Jim!' Charlotte blurted. 'What are you doing?'

He backed away quickly, like a scalded schoolboy. 'I'm sorry. I thought you liked me?'

'I do, Jim, but not like that. I thought we were just having a drink.'

'You were giving me all the signals.'

'No, Jim. Look, I'm sorry if it looked like that. I... I'm just not in that kind of place. I still have a lot of processing to do.'

'I feel like a complete idiot.'

'Sorry Jim, I didn't mean to react like that. I guess I'm just not ready. I need time.'

Jim stormed away into the darkness, leaving Charlotte alone on the veranda.

'Jim! I'm sorry. Jim!' she shouted after him, but he had gone.

23

NUTS

'I will break you if it's the last thing I do!' Charlotte said as she lay on the floor with her head in the cupboard under the sink. The hefty DIY book lay open on her chest, and with both hands, she was attempting to unscrew the U-bend. The sink had been getting worse, with the water barely draining. Above all, it was beginning to smell.

Getting both hands on the fixing at such an awkward angle was difficult. In addition, she was unsure of which way to twist it. In the book, the photo was from the top and, in her mind, she struggled to compute the orientation as she lay beneath. She recalled Peter saying something about how he fixed his. 'Righty tighty and lefty loosey,' she thought he said. And assuming it was as if you were looking at it, regardless of whether your head was rammed up against the stopcock and your feet in the vegetable rack.

With all her might, it started to revolve. She was sticking with lefty loosey, but it seemed to jam rigid. She hit it with a bottle of bleach, and water started dripping into her face.

'Jeez, this really can't be so difficult?' she murmured to herself.

She wedged her foot against a sack of potatoes, which gave her a better purchase and then gave it one last try. It moved a tiny bit and then, to her surprise, came loose. She smiled and gave herself a silent 'you're brilliant, you know,' and carried on twisting. The screw bit, nut or whatever it was, became completely free, but the pipe leading up to the plug was rigid. She wiggled it, and then the reality struck home as the foul-smelling water, hairs, and gloop cascaded directly into her face. Not able to see, she immediately wiped her mouth on the shoulder of her t-shirt.

She took to her knees. 'I'll show you who's boss, I'll show you,' she said, throttling the U-bend in her hand and waving a stern finger with the other. The next mistake was something she thought anyone could make. She started to rinse the U-bend out in the sink, forgetting that nothing was connected below, and completely flooded the cupboard, its remaining contents and her feet as the water gushed out onto the floor.

She couldn't move. She looked at herself and laughed. She couldn't stop laughing.

'What a pickle,' she said as she paddled her feet in the water and laughed until it hurt.

Eventually, she reattached the pipework and, with an air of smugness, rewarded herself with a cup of tea.

'Okay. What's next?' she thought.

'Tools! That's what I need.'

Then she disappeared into the shed.

Rummaging in a large wooden box, she found a rusty hammer and a drill with a manual handle. She rotated the handle. It seemed antiquated, like something an old fashioned dentist might have at his disposal. On finding the wood saw, she placed it to one side and carried on rummaging. Tape measure. Perfect. But no electric drill, which she hoped to find.

On leaving the shed, she climbed onto the dry-stone para-meter wall and, with the saw in hand, started cutting a branch off the oak tree which dominated the left side of the garden. It was a low branch of small diameter, about the size of her upper arm. Diligently remembering to make an undercut first so that the branch, on its departure from the tree, didn't tear the bark and cause irreparable damage. Peter had taught her so much!

After much sawing and using both arms, the branch crashed to the ground. Charlotte then trimmed smaller side shoots and cut off about two feet from the thickest end. She placed it in the kitchen for later, then set about measuring up for a shelf she planned to erect and had another cup of tea.

The timber for the shelf was a gift from Mr Frogatt. During an office clear-out, he dismantled it and offered it with the brackets.

She retired to the seat in the window and looked out over the garden. The oak to the left and the beech to the right offered a vista into the view beyond. Open fields, occasionally sheep, sometimes a horse or two, and mile after mile of lime-stone walls. The gap between the oak and beech tree was just enough to funnel her eye into the distance like an odd couple stood side by side, tilting their heads apart to create a gap.

Later, in the kitchen, she set about stripping off the bark from the oak branch with a knife. The peelings merely dropped onto the wooden floor. Then, gouged the knife into the wood to try to form a point at one end. She soon realised she may need to accomplish it over a series of evenings.

24

NATURE'S BRAMBLE JELLY

The late summer sun warmed the air, and the hedgerow's abundant offerings were too much for Charlotte to resist. She decided to explore the view. No official path, no ultimate destination, just to follow the view and see what she could find.

Fat, ripe blackberries soon started to fill her basket. She knew blackberries soon go over and become bitter and sour, so the timing was vital. She climbed numerous five-bar gates. Her wellingtons provided excellent grip, and her stride was purposeful as she followed the hedge line. The blackthorn almost buckled under the weight of sloes, which went into her backpack. Sloe gin was a favourite autumn tipple of hers.

Further ahead, she negotiated a series of badger holes, distinctive by the large entrances and heavily trodden pathways with piles of straw, grass and bracken. Old bedding, which the badgers had cleaned from their sets.

'Hello, badgers,' she said, acknowledging their presence, albeit hidden underground.

A little further, she came across a veteran tree. Instantly

recognisable by its upright demeanour and unique, grey and blocky bark, formed by deep fissures in between. The vast array of dangling fruit confirmation enough, this pear tree was old. Many of its upper branches had snapped off from the sheer weight of the fruit. This was, in fact, a great gift for Charlotte, as it made copious amounts available for easy picking, and she made the most of it. She produced an additional shoulder bag from the backpack, and it soon became full.

The basket and bags were now heavy from the haul, but she persevered. She could see that the land began to fall away and a rocky promontory accessible through the trees ahead. Placing her stash carefully on a rocky perch, she climbed the limestone, searching for handholds and using the sturdy sole of her wellingtons to scramble to the top. The rock, warm from the residual summer sun, felt smooth and accommodating, and then, unfolding before her, a patchwork of golden fields breaking up lush green grazing pasture, linear hedgerows and mature trees adding height and depth. True English glory and picturesque beauty and the shop floor of honest, hard-working people, all toiling in harmony, mutual respect of humans and nature, producing everything essential for survival. Flour, meat, cheese, milk, fruit and vegetables were all within her eyeline. Taking in a deep, deep breath, Charlotte consumed all the splendour to consolidate her heartfelt love for her newfound home. It was unexpected, that was for sure. She didn't think she would be in the Yorkshire Dales, surviving as a woman on her own, but that was life's way of shoving her in directions she never imagined. And the truth was, this was home now, and she had two options. Resist it or embrace it.

Her eyes couldn't get enough of all the detail below. Small farmsteads, tiny cottages, winding roads and arched stone bridges leaping over clear, meandering rivers. She sat and tucked her knees into her chest. A wave of melancholy filled her core, and the bittersweet taste of joy and utter sadness mixed together, making her shiver and rock gently on the spot. Why wasn't she able to share this with the one she loved? He was the one who had brought her to this place and then cruelly abandoned her. She recalled Peter telling her that trees spend a third of their lives growing to maturity, a third in maturity and then a third dying, and in between, all manner of different weather and stresses prevail.

'You just have to allow nature to take its course and grow strong enough to cope,' he'd say.

At the time, she dismissed it as another one of Peter's tree anecdotes, but he was right. She hadn't realised how bold and educated he was about life. He was, in many ways, not only an absolute ambassador for working-class culture and the inherent pride and knowledge within, but for the symbiosis of man and nature.

Her shiver slowly turned into warmth as the shadow of the trees behind her gave way to the sun.

'I feel you, Peter,' she said. 'I know you are here with me, and I'm grateful for everything you have taught me.' She looked up into the sky and the view beyond. 'Thank you from the bottom of my heart.'

An old rowan tree defied gravity and geology by apparently growing directly out of the rock. Its low branches enabled Charlotte to grab hold and swing down to where her pickings of the day were stashed. She gathered them together and headed along a deer track in the direction of home, but this time along a secluded valley. It was the right choice as the route offered more late summer produce. This time they were damsons and plenty of them. Ripe, and some of them oozing sugar from their flesh. Charlotte filled every available space in the basket and other bags until she was weighed down and barely unable to carry them.

The kitchen countertop was already awaiting with rows of sterilised jam jars. Charlotte immediately got to work washing and grading the fruit. Blackberries first into the giant pan on the stove. Some unripe to add more natural pectin, sugar and then lemon juice to help set. With the heat applied, Charlotte took a pen and started writing out the labels.

Nature's Bramble Jelly.

The overall plan was to jam the blackberries and damsons and stew and freeze the pear. Then, maybe a pear crumble for the Frogatts and one for Jim? As a way of an apology she thought.

Charlotte caught a glimpse of herself in the window as the daylight began to fade. She did a double take as she saw herself in denim dungarees, a white and blue checked shirt, and sleeves rolled up way beyond her elbows. Her hair up with a matching checked scarf, she chuckled to herself as she thought she looked like a land army girl following a long day in the fields. She grabbed a handful of blackberries she kept back for garnish, stuffed them into her mouth, and then carried on chuckling.

While the pot gently bubbled, she ventured into the garden before the daylight completely disappeared. Armed again with the wood saw, she pushed a ladder up against the beech tree and began sawing. A branch close in size to the oak one before, she found it hard going. The timber was tough. Much harder than the oak, it seemed, which surprised her. The undercut first, just enough to sever the bark and create a notch without the branch's weight trapping the saw. Then the top cut.

She hadn't realised that it was now completely dark. The light had faded quickly and gave an early autumnal feel. She sawed harder and faster. Maintaining balance on the ladder and saw with both hands was difficult. Of course, the saw was old and probably blunt, but she persevered. The branch began to make subtle cracking sounds, and then, without warning, it snapped off, and as it fell to the floor, it hit the base of the ladder, causing it to topple and Charlotte with it. She hit the floor with a heavy crash, landing flat on her back.

Unable to breathe, she panicked. Her head was in a daze, and her body was limp. She scrabbled with her hands on the bare ground, then managed to obtain a shallow breath and then another. She was alive. She knew that, but was unable to move. What about the blackberries? She tried again to push herself over, but the pain in her lower back inhibited the manoeuvre. A deep breath reassured her that she was okay. She was probably just winded, but she had to get to her feet. Her phone was somewhere in the house, and she had no way of contacting help.

The garden was now pitch-black, with no light on in the house. Another deep breath seemed to give her some strength, and with one arm, she wrapped it around the fallen tree branch and pulled her body so that she could sit. The lower back pain was excruciating. She gritted her teeth, got to her knees, and set off towards the house. She could make that all-important call if she could just get to the house.

Her agonising crawl seemed to take forever, but once in the kitchen, instead of plucking the thistle spines out of her hands and knees, she reached for the gas hob and turned off the pan of boiling blackberries. She knew the outcome without being able to see into the pan. The smell of burned sugar filled the air. Next, she grabbed her phone from the table and called 999.

She had no idea she had passed out, but the next she

remembered was the hospital ward and many faces looking at her as they transferred her from a stretcher to a bed.

'Ms Winterbourne. Ms Winterbourne,' a voice said. She gave a little nod. 'We are going to take you through to X-ray, just to make sure nothing's broken. Okay?'

'Yes. Thank you, doctor,' she replied.

Charlotte didn't have to do anything. Just lay there as she was pushed along corridors and then into the X-ray suite. Her mind rushed to the burned pan of blackberries, and her heart sank.

'Why did I have to tackle that tree so late in the day?' she said to herself.

Sitting up in bed drinking tea was not only a great relief but a testament to how headstrong she could be. She wasn't going to be held back by some stupid tree and was determined to return to full recovery as soon as possible.

'Do you have anyone to take you home, Ms Winterbourne?' the nurse asked while handing her a biscuit.

'Erm...' Charlotte thought for a minute. 'Erm... No. No, I don't have anyone.'

'Don't worry. Maybe a family member of a friend, perhaps?' the nurse replied.

'I could call the Frogatts, I suppose? But I think they are away visiting relatives. Mr Frogatt hasn't been at work for a few days.'

'Anyone else?'

'I'm not sure. Can I just get a taxi?'

'We prefer someone close to take you so we know you're leaving us in good hands.'

Charlotte's heart began to race. A wave of anxiety made her hands shake. 'I don't have anyone.'

The nurse perched on the bed.

'Not to worry. I can arrange for an ambulance, but it might not be possible the way things are. They're needed for emergencies.'

Charlotte nodded. 'Of course. I... I wouldn't want to take that away from anyone. God knows I'm grateful enough. There is one person who might do it.'

'Oh, yes? A friend?'

'Yes, a friend. Jim. Jim Buckley. He might be too busy, but I have his number in my phone.'

'I'll leave it with you.'

∼

'Jim, I can't thank you enough. Sorry for having to call you out all this way to the city.'

'Charlotte, I wouldn't have it any other way. What are friends for if we can't help each other?'

'Well, I'll pay you back, that's for sure.'

Jim turned to Charlotte. 'You don't have to do anything. That's not how it works out here. If I didn't want to help, I wouldn't be here.'

'That's one thing I have noticed about you northern folk. You say it as it is.'

'Is there any other way?' he said in earnest.

Charlotte laughed, said nothing, just shook her head and huffed. 'Thanks again, Jim.'

On opening the door to the house, the acrid smell of the blackberries hit them straightaway. 'Nothing to worry about, Jim. I was doing some cooking when it happened.'

'That's a relief. You walked from the car well, so I think you'll probably be okay.'

'I think so,' Charlotte replied while struggling a little to get through the door. 'The doctor said, just some bruising and it will ache, but a couple of days and should be back to normal.'

Jim acknowledged with a helping arm and switched on the house's lights as he led her into the kitchen.

'What about food? I guess you haven't eaten?'

'I have some bread and cheese. I'll be fine with that. Oh, and some caramelised blackberries.'

She laughed.

Jim inspected the pan, which was still on the stove. 'Crikey! You really did burn them. Welded to the pan by the look of 'em?'

'I don't do things by halves.'

'No! Look, how are you going to get upstairs and... you know... the bathroom and things?'

'I hadn't thought about that.'

'Okay. Well, this is where I take charge. I'll make us some bread and cheese. What else do you have in here?' he asked, peering into the fridge. 'Okay, some tomatoes as well, and what's this? Caviar?'

Charlotte's face turned bright red. 'Oh, erm, yes. I do love a bit of caviar. I had a few tins from the old house. I brought them.'

Jim gathered the items and closed the fridge door. 'Blimey, you are posh. I've never had caviar. Fish eggs, isn't it?'

'We don't have to have it now, Jim, just the cheese and tomato.'

Jim shook his head. 'Right. I'll fix this, then get you upstairs. Do you want me to stay the night just to make sure you're okay?'

Charlotte's face instantly went from bright red to pale white. 'Oh, no, Jim. I wouldn't dream of it. I...'

Jim intervened swiftly. 'I mean to sleep on the sofa. I don't have to get back to anyone. I may as well kip here, and then if you need help in the night, I'm, well, you know... here.'

Charlotte mustered some defiant energy and tried to stand. 'I'll make that bread and cheese,' she said and then dropped back onto her chair.

Jim watched her and paused for a moment. 'I'll take that as a yes, then?'

'I don't want to put you out, Jim.'

'Charlotte. Stop being so proud and accept some help when you need it.'

The pair instantly started laughing together and couldn't stop. 'Stop it, Jim, you're making it hurt.'

'Serves you right. Anyway, where's the Bollinger to go with this caviar?'

He returned with two plates laden with torn bread chunks, wedges of cheese and dollops of black beluga caviar spilling over.

'There are some blankets in the airing cupboard. Grab them when you take me upstairs.'

'Okay, Ma'am,' he said, doffing his pretend hat.

THE ROYAL WE

J im had discreetly left by the morning. She'd felt safe while he was there, and her back, although painful, could move. Taking her prescribed painkillers, she tentatively ventured downstairs to find a note from him, offering more help should she need it.

Something was changing. She didn't know whether it was her mind, her attitude, or whether it was just down to the goodwill of the people around her, but she felt different.

Clearing out all her designer clothes felt cleansing. Yes, she could have sold them, which would have taken some pressure off the finances, but the act itself felt liberating.

Thoughts back to her privileged lifestyle and being able to have everything she wanted were starting to leave a sour taste, and she was now grateful for everything. Not that she wasn't grateful before, but now she was noticing the smaller things and coming to terms with the basic necessities of life.

A text from Sam.

'Charlotte, we are coming to visit. Jojo and I. In fact, we are already here. Call it a surprise. Just struggling to find the house. Narrowed it down to two. The huge farmhouse on the left with the horseboxes and a menage? Or the one with the black wrought-iron gates leading up to the mansion on the hill. Either way, we didn't want to just knock on doors. Sx.'

Charlotte replied.

'You are a tonic. It's neither. I'm in Holm Cottage. Right at the end of Stone Ghyll Lane. Turn left at the church, and if you end up in a forest, you've gone too far. Cx.'

'Oh! Well, we're at the church now. See you in two. Sx.'

'Mwah mwah, darling, it's so nice to see you. What a funny way of spelling home? Why do Yorkshire people put an L in it?'

Charlotte smiled. 'It sounds similar but means something completely different. Think of it as Holly House. Because of all the holly trees overhanging the lane.'

Sam still looked bemused. 'Anyway, darling, you're definitely missed in London. I keep saying, we should get Charlotte back in town, so she can let her hair down, but time moves so quickly. Anyway, here we are, the royal we!'

Charlotte finished kissing and hugging both. The painkillers helping to mask her pain, she invited them in.

Sam hesitated in the hall.

'Let's address the elephant in the room. We're so sorry to hear your news. It's one of the reasons we came. You must be devastated.'

'He was a good man. I struggle at times without him, and I'll never fully recover. You can't understand how it feels to lose someone you were so close to until you do. I realise he taught me a great deal, and I'm grateful. Very grateful. I'm hurting inside and I don't think the pain will ever go away, but strangely, I'm starting to feel… different with every new day.'

'Different? What on earth do you mean?' Jojo replied.

'Like things happen for a reason? I don't know. Despite losing a wonderful man, I feel he left me with something powerful. Like I'm more at one with myself. I feel kind of… genuine. Does that make sense?'

Sam and Jojo looked at each other, and Sam spoke for both of them.

'Not really. You're obviously still in shock. As you say, time is a good healer, and maybe a trip to London might just help you remember the good times again?'

Charlotte stopped, looked at them, and realised she was probably growing away from them too.

'Ignore the floor. I ripped up the old carpets and found the original wood. You only have to watch the splinters in bare feet. Mira not with you?'

'No. We hardly see anything of her these days. She's gone and grabbed herself a little American man. Into jewellery or diamonds, I think she said. Anyway, she's hardly ever in town.'

'I'm glad she's happy. I call and leave messages, but she barely ever replies.'

'She's besotted with him,' Sam replied. 'She travels with him everywhere. If it isn't New York, it's South Africa or somewhere in Asia.'

An uncomfortable silence allowed them to follow through to the kitchen.

'So… this is an interesting place. I always wanted a rustic property myself, but apparently, they're damp and infested with rats? You seen any rats?' Jojo asked, scouring the floor.

Charlotte laughed. 'Not the rodent type!'

Jojo looked at the whittled oak branch on the table. 'You making your own chair legs?'

'No. It's... nothing, just an old stick.'

'Anyway, Mrs Hathersage sends her love, by the way. Bumped into her somewhere... anyway, I can't remember just where. She left Loxley, couldn't stand the man, by all accounts, you know, your brother.'

Charlotte picked up the tree branch and started pointing it.

'He's no brother of mine. I never want to speak of him again. He's a cruel, cruel man.'

Sam intervened quickly. 'Sorry, Charlotte. She didn't mean to... you know. Anyway, we brought you a food parcel, look. In fact, let's call it a hamper. It's from Fortnum and Mason. Look, there's jam... olives and biscuits...'

Charlotte gave a courteous glance at the bag.

'I make my own jam. Blackberry, from the hedgerows and damson. We're making biscuits at the WI next week too.'

Sam and Jojo were stuck for words. Jojo smiled and stood rigid with her hands behind her back, and Sam pretended to carry on rummaging in the bag.

'Look, girls. I'm sorry. You just caught me at a bad time. I don't mean to be ungrateful. The hamper is lovely. A hammer drill would have been perfect for the shelf I'm planning, but jam and olives will do just fine. We go back a long way, and I appreciate your kindness. Come through to the sitting room.'

Sam and Jojo sat side by side on the couch while Charlotte perched on the seat in the window to relieve her back. She didn't want to tell them about her visit to the hospital.

'Have you seen the view?' Charlotte said, pointing out across the fields.

'Yes,' they said simultaneously without bothering to stand and look.

'There's something strange about you two. Come on... what is it?'

'We just couldn't wait to tell you, and that's why we wanted to see you in person,' Jojo said with a giggle.

Sam and Jojo brought themselves to the edge of the sofa and held out their left hands together.

'We're getting married.'

Charlotte couldn't believe her eyes. 'What, together?'

Sam looked at Jojo. 'No, silly, not to each other. To separate men. Well, actually, they're brothers.'

'You have to be kidding? How did that happen?'

Sam again took the lead. 'Well, I had a date with Marcus and fell for him straightaway, and then...'

Jojo took over the reins. 'Then Sam asked me to accompany her to an event Marcus was hosting, and that's where I met Monty.'

'Monty and Marcus?'

'Yes, they're twins.'

'Not triplets, then?' Charlotte quipped ironically. Sam and Jojo looked at each other, not realising the joke, and then, in complete synchronicity, held out their hands again to show off their rings.

Charlotte held them together. 'They're beautiful. You really deserve it. I did think that you would become two old spinsters living alone in ramshackle cottages.'

They all looked at each other and burst out laughing. Charlotte took the brunt of the joke and over-emphasised looking around the room at the peeling paintwork and damp patch in the corner.

'I'm really pleased. For both of you. Do you have dates?'

Sam once again spoke for both of them. 'Well, that's the other thing. We're having a combined wedding.'

'It was the brothers idea,' Jojo chirped.

'It makes practical sense,' Sam said, nodding. 'And we want you to be head bridesmaid to both of us.'

Charlotte took a moment to think. 'Me?'

'Yes. You'd be doing us both the greatest honour. Please say yes?'

'When is it?'

'It's six months away. There's a lot to organise, you know, both families, etcetera, but we do need a decision on some things.'

They both looked eagerly at Charlotte.

She remembered when Peter and she were thinking about their wedding, and a rush of anxiety ran through her veins as she stared into space.

'Are you all right?' Sam asked, looking concerned that she had said the wrong thing again.

'I can't believe what I'm hearing. Of course I will. You are my dearest friends. I'm going to wear my wellingtons, though.'

'What do you mean?'

'Oh, nothing. Yes, I'd be delighted. Congratulations. I think I have a bottle of something sparkly in the kitchen.'

Charlotte left the room to search for the wine, and Sam and Jojo hugged and shared a tear.

26

YOUNGER SELF

Droplets of condensation ran in competition down the window and then joined forces to speed their way to the bottom and pool on the rotting windowsill below. Charlotte followed each drop with her eyes as she lay in bed. The air was cold, and the only warm section of the bed was where she was huddled up within the duvet. She despondently stared at the decaying windowsill and prodded it with the handle of a spoon, which was in her coffee mug and now forming an island in the water.

Despite her moments of positivity and integration into village life, some days, she lapsed. A reminder that healing was a slow process. A restless night had her dwelling on her loss of Peter. She tried her best to move on and, most days, managed to convince herself she was doing well. But today, she felt sad. Simple as that. Sad, lonely, cold and despondent. That's how it was sometimes.

To make things worse, there was no hint that the boiler had kicked in. Its temperamental behaviour becoming a more regular feature. Charlotte poked her leg out from the warmth of the bed. The cold instant, and her breath could be seen in the air. Her dressing gown and slippers gave mild comfort as she made her way to the cellar. Spider's webs tangled on her face, catching her off guard on the steps. She hated the cellar and its dark, damp atmosphere. In her mind, it was the set of The Blair Witch Project and despite telling herself, it was just a cellar, it made no difference to her irrational fear that she was about to be murdered.

She thought the boiler appeared like an industrial furnace, like something from a redundant hospital or children's home. It had a creepy look about it, which added to the speculation of terror.

She tentatively approached and gave it a kick with her slippered foot. The solid equipment didn't respond. She checked the fuse, and the switch was live. Then pushed the button to fire it up it and failed to ignite despite an array of clicks. A mouse scuttled over her foot. Its tail flicking uncontrollably made her jump as it touched her leg. Even the mice were disgruntled at the lack of warmth. She added mouse-catching to her mental to-do list and sighed. In fact, it was more than a sigh. A whimper, a sorrowful whimper. She kicked the boiler again. The pain of her stubbed toe barely registered as she once again pushed the button to no avail.

She plunged her hand into her pocket for her phone and sank to the floor. There was hope in the boiler man. He'd been before and seemed to have an affinity with the ancient machine. It rang and rang, but no one answered. The despondency within her mind crept into her body, and as she sat in a heap on the dirty, damp floor, she started to shiver.

It just wasn't fair. How was she meant to cope with such a decrepit old house? She compared it to her past life and the myriad of house staff, who would make sure everything was perfect, the warmth of the Aga and amazing Mrs Hathersage, who seemed to have everything under control. Her shivering became worse, and she realised how it really was to feel lonely.

'It just isn't fair,' she said to herself.

Her eye was drawn to the blade of a knife, which was dangling on a piece of string from a large rusty screw in one of the rafters. Its blade, stout and of thick steel, and the handle, carved wood, like a butcher's boning knife. She'd seen them in the kitchens at Loxley.

Several attempts to call the boiler man remained futile. She knew his wife was not so well and assumed he might be busy with much more important things and that her plumbing catastrophe would be the least of his worries. She took to her feet and headed back up the stairs into the house, where she donned her wellington boots and assembled various items into her foraging basket. A small photograph of Peter in a driftwood frame. His impish smile, radiating and almost too big for his face, was one of her favourites. Next, the painstakingly harvested and whittled pieces of oak and beech wood, some string, a patchwork blanket and the knife.

The bitter northerly wind made Charlotte's face turn pale and icy cold. The lacklustre winter sun was attempting to warm the air with little success. Everywhere was wet from the persistent rain which had lashed the Yorkshire Dales several days previously. The grass was sodden, the rivers almost bursting their banks and the air heavy and foreboding. Charlotte slammed the door and didn't bother to lock it. She walked a few paces and then turned back to look at the house with mixed feelings. Kicking the back gate open, she proceeded on her usual summer foraging route, now bare and seemingly lifeless, and into the view beyond.

The rocky outcrop was somewhat drier as the clints and

grykes of the limestone pavement allowed water to permeate deep below into the underground streams. She took a moment to take in the view. As far as the eye could see, stone walls, pastures, small barns and tree-lined valleys. Then she laid out the blanket and sat cross-legged, looking out across the river below, the basket beside her and a numbness inside she was reluctant to shake.

First, she wrapped the string tightly around her wedding ring finger. Her engagement ring was safely stowed away and not on visual display. Her finger felt bare. Why didn't they marry before? She regretted not having his ring to wear and felt, somehow, it would have felt like she hadn't completely lost him. She wound it tight until the end of her finger turned pale. Then, leaving it to unravel naturally, she took out the two pieces of wood and held them in each hand.

Oak, strong, dependable, masculine and wise. 'This is you, Peter!' she shouted up into the bleak sky.

Beech, feminine, delicate leaves, sometimes brittle.

'This is me,' she shouted and held them both side by side, thrusting them up to the heavens. Tears ran uncontrollably down her cheeks as she reached for the knife. Its tarnished blade edged with a pristine sharpness and a point designed for separating flesh from bone felt empowering in her hand.

'This is for you', she shouted at the top of her voice.

The echo resonated in the air and then petered out to melancholy indistinction.

She held the knife tightly and forced it into the rustic but flat beech wood surface and began to carve.

P.

She pictured his smiling face again and took reference from the photo within the basket.

E.

Closing her eyes momentarily, she remembered their bodies entangled in passionate joy, which made her shiver.

T.

The blade now honed the letters effortlessly and enabled her to revel in his tender attentiveness.

E.

Entitlement. She didn't deserve him. She had been selfish, self-absorbed and judgemental. She was now paying the price, and it hurt.

R.

She couldn't take away his relentless honesty and pride. Her previous doubting was now a constant cause of regret and guilt. She owed him everything and felt ashamed of her previous self.

Taking her time to make his name as presentable as possible, her hand began to cramp, but the finished article had to be worthy of him. She pushed the whole thing away from her to let the light catch each letter. It was done. Some of the letters were not quite level, and the R squashed in at the end as it rivalled for its own space.

Cutting the string with her teeth, she draped it over her arm, took the oak branch, and eagerly sharpened the point.

The woody, earthy smell of the exposed beech wood made her put the point to her nose and took in its natural scent.

'This is me,' she said, thrusting it up again to the sky before clamping the two into a cross shape. Holding it steady with her thumb, she began wrapping the string around both of them. Tightly lashing them together like a girl guide's tent pole.

It was done. The final memorial to her dearest love. The only person who really understood her. The only person who truly had faith in her and the only man she had unreservedly given her heart to.

Taking to her feet, she located a patch of earth within the rocky outcrop and stabbed the cross with such force it stood of its own accord. Then, grabbing a large but manageable stone, bashed it further into the ground. Beating it harder and harder, the tears rolled down her face.

'I'm coming to you, Peter, I'm coming,' she shouted.

Her loud voice was tempered with despair. She wiped her grubby hands across her face in an attempt to clear her vision.

She looked back toward the basket. The tarnished blade of the knife stared at her, goading her.

'I'm coming to you, my love,' she whimpered, calmly picking up the wooden handle and bringing the blade to her face. 'I didn't deserve you, and I don't deserve myself,' she said, raising her voice again. 'Do you hear me, Peter?'

Gripping the knife with both hands, she pointed the blade towards her stomach and closed her eyes...

'Peter? Is that you?' She said dropping the knife.

Her attention was diverted to the sound of someone singing. Someone nearby. The singing became louder. She crawled to the edge of the rock and listened intently. She heard the voice again, and then a young girl appeared down by the river. No more than twelve or thirteen in age, she ran carefree along the water's edge, appearing not to care about getting her feet wet as she ran along, jumping from rock to rock. Seemingly tomboyish and defiant and enjoying the risk of potentially falling into the fast-flowing torrent, she gathered pace and continued to sing out loud.

Charlotte couldn't take her eyes off her. Who was she? Long chestnut-brown hair billowing behind her, dressed in jeans and sneakers and with an innocent look on her face. She looked familiar. Creepily familiar, the song now resonating in her mind, like a tune from an old movie she had watched repeatedly. Charlotte watched with great interest, staring at her youth and buoyant demeanour, and then, suddenly, the girl stopped dead in her tracks and stared back. The look on her face, now, ambivalent.

'Who are you?' Charlotte asked.

The girl stared back, motionless and silent.

Charlotte upped her tone. 'Who are you?'

The girl remained motionless, except for shaking her head. 'Who am I?' the girl said. 'Who am I?'

Charlotte shrugged and couldn't believe this stranger seemed to be confronting her.

They stared at each other in silence. Their eyes fixed on each other's, and Charlotte could feel her heart pounding deep within her core.

'What do you want?' Charlotte said with unease.

'What do I want? You need to think about what you want, the girl said, matter-of-factly. 'You're feeling sorry for yourself. Yet again, poor Charlotte feels sorry for herself, and everyone's against her.'

Charlotte could do nothing but listen.

'It's all too much, life's not fair, and I'm going to wallow in my own pitiful sorrow,' the girl said with a condescending tone, mocking her. 'You're no role model for a young girl like me. You're gross. A joke, a disgusting mess. Take a good look at yourself. Life doesn't owe you anything. The silver spoon world you were born into has abandoned you; no longer able to click your fingers and summon luxury to hide your fears.'

Charlotte continued to listen. Who was this impudent youth?

The girl sneered. 'You need to look deep inside that tormented brain, and work out who you are, instead of hiding from yourself. Life is tough, it's tough for everyone, and there's only one person who can rescue you from your self-pity.'

Charlotte started to nod. The girl's words hit her like repeated slaps in the face, but, somehow, she knew she was right.

The girl took her gaze to the fast-flowing water beneath her, held it momentarily, and then fixed her eyes once again on Charlotte.

'To look within oneself, try looking further than yourself, look beyond your immediate pain and find your own truth. It's out there. It's waiting for you.'

Charlotte took a series of shallow breaths. Her own truth? What did she mean?

Her eyes were drawn to the photo of Peter in the basket. She took a deep breath and bit her lip.

'But what...'

She looked up to see the doubled-over back of the haggard old woman she'd encountered before walking away from her. She looked back, and Charlotte was again drawn in by her knowing eyes.

'Hey!' she shouted, but the woman turned and carried on walking until she disappeared into the view beyond.

27

WOMEN'S INSTITUTE

C harlotte was determined to be able to attend her first WI event the following Saturday. She felt privileged to be invited and didn't want to let anyone down.

Anytime, Guilt-Free Biscuit-Making was the title, and they would all be making their own biscuits at the school as it was the only place with two ovens and all under the instruction of Izzy Beckwith-Smyth. Izzy, who was formally from the village, had subsequently moved to London and was now a food blogger and influencer. She was back on her old stomping ground to help the ladies with new culinary thinking and how to make biscuits without flour, butter or sugar.

Charlotte's mind was boggled about what could be used instead. Still, she was more interested in forging more friendships within the village. By Thursday, she was back at work and, that evening, made pear crumbles in three separate tins and used flour, butter and sugar for the topping.

Her apparition the previous day with the girl had unnerved her. She couldn't quite understand what had happened? The girl appeared to resemble her younger self, yet, was worldly wise, and talking as if she were the grown-up. Mysterious. And then she seemed to turn into the haggard old lady. It was bewildering and surreal, yet incredibly tangible, as if it were meant to be. She resented being challenged in that way, but at the same time, she was glad she had. It was bizarre, but made her think twice about feeling sorry for herself, and in doing so, opened a new door in her mind. A door to wider thinking and a door to her inner self.

It was announced that Amanda had given birth to a beautiful baby boy and would not be returning to work as Mr Frogatt's assistant. Charlotte had therefore been offered the full-time position with a view to training as the vet's assistant. She was overwhelmed by the offer and willingly accepted. She was a working woman now. A necessity for sure, but she was actually enjoying working. Previously, she was preoccupied with lunch and dinner engagements, fundraising galas and family commitments. All in the distant past now, but somehow, she didn't miss it, and her work with Mr Frogatt seemed to have a real purpose and gravitas. She had always relished her involvement with her animal charities, and although no longer in a fortunate enough position to contribute financially, she felt she was actually working at the coal face of animal welfare and was, literally, sometimes a matter of life or death.

It was a bright morning, and a brisk walk into the village was what she needed to stretch out her back. She was feeling good, so she packed one of the pear crumbles with the intention of calling in on the Frogatt's as a thank you for all they had done for her. Turning right just after the church, she headed up the high street, and as she passed the old bric-à-brac shop, something caught her eye. An old, but beautiful bike. A woman's bike with a very handy basket on the front and, more importantly, a worn but comfy leather saddle. She entered the shop to enquire.

'Mornin'', the shopkeeper said. He was unloading even more items onto the already crowded shelves and floor. There was barely room to walk, and Charlotte had to pick her way through the antiques and junk, which appeared to have been there, by the thickness of the dust, for decades.

'Hello, I'm Charlie. I'm down at Holm Cottage.'

'Oh yes. Holm Cottage. Is that place still standing?'

He didn't seem so friendly, so she got straight to the point. 'I'm interested in the bike you have out front?'

He said nothing, just continued rummaging in the boxes.

'I'm assuming it's for sale?'

He looked up. 'Everythin's for sale in 'ere love.' His accent was one of a true Yorkshireman, either missing letters off at the end of his words or, with equal regularity, the beginning too and when he couldn't be bothered with any letters, he remained silent.

'In that case, I'd like to buy it. I'm on my way to see friends now, but I'd like to pick it up on my way home if that's okay?'

The man stopped rummaging. 'It'll need some oil on them there gears and the front brakes got an intermittent squeak.'

Wow, quite a few letters there and all were delivered at the right time, she thought. Must have been the pound signs in his eyes, perhaps?

'Lovely, I'll pay you now and pick it up in about thirty-five minutes?'

'Right you are. Twenty-five pounds cash.'

On leaving, it did cross her mind that there must be some old tin of oil in that shop he could put on the gears to help her out. Anyway, she had a pear crumble to deliver and all before the *Anytime, Guilt-Free Biscuit-Making* session at 11.30.

The Frogatts were delighted with their crumble and reciprocated with a box of six eggs from their own chickens. On remembering she was collecting the bike, Charlotte nearly refused but then thought carrying the eggs in the basket was a fabulous first test of worthiness. She noted that Mrs Frogatt looked a little unwell again. Her face was thin and pale, and she trembled as she handed over the eggs, but she mentioned her high blood pressure and a recent stomach bug, which put Charlotte at ease.

In view of the bric-à-brac shop, she noticed the bike was still out front and the price ticket still attached to the handlebars. No puddle of oil on the floor too, but she was happy. If all went to plan, this could get her around the village a little quicker, including to and from work.

A quick adjustment of the handlebars, and she was off. The bike had a comfortable upright position, and the saddle, already living up to expectations. The gears did crunch somewhat when passing the church, but it didn't hold her back. The squeaky brake was a novel distraction that would have to get fixed sooner than later.

With no time to waste, she unloaded the eggs, packed her apron and rolling pin (as requested), and headed off to the school and the biscuit session. Squeak, squeak, squeak...

'Lovely to see you again, Charlotte,' Margaret said, stepping out of her car.

Charlotte propped her bike against the wall, just inside the school gate. 'And you, Margaret. How are you?'

'Oh, you know. Trying to fit everything in. Both my children are at university, but at different ends of the country, so

Simon and I feel like long-distance lorry drivers at the moment.'

'Where are they?'

'Millie is at Edinburgh and Phoebe, Brighton.'

Charlotte shook her head. 'Wow, they really have spread their wings.'

'Well, it's only when they move accommodation or back home for the holidays it becomes interesting. Simon said, the other evening, we are like ships in the night.'

Charlotte smiled graciously. 'Relationships are never easy, are they?'

The two of them were greeted with the lovely beaming face of Izzy Beckwith-Smyth and shown into the school kitchen. Margaret instantly knew the other ladies present and introduced Charlotte as a newcomer to the village.

Izzy showed them immaculate, individual stainless-steel tables already set with ingredients and apparatus. Charlotte produced her rolling pin and tied her apron with enthusiasm.

'We're just waiting for one other,' Izzy said, addressing the whole group. 'Seven is my lucky number and should work well in here today.'

Charlotte unloaded the bag in front of her and examined the contents. Margaret did the same. 'So, you never said whether you have any children?'

Charlotte replied while pausing with the ingredients. 'I have a lovely daughter, Lucy. She's living with her father at the moment.'

Charlotte was cut short as Izzy suggested they get the ovens lit and warming while they wait.

The kitchen was modern yet set within the Victorian-age school. The fabric of which had barely changed. The walls, floor to ceiling in white ceramic tiles, and a wooden parquet herringbone floor that was stained and weathered from the years of use. Modern appliances and gleaming stainless steel consolidated the canteen feeling along with gigantic pans, ladles, and baking trays, the size you would imagine from a large prison.

'Okay, ladies, apologies for the wait. We'll give it another few minutes, and if our other attendee doesn't show, we'll make a start. While we're waiting, I'll introduce myself. I'm Izzy. I originate from the village, and my parents, you might know, are still here, up at High Brow Farm.'

Everyone nodded, and Charlotte smiled.

Izzy continued. 'As you may know, I stayed in London after my studies and write for various food magazines as well as my own blog, which is growing from strength to strength. I came across this fabulous recipe in a little café off the King's Road and, if you're like me, I love a biscuit, or two, but can never really feel like I can indulge.'

Everyone nodded and laughed.

'So, today, we're making guilt-free...' she paused. 'To a certain extent. But no flour, butter or sugar is not only good on your waistline, but gluten and dairy-free too.'

'Sounds good to me!' Charlotte said with raised eyebrows.

Izzy smiled her young, exuberant smile and looked at the huge clock on the dining room wall through the open hatch.

'It doesn't look like our other lady is coming, so I'll make a start. So, welcome, ladies. As I said, my name is Izzy, and today we'll be making gluten-free...' She was abruptly interrupted as the door flung open, and in marched the latecomer.

'Gluten-free! It's hard to believe. A biscuit without flour? I was too intrigued not to attend,' the lady said loudly as she bustled in and took her place at the spare table.

'Is this my place?' she declared assertively.

'Hello, Lady Mountjoy,' Izzy said, not showing any kind of dismay she had been interrupted.

Lady Mountjoy acknowledged the other ladies with a courteous yet distant widening of her closed mouth. She lingered slightly when she saw Charlotte, and one eyebrow raised as if to question why a newcomer was invited.

Charlotte smiled back but remained silent. Then Margaret turned her head and gave Charlotte a knowing look before continuing to unload her ingredients from the bag.

Izzy went through her opening introduction, especially for Lady Mountjoy, and everyone held in their frustration as they listened one more time.

'Okay. Has everyone brought their rolling pin?' Izzy asked.

Lady Mountjoy immediately responded, 'Rolling pin! Am I wrong in understanding we will not be using flour?' Everyone else raised their rolling pins with glee. 'Well, what on earth are we using rolling pins for?'

Izzy held up a plastic bag in one hand and her rolling pin in the other. 'Almonds! We will be making our own almond flour. Ladies. I find it best to imagine someone you really don't like and give it everything.'

Charlotte and Margaret immediately started bashing their pins onto their bags of almonds. Lady Mountjoy appeared despondent, but Izzy came to the rescue with a spare one she had brought, and the kitchen was soon filled with grunts, groans and the occasional *Take that!* as they proceeded to pulverise their contents. Charlotte and Margaret occasionally shared a glance as their almonds turned finer and finer.

'Who are you imagining?' Margaret asked Charlotte.

'But what is the recipe?' Lady Mountjoy asked as she let Izzy take most of the responsibility for her almonds.

'Great question. Of course, your fabulous almond flour, a

pinch of salt, coconut oil and honey. Some of nature's best,' Izzy declared proudly, then gave Lady Mountjoy's bag another pounding.

'Genius,' Charlotte said. 'I suppose you could use maple syrup too?'

'Exactly! Yes, I've used maple syrup, and it works just as well, and even the two together,' Izzy replied.

Lady Mountjoy took a step back and examined her immaculate nails, as she allowed Izzy to continue with her almonds.

'We have our own honey, of course, but where does one find maple syrup around here?'

Margaret wasted no time replying. 'At the Co-op.'

Charlotte added a pinch of salt and then combined her almond flour with the oil. Using a spatula, she pressed and needed it into a dough.

'It does look like a biscuit dough,' Margaret said, looking surprised.

Izzy smiled and went to further assist Lady Mountjoy but was instantly dismissed as she scrutinised the bottle of coconut oil.

'Didn't we use that for sunbathing back in the 80s?' Charlotte said, laughing.

Lady Mountjoy's nose seemed to curl up at the nostrils.

'Not in St Tropez darling,' Margaret replied, with both her and Charlotte bursting out in uncontrollable laughter.

Lady Mountjoy pretended not to hear, but by the way she poured in the oil and began beating the mixture, they knew she was on to them.

The other ladies followed suit. Then Izzy showed them how to roll the mixture in their hands to form a ball and then place it on the backing tray, ready for a little flattening with the back of a spoon and then into the oven.

'Ten to fifteen minutes, ladies. That's all. I've organised tea and coffee outside in the sun while we wait,' Izzy said, ensuring there was enough oven space for everyone.

They all gathered outside and chatted about their previous baking encounters. Lady Mountjoy stood next to the children's sandpit and by her stern voice, seemed to be ordering someone about on her phone.

'That's time, ladies,' Izzy said, rounding everyone up.

Charlotte and Margaret's faces lit up as they opened the oven door to find golden brown biscuits all plump and smelling divine. They quickly removed them and placed them individually on a wire cooling rack; both couldn't resist trying one each. They fanned their mouths as they nibbled on the hot treats.

Lady Mountjoy appeared and, still on the phone, tried attracting the attention of Izzy to retrieve her biscuits and enable her ordering to continue. Izzy was busy helping the other ladies with their baking trays, and when Lady Mountjoy eventually put her phone down, found an oven glove and retrieved her tray, she gave an almighty high-pitched shrill.

'These can't be mine?' she said, holding the tray at arm's length as if it were radioactive. 'Someone must have swapped them?' she continued as everyone looked at the very flat and very overdone biscuits in her hand.

'Maybe a little too much oil?' Izzy said positively.

Lady Mountjoy turned her head slowly and purposefully. Her chin raised, her lips pursed, and her nose flared at the nostrils. 'Impossible. I followed your instructions to the letter!' she said, disgustingly casting the tray onto the table.

Charlotte and Margaret enjoyed a few more *let's just try another one*, bites as they exited the building and chatted by the gate.

'Thanks for inviting me,' Charlotte said, loading the parcel into the basket of her bike.

'It was a pleasure, Charlotte. It is a shame Lady Mountjoy always seems to steal the show. The thing is, she contributes, financially, so much to the community she thinks she owns the place. I think she needs to step down from that ivory tower and realise she is just a woman like the rest of us.'

Charlotte gave Margaret a kiss on the cheek.

'It's been a real tonic. Thanks again. I haven't laughed so much in a long while.'

28

DRILLS

T he sound of heavy rain lashing on the bedroom window woke Charlotte. It was barely light, but she wasted no time striding into her denim dungarees and red-and-white checked shirt. She'd bought them for a barn dance party Jojo had for her 40th. Along with the almost compulsory wellington boots, she felt the apparel fit for the day.

She exited the back door and entered the covered yard adjacent to the wooden shed. The ramshackle lean-to against the house, by the looks of it, had been the log-splitting zone for many years. A prominent and impressively sized section of tree trunk provided the centrepiece and sturdy block on which to chop. Surrounded by stacked logs and a plethora of offcuts, bark and sawdust, it had the sweet smell of the forest and productivity.

Embedded in the middle of the block, an axe, like King Arthur's sword, protruding magnificently as if its sole intention was to do business. Charlotte grabbed the hickory handle with purpose. She'd heard the term hickory before but had no idea what it meant. She said the word again in an American southern drawl as she read the branded lettering on the shaft.

'I'm huckleberry, hickory, hackwood,' she said out loud while chuckling and slapping her thigh.

What was strange was she was smiling. She hadn't remembered the last time she caught herself smiling and giggling on her own.

Straightening her back and adopting a more serious face, she took hold of the shaft and pulled. It was stuck fast within the solid block. She clamped her teeth together and forced it to move. A little at first, and then pushing and pulling it, managed to encourage it out of its resting place. It weighed a ton. The partly rusty head was like a block of iron.

Lifting it above her head, she realised, with a bit of encouragement, the axe would be more than capable of processing the timber before her and proved to herself she could see the job through.

Round offcuts of a tree branch, no thicker than her leg, looked easier to work with than some of the whole tree trunk sections. She placed the first one on the block, drew a deep breath, and took the axe in both hands. The blade looked dull, not sharp like a knife, but enough to bludgeon anything to death. Once again, the tool took some lifting, but once in the air, she let it fall towards the log. She hit it, but instead of splitting, the axe glanced off and imbedded itself back into the block. Charlotte pictured the wood burner in the kitchen in her mind, alive and providing warmth to the house. She would not give in and grasped the hickory handle with gusto. Once again, lifting it high and letting the sheer weight of the thing drop onto the log. Bullseye. A direct hit and a satisfying split right down the centre. She preened with joy and stuck her thumbs into the straps of her dungarees.

'Yep!' she said and placed another ready for execution.

The satisfaction of each split felt amazing. She wondered how, so much joy could come from such a simple task. Maybe she was turning into a country bumpkin? The joy seemed to have meaning. The fact that the process felt like a means to an end and that the end result, potentially life-saving, gave it gravitas and purpose. With the boiler still out of action, she was even more determined and lifted it again and deployed the fatal blow. She already had enough to keep her warm for an hour or so, and the excitement of generating more heat spurred her on even more.

She wiped the sweat from her forehead with her sleeve. Her back ached, but she still had enough energy to persevere. The pile of logs soon started to look substantial, and sweat dripped from her forehead. If the girls could see her now, she thought, Mira would have a meltdown at the sight of a woman harvesting her own fuel. She gave another solid blow on her account, and it yet again produced two mighty fine pieces of fuel gold.

Her basket loaded to the brim, she transported them into the house and placed them by the stove. Before long, an impressive stack surrounded it. With copious amounts of scrunched-up paper, egg boxes and almost depleted candles, she assembled a fire fit for a queen.

Striking the match and watching the flame take hold was something magical to observe, and Charlotte took a moment to watch the flame start small and then gather enthusiasm and strength as it set a sure foundation. In her mind, it symbolised new beginnings and a fresh start for her. It felt natural, and having supplied the logs herself, rewarding and satisfying. She knew she would now be warm, despite the boiler letting her down. As long as she had a supply of timber, she could make the place liveable and as homely as possible, and she would be grateful. She opened all the vents on the stove to let it breathe and stood back, marvelling at her handiwork as the fire raged.

Thankfully, the rain had eased when she mounted her bike and headed out. The fire was on, and she would leave it to settle in while job number two was put into action. Off she sped into the village. The vicar gave her a wave as she passed the church. He was pinning a notice to the board by the gate. On entering the high street, she avoided a large puddle, de-mounted and propped the bike against a lamppost by the hardware shop. At that moment, Lady Mountjoy came speeding past in her blacked-out Range Rover. The large, unforgiving wide tyres hit the puddle with such force the water shot up into the air, seemed to double in size and then deposited itself directly upon Charlotte. Her friendly wave extinguished immediately as the vehicle disappeared with blatant disregard.

'And good day to you too, Lady Mountjoy!' she said, watching the cold, filthy water drip from her clothes. Charlotte stood there, a distasteful look on her face and a feeling things surely had to make a turn for the better.

The hardware shop was a testament to bygone days. Shelves packed with household goods, jars, bottles, paint, nuts, bolts, and screws, plus animal feeders, pitchforks, gate hinges and even horse saddles hanging from the ceiling.

'Hello, Bob.' Charlotte sloshed her way up to the front door, water dripping from her and her wellingtons squeaked. Bob was up a ladder, adjusting the shop's ageing and heavily rotten wooden sign.

'Hello, Charlotte. By the look of you, I'd say you're in the market for some wet weather gear? Waterproof trousers, is it, or just the whole sealskin look?' He laughed.

'If I wasn't so defiant today, Bob, I'd be crying,' she said, smiling.

Bob descended the ladder. 'I saw what happened.'

'Lady Mountjoy —'

Bob stepped in and cut her off. 'Say no more. It's a different world up there at Mountjoy Towers. She doesn't care about us second-class citizens down here. I'm still waiting for her to settle an outstanding bill from months ago. Doesn't understand I have children to feed and a wife with a handbag fetish,' he said with a wry smile. 'She thinks she's better than all of us put together. But I'll tell you one thing.'

'What?'

'I don't think all that money makes her happy. Was she smiling when you saw her?' he asked, leading her to the huge wooden counter.

'Well, erm, no. I suppose not,' Charlotte said.

Bob turned and placed both hands on the counter. 'Well, there you are then. And look at you. Coming in her, like a drowned rat, and you're beaming from ear to ear. Now, what can I get you?'

Charlotte stood, hands on hips. 'I need firelighters, lots.'

Bob immediately slammed three packs down on the counter.

'I need sealant.'

'What kind of sealant?'

'Sealant, sealant. For stopping water coming through the window frame.'

Bob turned to face a huge shelf to his left and then looked back. 'Lots?'

Charlotte nodded and smiled.

Bob returned with three tubes of silicone sealant and placed them on the counter.

'Do you need a gun?'

Charlotte's face dropped. 'Erm, a gun? No thanks. I didn't know you sold weapons here too?'

Bob laughed. 'Well, we do. Shotguns and all, but I meant for your sealant.'

Charlotte laughed with him. 'Oh, yes, the squidgy thing. Just the one, please.'

'Anything else?'

'Yes. A windowsill.'

Bob paused for a moment. 'A windowsill?'

Charlotte raised an eyebrow. 'Don't you sell windowsills?'

Bob took his hand to his chin and stoked his beard. 'Half inch or three-eighths?'

Charlotte made an arbitrary measurement with her thumb and index finger.

'Windowsill,' she said, reiterating with her hand.

'Are you in your car?'

Charlotte shook her head. 'I'm on my bike.'

'Mmm. I'll cut you one from a piece of larch I have out the back and drop it around when I finish after work. Just the one?'

'Yes, please.' Charlotte said, feeling proud of herself and grateful he would save her from trying to strap it to the bike.

Bob chuckled. 'A windowsill!'

Charlotte chuckled too, and for a moment, they shared one of those rare chuckling moments in which no one really knew why they were.

'Anything else?' he asked.

'Yes. Some drills. For the drill.'

Bob gallantly disappeared into the bowels of the shop. Then appeared two minutes later. '6mm or 8mm?'

Charlotte looked puzzled. 'Why have you gone metric all of a sudden?'

Bob looked a little exasperated. 'We do timber in imperial and drill bits in metric. Coal by the ton, nails and screws in pounds and ounces and potatoes by the kg. It's a mixed-up world. Now which is it to be?'

Charlotte thought for a moment. 'I'm not exactly sure. I'm going to put a shelf up.'

Bob disappeared once again, and Charlotte marvelled at the sheer variety of goods on display in the shop and spied a mousetrap.

Bob returned with a smile. '6mm drill bit and wall plugs to match. I assume you want those too?'

'Thanks, Bob, sorry to be such a pain. I'm sure I'm your worst customer.'

Bob rested his elbows beside her equipment. 'Charlotte, you wouldn't believe the people I get in here. You're an absolute delight, I can assure you. Just be sure to start the drill off slowly, or you'll chew an almighty hole in the wall.'

Charlotte put her hand on his. 'Thanks again, Bob, and thanks for delivering the windowsill.'

Bob nodded. 'Do you have a drill for the drills?'

Charlotte laughed. 'I'd forgotten about that. Why do they call the drill for the drills a drill and the drills for the drill, drills?'

They shared another wonderful yet bizarre moment of chuckling.

'I don't know,' he said, raising his eyebrows. 'I guess we call them drill bits these days.'

Charlotte shrugged. 'Whatever.'

'Right you are,' he said, placing a cordless drill on the counter. 'Is there anything else?'

Charlotte hesitated. 'Yes. A mousetrap.'

Bob opened his mouth, about to speak, and Charlotte butted in. 'Humane. Please.'

Bob courteously nodded and bagged up the selection. 'You doing up the old cottage then? Looks like you're planning on staying.'

Charlotte looked Bob straight in the eye. 'Looks that way, doesn't it?'

29

CAKE AND CHEESE

The letterbox slamming woke Charlotte. Probably the electric bill, she thought as she lay there admiring her brand-new windowsill. Bob had gallantly cut it to size and helped her install it. The plan today would be to varnish it and then hopefully seal the edges while the rain held off.

Downstairs, the wood stove was still warm and the embers within, enough to tend and encourage back into a blazing fire. Charlotte loaded logs carefully as she remembered splitting each individual piece personally. She would have to split more later, but first, some coffee. She headed towards the kitchen and spotted a brown envelope by the front door. The franking was in clear black ink.

Hong Kong.

Another letter. Another reminder.

'I don't need this,' she thought as she sighed and placed it on the kitchen table between the Italian marble salt and pepper pots they had bought in Venice.

The smell of fresh coffee soon filled the kitchen, and a couple of crumpets placed on the wood stove slowly sizzled with anticipation. It felt like a Sunday morning. Quiet and still outside, no one rushing around with loud exhausts or leaf blowers, and it was dry for a change. Stirring her coffee, something caught her eye in the back garden. A deer. A solitary roebuck nibbling on the grass. She stood completely still and watched him. Such a beautiful, gracious, bold animal, yet wary and ready to bound away at the slightest hint of noise or human. She thought he might be a youngster from his short, velvety antlers, but his stature was of a leader in the making. She gave no direct comparison but knew she had Peter in the fore of her mind. She wanted him to be her inspiration now. Cast away all the unhappiness and move on, although the letter on the table was not helping. No longer was she eager to find out whether he was still alive. Too much time had passed, and the agony of opening up to those thoughts again frightened her.

On a positive note, the apparition of her younger self down by the river had seemed to jolt her out of her eternal misery. Realising that self-pity was not the answer. It was time to dig deep within herself and find the inner spirit she once had as a young girl. But no itching powder in the school bullies' beds now, instead a more considered approach to the life she had been dealt. Removing the crumpets from the stove, she spread a thick layer of butter and watched it melt with ease. She took a bite and enjoyed the warm, savoury taste as she continued to watch the deer. He was nervous. She could see it in his quivering muscles and the frequent lifting of his head to check for danger, but he lingered.

For some reason, she remembered the words of her shrink back in London. He often said that seeking happiness should not be your main goal in life because you would only be disappointed. Instead, get on with what is thrown at you and hope that some happiness will come your way as a result. Profound words indeed and, somehow, easy for him to say, especially as he wasn't living her life. Anyway, she was beginning to take comfort in his words. It didn't seem practical to be happy all the time, and being miserable just because you resented not being happy was totally defeatist.

The little things were beginning to make her feel good. Chopping the logs and fixing the windowsill, significant achievements and, somehow, a feeling of gratitude from doing it herself felt energising. Not only had she given up all hope of the boiler man returning her call, but she'd also given up on the thought of a court appeal. With Mr Scrivener had now retired and the new solicitor refusing to continue without adequate funding, plus, any hope of finding evidence in Hong Kong, probably shark's fin soup by now, and a letter waiting on the kitchen table, inevitably the nail in the coffin.

On went an old t-shirt and her dungarees and into the garden she headed. Creeping quietly and slowly, she hoped she might get a glimpse of the deer without glass between them. Poking her head gradually around the corner, she spotted him. The texture of his velvety antlers more tangible closer up. Then, without warning, a stamp of his back legs and he was off. Bounding away across the garden and out into the view beyond. A free spirit, free to roam, free to live and free to grow.

Axe in hand, Charlotte began to hone her swing and perfect her log-splitting action. Her muscles ached from the previous day's session, but she felt her back was stronger, and although she knew she couldn't sustain a whole day of chopping, the exercise was doing her good, physically and mentally.

Logs were transported into the house and stacked. She helped herself to another coffee. Then descended the steps to the cellar. It didn't matter what time of day it was, The Blair

Witch was still a distinct possibility, so a swift visit to grab paintbrushes, another futile yet somehow necessary press of the boiler button and the all-important setting of the mouse-trap, all carried out with the greatest of haste. All done, she set about varnishing the windowsill. The sun now streaming in through the window, her body felt the warmth right through to her bones. She put on some music. The Jam, Eton Riffles, Peter's favourite, and the song they listened to together, out on their bike adventure on their second or third date. She couldn't remember, but it was a happy day. She always thought The Jam a little working-class and rebellious, but as she listened more, it sounded upbeat, definitely rebellious, but nevertheless appropriate, and she smiled.

Dancing on the spot while applying the varnish and singing at the top of her voice made her smile. She was doing it. Making it work, and for the first time ever, her life felt meaningful and somehow, tangible.

Next was the shelf. She took a seat by the stove and finished off the dregs of coffee, which she'd left to keep warm on the top. Opening the hefty DIY book, she turned to the drilling holes section. A drill always looked intimidating. Lots of noise and the appearance of a sawn-off shotgun. It was something she was determined to conquer. It was only four holes, after all.

The name, chuck key, made her giggle. She didn't know why, but it did what the book said it would do, and she tight-ened the jaws around the 6mm drill bit and pulled the trigger. It made the tool burst to life, and as she remembered what Bob had told her, she felt her rebellious streak kick in, and revved it provocatively, pointed it at various objects in the room.

Firstly, she held the timber against the wall. She offered the bracket to the underside and marked the two holes with a pencil she had lodged behind her ear. A proper tradesgirl, she thought, as she stuck it back behind her ear and picked up the drill. Starting slowly, she positioned the end of the bit to the mark and began to excavate the hole. The book said to mark the drill bit with a piece of masking tape to show the depth of the wall plug. It went in a breeze, and the second to follow.

She knocked in the wall plugs with the back of a ladle. She'd abandoned searching for the hammer when the spider's webs increased in density and the residing spiders in size. A ladle did the job perfectly. One thing she did have was a screwdriver, and although a little bit hard to finish, the screws felt solid and the bracket too. The next bit was tricky. She had to hold the shelf in place while offering the second bracket, mark the holes and make sure it was level. She used the spirit level app on her phone. This whole manoeuvre involved balancing the shelf and phone in one hand and the bracket in the other, while scrabbling for the pencil and making the marks. It was all going as well as it could when there was a knock at the door. Everything fell to the floor, including her phone.

'Damn the door,' she said, rescuing the phone and checking it wasn't broken.

She opened the door.

'Hello, Charlotte, hope I didn't interrupt anything important by just calling in unannounced?'

'Jim. No, no, not at all. Come in, come in,' she said, secretly resenting his timing.

'I brought you some homemade cheese. Thought you might like some to put on your Christmas cake.'

'Have a seat, Jim. Tea?'

'Yes, please.'

'Christmas cake?'

Jim pulled up a chair in front of the wood stove. 'Yes. You

know it's a tradition to have Wensleydale cheese on your Christmas cake.'

'Are you winding me up, Jim? I know I'm a newbie in town, but I don't want to be the laughing stock.'

Jim presented her with the cheese. 'I wouldn't do that to you, Charlotte. You know I think a lot about you.'

Charlotte looked at him sitting on the chair in his smart jeans, the ones without frayed legs. He'd clearly made an effort, and that was compounded by his best 1970s heavy-knit brown jumper. He was kind, thoughtful, and well-meaning, but he carried a look of desperation, which wasn't sexy.

'Thanks, Jim, that's a lovely thought. Who knew? Cake and cheese.'

'Well, Christmas is nearly upon us, and it's a time for sharing.'

Charlotte remained standing. 'It's weeks away yet,' she said, trying to deflect the dreaded 'C' word.

'Well, you have to plan ahead for these things. Anyway. Hope you don't mind me saying but thought you might be a bit lonely down here on your own, and I'll have plenty of cake for that cheese.'

'Oh! Erm. No. Erm... I won't be. I'm invited to the Frogatts. Yes, they've already invited me. I'm also hopeful Lucy might visit too. Sorry, Jim, I wouldn't want to let them down.'

Jim took a swig of his tea. 'Of course. They're great people, the veterinary and his wife. Who's Lucy?'

'My daughter. She lives in the US with her father, and, yes, the Frogatts have really helped me in many ways, and they asked me ages ago.'

She was lying through her teeth, and behind her back, she crossed her fingers in the hope she would be spared any consequences. She just hoped to God that he didn't speak to them before she did.

'Not a problem at all,' he said. 'I have my sister and her family coming. Nine of us if her eldest son comes too. We can always make another space at the table.'

Charlotte instantly felt terrible. She imagined just the two of them huddled in the cowshed, stinking of sour milk, eating cake and cheese. Her heart sank to her feet, and the guilt of lying to him made her feel ashamed.

'That's very kind, Jim. Maybe I'll pop by in the afternoon?'

Back-pedalling was not her forte, and she knew, he knew, she was on the back foot.

Jim gracefully moved the conversation on. 'So. You look busy. Doing a bit of DIY?'

'Oh, you know, Jim, just making the place feel like home. A shelf here and a... windowsill there,' she said jovially.

Jim replied instantly. 'I'm a dab hand with shelving if you're struggling.'

Charlotte knew a second pair of hands on the shelf would be most useful, and she felt bad for rejecting his Christmas offer. She paused and thought carefully.

'I'm fine, Jim. Thanks for the offer. I'm pretty much done now. But before you go, I have some more jam in exchange for the cheese.'

She didn't want to offend him in any way. The problem was she was immensely proud of her DIY skills, and although it was easy to let Jim take control, she wanted to prove to herself she could finish the job.

She handed him a jar of jam, and Jim paused, came close to Charlotte and then held out his hand and shook her by the hand. It was a strange gesture. They were friends, no need for handshaking, but she could see he was awkward in his movement.

'I'll be off then.'

'Thanks, Jim, lovely to see you and thanks again for the cheese.'

Jim nodded and exited without another word.

Charlotte sat at the table, placed her head in her hands and sighed deeply. She was a bitch. A callus, cold bitch, and she could feel she'd hurt him.

She returned to the shelf and again assumed the octopus stance, balancing shelf, phone, bracket and pencil, and marked the holes as quickly as she could.

The drill, once more, chewed into the wall effortlessly and, this time, probably a little too aggressively, as the hole went deeper than the tape, and it wasn't so clean going in. The result was a wider hole than anticipated. The second hole had to be perfect so as not to merge with the first. They were relatively close together, and this was make or break.

'Start off slowly,' she said, and she did just that.

It was difficult to be slow enough to be controlled yet fast enough to actually form a hole. With absolute concentration, the drill progressed into the wall.

She removed the drill and stood back while crossing her fingers. The second hole accommodated the wall plug perfectly, but the first seemed to swallow it, and it disappeared into the wall. She pushed another one in, and it followed it into the cavity behind.

'Damn.'

Three pretty much perfect, and one the size of Gaping Gill. Then, she had an idea. Thin slithers of wood strewn over the floor, left from the log chopping maybe, packing the hole first might be a solution?

She placed a slither in and managed to wedge the wall plug. It needed a whack with the ladle, so she was hopeful it would be tight enough. She screwed the bracket in place and tentatively applied her weight. It held tight.

Then the timber shelf was placed on top, and it looked good. In fact, it looked really good. She tested it with the spirit level, and it was perfect. Not one degree out, perfect. She took the pencil from her ear and smoked it like a celebratory cigar.

'Oh yes, Charlie girl,' she said while jumping up and down and clapping.

This shelf was mainly for her books. But first, a photo of Lucy in a silver frame. Taken on a rare occasion when she was smiling on her birthday some years ago. The books were the ones she needed most. The DIY manual was followed by Jam Making for Beginners, a Yorkshire dialect book loaned to her by Margaret and a few novels that were on her TBR list. She left space for lumberjacks and log splitters weekly. Well, she thought about it and laughed to herself.

'I'm doing it, Peter, I'm doing it. See. I'm not a spoiled, toffee-nosed idiot. I can do shelves and screwy things.' Her voice wobbled, and a tear dribbled down her cheek.

'I'm doing it for you, Peter.'

To celebrate, she made a pot of mint tea and sat at the table with a bone china cup and saucer. Tea always tasted better out of bone china. She sipped it and looked at the envelope before her.

'I'm doing it for you, Peter,' she said again and then reached for the letter.

Dear Ms Winterbourne,

I hope this letter finds you well?

I write to inform you that we have now concluded that the death of Mr Peter Heath was caused by a rare shark attack and that no foul play seems to be implicated. We are therefore closing the case and have dealt with the ashes as you requested. Yesterday they were scattered within the Tai Po Kau Nature Reserve, among the ancient trees, as you wished.

Enclosed is the coroner's report and death certificate.

Please accept our sincere best wishes, and should you wish for any further assistance, please do not hesitate to contact me.

Mr Chang

'Tai Po Kau. I'll remember that,' she said as tears streamed down her face.

She could barely breathe and shook uncontrollably while tearing up the letter and throwing it into the stove to watch it shrivel and crumble into tiny pieces.

30

HOME

'Charlotte, I'll pick you up in ten minutes. We have a barn owl, which looks like it's been hit by a car. Mary Jenkins at Dean Clough Farm has it in her kitchen.'

'I'll pick you up in ten minutes.'

'Have you looked outside?' Mr Frogatt said, laughing.

Charlotte peered out of the window. A deep white carpet of snow covered everything, and the snowflakes were thick and falling rapidly.

Thick socks and tights, wellingtons, hat, gloves and scarf, she thought, as she finished her coffee and loaded the fire in anticipation of her return later.

She heard the Land Rover approaching and watched it ploughing through the already drifting snow. She'd never seen a barn owl up close and was excited to be, once again, on another adventure with Mr Frogatt. Thankfully, his arm was out of the cast and functioning as normal, although she secretly hoped she would be the driver again, especially in such demanding conditions.

The drive to Dean Clough Farm filled Charlotte with

amazement and joy. Snow stuck to the trees and capped the dry stone walls, like something from an artist's winter landscape. The road was treacherous in places, but open fields of pristine snow were like nothing she had seen. Of course, the alpine hotel she once owned had a dramatic backdrop, and the frozen lake and high peaks were nothing but magnificent. But the English countryside carpeted in brilliant white with its rugged stone walls, remote farms and limestone escarpments was infinitely more enchanting.

Mrs Jenkins had found the owl at the side of the road when she was returning from taking hay down to the sheep in the valley. It was the only road in and out of the village that had been gritted, so a car or a lorry had probably caught it as it was flying low. Searching for food in the snow was difficult, but the roadside offered some potential for a vole or smaller bird, perhaps?

Mr Frogatt examined the bird. It seemed it knew it was in capable hands and didn't flinch.

'It's a broken wing. But I'd say it's been a day or so. The animal looks weak. Do you have some cat or dog food?' he asked Mrs Jenkins.

She scurried off to the larder.

'Charlotte, get the blanket from the Land Rover.'

Mrs Jenkins offered the bird some cat food, but it was too weak.

Charlotte returned with the blanket as Mr Frogatt held the owl close to his chest.

'Wrap it carefully in the blanket, Charlotte. We need to get it to the animal sanctuary in the next valley immediately. They'll have everything it needs, but we need to hurry.'

Mr Frogatt thanked Mrs Jenkins for her sterling work and

exited the house, followed by Charlotte. He passed the swaddled owl to Charlotte.

'I'll drive. You hold the bird.'

Charlotte started to panic. 'I'm frightened I might crush it.'

Mr Frogatt climbed into the driving seat. 'You won't.'

All Charlotte could do was look at the beautiful face of the owl. Its feathers were as white as snow, and its eyes were deep black.

'It can't move its eyes like us,' Mr Frogatt said as he turned off the main road and into deep snow. 'They move their heads instead and almost all the way around. Monitor the eyes, Charlotte. We don't want it dying on us.'

'I can't do anything but.'

Mr Frogatt looked at her. 'Are you all right? You seem on edge today.'

Charlotte sighed. 'I received a letter confirming Peter's death. It wasn't a surprise, but it just seems so final.'

'But you seem to be coping?'

'He taught me to just get on with things and count my blessings, no matter what life throws at me. I've taken comfort from his words and grown stronger over the last few months, which is a surprise. Adventures with you help take my mind off things.'

Mr Frogatt smiled while keeping his eye on the road. His driving skills were being tested to the limit as the vehicle negotiated the narrow roads, often spinning the wheels and sometimes blasting through snow drifts. Eventually, they approached the animal sanctuary. Mr Frogatt had asked Mrs Jenkins to phone ahead, so hopefully, Mr Hawkins would be ready for them.

Mr Frogatt led the way in between various cages containing badgers, a fox, other birds of prey and what looked to be an otter. Charlotte was preoccupied carrying the owl to notice, and once in the door, they were greeted by Mr Hawkins.

'What do we have here?' he asked in his deep, commanding voice.

Charlotte handed over the owl and was drawn in by his smoky brown eyes and defined cheekbones.

'It's an owl,' Charlotte said in a state of fluster.

'I see,' he said, taking the animal and then looking straight back at Charlotte. She was caught off guard. He was very charismatic and ever so handsome. Dark hair with salt and pepper stubble. His liquid voice, like drinking audible Baileys Irish Cream.

Charlotte couldn't say anything else. She just blushed and folded the blanket so many times it continued to unravel.

'Broken wing, you say?' he said, examining the owl with his huge hands.

'Yes,' Charlotte said, looking at Mr Frogatt.

He opened the wing and confirmed it to be true, showing the fractured area to Charlotte and then reaching for a syringe and a glass container.

'It's weak. I'll give it some antibiotic and a steroid.'

She watched him administer the dose and marvelled at how purposeful and attentive he was, yet delicate in his handling of the owl.

'You did a great job,' he said, looking at Charlotte.

'Oh... erm... I didn't really do anything,' she said, looking at Mr Frogatt, who smiled.

An assistant entered and took the owl. 'I'll put her in the emergency bay and connect a drip. Hopefully, it will heal and make a full recovery,' she said, taking the bird through the door.

Mr Hawkins washed his hands and thanked them again.

'You think it will make it?' Mr Frogatt asked.

Mr Hawkins looked at both of them. 'It's a 50/50 chance, but we'll do all we can. You did the right thing, bringing it here.'

'Will it be able to fly again?' Charlotte asked.

'I can't see why not. If it pulls through. Acting as quick as you did will probably save its life. It's Charlotte, isn't it?'

'Yes,' she said, reaching out her hand.

'Call me Hunter,' he said while his manly hand took hers and firmly shook it.

Charlotte smiled and felt ever so nervous. What was wrong with her? How could someone make her feel so vulnerable and off guard? And Hunter Hawkins. What kind of a name was that?

'I'll keep you posted and feel free to call or drop in if your curiosity gets the better of you.'

'Erm. Okay,' she replied.

Her voice was like that of a ten-year-old schoolgirl.

The drive back was less frantic. The snow, easing, and various tractors could be seen delivering essential hay and food for a variety of animals. The ford into the village, where the road ran through the river, was beginning to ice over at the edges. The temperature had plummeted, and Charlotte hoped the fire was still alight at home.

'How's everything going at home? I bumped into Bob the other day. He said you'd started to do up the old cottage.'

'Oh, he did, did he? Well, he's right. Just trying to make it as liveable as possible. I'm learning. You know... slow but sure.'

'You're a very capable woman, Charlotte. You want it nice for Christmas?'

'Ah! On that note, I meant to ask you something. I did a

terrible thing yesterday. It's unforgivable, but I need to tell you.'

Mr Frogatt raised his brow. 'Go on.'

'Well, Jim invited me to his house for Christmas Day. You know I'm fond of him, but I don't want to take it any further and give him the thought I was interested.'

'Go on?'

'It's just... I said you and Mrs Frogatt had already invited me and I didn't want to let you down.'

Mr Frogatt lowered his brow into a stern face and looked at her.

'I'm so sorry. I feel ashamed lying to him and putting you in such a position.'

Mr Frogatt slammed his hand on the steering wheel, and Charlotte jumped.

'Hahaha, I don't blame you at all. I imagine it's pretty bleak up there at Jim's. We were going to ask you, anyway. Christmas is a difficult time of year for us.'

Charlotte was relieved to hear his laugh but could sense something deeper.

'Why's that?'

'My late wife... She took her own life on Christmas Day. I try remembering the good times, although Mrs Frogatt doesn't find it easy. She feels guilty enjoying the day, and I feel guilty that she feels guilty. In fact, we don't really do Christmas as a result. We'd appreciate your company.'

Charlotte stared straight ahead, and a silence ensued.

'Why don't you come to mine? Lucy, my daughter, may be coming. As I said, she lives in the US with her father, but I suggested to her that it would be nice to see her at Christmas. It would be a pleasure having you two in my house and give me an excuse to get all my DIY finished.'

Mr Frogatt grinned. 'I'll put it to Mrs Frogatt, and I won't mention anything to Jim if I see him.'

'Thank you. I'd like that.'

'She does make a mean Christmas cake, though, Mrs Frogatt. We'd have to bring that.'

'Do you have cheese on it?' Charlotte asked.

Mr Frogatt kept his eyes on the road. 'Yes. Of course!'

Charlotte pursed her lips and smiled. 'I'll put up a tree and get some lights.'

'Well, hang fire until I've put it to the boss,' he replied.

'Okay,' she said eagerly.

'So, it looks like you're hanging around for a while? Wasn't sure if you were going to stay.'

Charlotte looked out of the window at the stunning snowy landscape and the river valley stretching as far as the eye could see.

'This is my home now.'

31

SPECIAL DELIVERY

Alpine conditions could only describe the week leading up to Christmas. The snow had lingered and even topped up on occasions, and the blue skies accentuated the glistening white blanket which was now high on the rooftops and deep in the valleys. It was a light, dry snow, not like the usual wet, heavy and slushy snow of winters gone. It had a beauty, a calming effect and an optimism, Charlotte thought.

She had popped in to see how the owl was getting on, and fortunately, the devilishly handsome Hunter Hawkins, the wildlife's answer to Crocodile Dundee, wasn't there. He was rescuing a squirrel that had managed to get itself stuck in someone's bird feeder.

The owl was making good progress, and with increased strength every day, it was scheduled to make a full recovery.

Mr and Mrs Frogatt were confirmed for Christmas Day, the turkey was ordered, the cheese maturing and eagerly awaiting the cake, and Lucy was due in from the US for two days before flying out to Dubai for Christmas with her father and his new wife.

Charlotte trudged through the snow into the village. Crackers, lights, tinsel and baubles were ordered and waiting at the hardware store for collection.

'Hello, Charlotte.'

'Hello, Bob, is my special delivery here?'

'Sure is. It's quite a load. You on your bike again?'

He laughed.

She chuckled with him.

'No, but it does look cumbersome. I could do with a sledge,' she said, tongue in cheek.

'Well, it's your lucky day. We have sledges.'

'No way?'

'Yes, way.'

Charlotte had a mischievous look on her face. 'Do you have two?'

'Absolutely, but why two? The package isn't that big!'

'I'm excited that Lucy is coming home for a few days. She hasn't visited the house before, and I want it to be perfect for her. The decorations, the tree, and another sledge would be so much fun out of the back gate and down the fields.'

'We can stack them, they're plastic and will fit together, then put your box on top. You should be able to grapple them home together.'

'Perfect,' she said, clapping her hands.

Normally, she would only see a couple of other people on her way back from the village, but today, it seemed everyone was out to spectate her sledge antics. Margaret gave a friendly wave from inside the butcher's window. The postman, who was bravely still wearing his shorts, greeted her with a cheerful good morning. Two ladies from the WI shouted encouraging noises and offered a lift from their car, but she declined. In a way, she was revelling in the adventure. The vicar, as usual, was painting another measly millimetre of red paint on the thermometer at the gate. 'Good day, Vicar.'

'God bless you, Charlotte. You have a heavy load there.'

'I'm thinking of getting a horse and making this a regular feature,' she said, laughing.

'Could you make it a donkey? We're short for the nativity on Christmas Eve,' he said with a straight face.

Many a truth said in jest, Charlotte thought. 'I see there's a carol service and midnight mass on Christmas Eve,' she said, observing a notice on the board.

'You'd be very welcome, Charlotte, and anyone else or thing you wish to bring along.'

He was still obviously going on about a donkey.

'My daughter will be here this afternoon, but sadly won't be for mass. It'll just be me, I'm afraid.'

'Lovely to hear your daughter will be here for a short while at least. God bless you both.'

'Thank you, Vicar. I'm so excited. Much to do. See you for mass.'

The cottage looked much more homely, and the boiler, at last, had been fixed. A mouse had nibbled through a wire at the back and was shorting the ignition. Anyway, good results from the trap meant that the issue was likely resolved.

Charlotte set to work hanging the tinsel and putting up all the cards on display. Margaret had given her a beautiful wreath with pinecones, holly and willow for the front door.

She stoked the fire. It was still nice to have the stove on, despite the boiler being back in action. It gave a lovely cosy feel, and the smell of the wood, rosemary, and lavender she placed on the top added to the rustic feel.

She wanted it to be perfect for Lucy, and there was one last thing to make things complete.

The tree.

Mr Bickerdyke, the owner of the woodland to the side of the house, had given her permission to harvest a tree, and there were many small Norway spruce trees along the near bank, which she had her eye on.

Off she set with her trusty saw in hand.

The snow on the slope made it a slow process. Beautiful as it was, it was two steps forward, one step back. Her first choice of tree was a little lopsided, with a couple of branches missing, so she climbed higher where a near-symmetrical specimen stood. It was the right height, too, about 5ft.

Scraping the snow away with her bare hands was something she had not planned for. A shovel would have been very useful. Nevertheless, she persevered, knees in the snow and her hands beginning to numb. She had to excavate it to be able to expose the lower stem. Reaching into the hole, she started the cut. What seemed ridiculous to her was the size of the saw. The handle of it kept catching on the floor and also scraping in the snow, causing it to cascade back into the hole. It was much harder work than she had anticipated. Wood was so solid, despite the aggressive teeth on the saw.

'You're doing a great job,' a distinct voice said behind her.

She stopped sawing immediately but daren't look around. It couldn't be?

His masculine voice spoke again, 'That's a mighty fine tree. You chose well.'

Gosh, that tone was so familiar and one she hadn't heard in a very long time.

'Don't stop now. You're nearly done,' his voice encouraged her.

Her heart thumped into action. She could feel it in her temples and feet at the same time.

'Please tell me it's you?'

She was scared to look.

'It will look mighty fine in the cottage,' his voice was so definite and tangible.

Turning her head slowly, she caught sight of his legs. His sturdy boots were embedded in the snow. Her heart thumped harder and harder. Her freezing hands and knees were now completely forgotten about.

His body's unmistakable shape was right in front of her, and then his face. Smiling from ear to ear.

'Peter!'

Her breathing was rapid, and her heart was almost exploding with excitement.

'They told me you were dead?'

Peter stood strong, his hands on his hips. 'Don't stop for me. You're doing a fine job,' he said, still smiling.

'I can't believe you're here. After so long.'

Peter leaned forward. 'I've missed you.'

'And I've missed you so much. Do you know how bloody hard it's been without you? I've put shelves up, caught mice, and chopped enough logs to heat a whole city. What the hell were you doing out there. I can't believe you left me like that? I need to know everything. Every last detail, you hear me?'

She instantly felt guilty, giving him such a dressing-down, and then just stared into his deep blue eyes.

They stood looking at each other, not moving, just taking in the incredible sight.

'Don't just saw from the back. Do an undercut, or the bark will tear,' he said, dropping his smile. Charlotte turned her head to look at the saw, still engaged in the cut. She shook her head. This was so typical of him out of all the things he could have said right then.

She turned to look at him.

'Peter?'

He was gone. The only footprints were her own, and his smile was no longer present.

She collapsed into the thick snow. Another disturbing apparition she could well do without.

He was gone, and the dreadful, intestinal-wrenching feeling of utter, bitter cold loneliness engulfed her soul like an icy black cloud.

'Peter...'

32

ANGEL

Charlotte completed the felling of the tree with bitter disappointment deep within her heart. She felt she was going out of her mind. The sheer anger and resentment now driving her energy, she hauled the tree to the back gate and burst into tears.

Her apparitions were beginning to frighten her. She was so sure Peter was there right in front of her. It was so lovely to see him. He looked happy and healthy. But she was living in a dream world. He wasn't coming back, and she had to face the truth and clear her mind of any hope. Lucy was coming, and that was real and dreadfully important. She dried her eyes and shook her fist at herself.

'Come on, girl,' she said. 'Pull yourself together and show the world you are strong and capable. Your daughter needs you, so get a grip.'

Her face turned from despair to determination, as she grabbed the tree by the trunk and dragged it through the gate, up the step and into the house.

It was a struggle to lift the tree in its entirety, but she

dropped it into the stand, and it flopped to one side. Same plan as the wall plug, she thought, and fetched a large slither of wood and, using the same ladle technique, battered it in, and the tree stood tall and solid.

'Right!' she said, having another strict motivational talk with herself. 'Let's do this for Lucy.'

The lights went on first. Thankfully, they worked the first time. Then the new baubles. There was no theme, just random red, silver, gold and sparkly tinsel and the finishing touch on top, a very special keepsake, she had managed to hold on to, which was an angel Lucy had made at school when she was six years old. A recycled toilet roll tube, with ping-pong ball head and wire halo all sprayed in gold and a face in pen with a huge lopsided smile.

All she had to do was slide a pre-prepared seafood linguine, Lucy's favourite, into the oven with some garlic bread, and everything was ready.

She'd just finished her shower, and the sound of the taxi alerted Charlotte of Lucy's arrival. As she put on her jeans, she could see the car approaching.

Charlotte dashed to the front gate. The taxi door opened and outstretched a long stilettoed leg, followed by another and then a woman in a fur coat.

Charlotte looked in amazement. No longer was Lucy a little girl. She was a woman and inappropriately dressed for a rugged Yorkshire life.

'Darling, I'm so pleased to see you. How was your trip? Were the roads clear? Do you have any warm clothes?'

Lucy's heels sank into the snow.

'Mama, stop all the questions. Just get me to solid ground.'

Lucy hobbled precariously to the front door. The taxi driver unloaded two suitcases and politely dropped them inside the hall.

Charlotte took Lucy in her arms and squeezed her tight.

'My love, I've missed you so very much.'

'I've missed you too. Sorry I haven't been in touch much. Life in LA is just hectic. So many parties.'

'You don't have to apologise. I'm your mother. I'm happy that you have a busy life. Come through to the kitchen.'

Lucy followed Charlotte, and as they reached the top of the cellar steps, a mouse ran right in front of her.

'Oh my god, it's a mouse!' Lucy said, jumping up and down and then screaming.

Charlotte watched it scurry under the door.

'I think that's the one that got away.'

'You mean there are more?'

'I'm not sleeping where there are mice.'

'Come through. I'll set the trap again tonight, and you can help me release it into the field tomorrow.'

'You have to be kidding!' Lucy said, raising her tattooed eyebrows.

Charlotte laughed. 'I'll make some tea. So, what are you doing with yourself in LA?'

'Well, Daddy keeps saying I have to get a job, but I just don't have the time to look. I've been doing some modelling for Vogue, but that was just fun.'

'Wow, that sounds exciting. So, Christmas in Dubai?' Charlotte said, pouring the tea, pulling up a chair from the table, and knocking the back into its socket. 'The back is a bit loose, so don't learn on it,' she said, gesturing with her hand and smiling.

'Yes, I'll be there for a month with Daddy for the wedding, but there's a boy.'

Charlotte gasped and pulled her wooden stool closer. 'Who is he?' She purposefully focused on the boy and not the wedding.

'Prince Mohammed Atchuri. Remember? They came to stay at the Alpenblick. When we still owned it.' She sighed. 'Why did you give it away?'

Charlotte's face sank, and she cringed. 'Lucy, I didn't give it away. It was taken from us. You know full well. Do we have to go over all that old ground? It was painful for me too.'

Lucy looked around at the rustic kitchen. The small cooker with the handle hanging down. Half the cupboard doors were painted, and half bare wood. Some without handles and the spice rack hanging from a rope.

'Do you like that? I call it my freedom spice rack.'

Lucy raised her sluggy brows even more.

'Do you actually live here?'

Charlotte looked at Lucy. 'Yes. I actually do. And you know what? It's my home, and I'm very proud to have hung that spice rack, started painting the cupboards, and only half finished them, chopped the goddamn logs which are keeping you warm, successfully banished most of the vermin and kept this life together despite having no help from anyone, especially you.'

Her heart was racing, and her cheeks were red hot. 'Sorry! It hasn't been easy, especially since Peter...'

Lucy cut straight in. 'I did warn you.'

Charlotte rose to her feet.

'How dare you? How dare you insult Peter like that and come here and talk to me like a second-class citizen? I thought

I brought you up to respect people and not look down on anyone. Especially your own mother.'

Lucy froze in her seat, and Charlotte stormed out of the back door and into the yard. She perched on the chopping block. How dare she? Her father was obviously not doing a fantastic job, and Charlotte realised the blame was also on her for being absent from her life. She should have brought her to the cottage earlier, and then she would not be so self-centred.

Charlotte's cheeks cooled, and so did her temper. She took to her feet and re-entered the house. Lucy was texting on her phone.

'I've made linguine and garlic bread. I'm sure you'll be hungry.'

'I am hungry,' Lucy said as she came over and flung her arms around Charlotte.

They both started to cry with their foreheads resting on each other. 'You were always the same when you were hungry as a little girl.'

'I'm sorry, Mama.'

'It's okay. I understand you have your own life now and don't need your old mum.'

'We just live in different worlds now, that's all. I'll always love you, Mama.' Their tears became one as they held each other tight. 'I'll stay tonight, but I've ordered the taxi to pick me up in the morning, and I'll catch the earlier flight to Dubai.'

Charlotte broke the embrace gently.

'You know what you want. I respect that. Do you still have your locket?'

Lucy reached into her collar, produced the gold heart-shaped locket, and opened it to show the tiny photo of them both laughing together.

'It's always with me.'

'I love you, Lucy. Go and find your destiny and send my regards to Mohammed and your father.'

With gigantic lumps in their throats, they wiped each other's tears from their cheeks.

'You'll be at the head table at the wedding. If he proposes, that is.'

'I won't let you down,' Charlotte said, turning away, gasping for air and opening the oven door.

Charlotte woke early. She put the coffee on and went out to chop logs. She'd had a restless night. Thoughts about her life now and how much Lucy had grown up in what seemed to be no time at all. It would take time to come to terms with it, but she realised that Lucy hadn't changed much at all, and maybe it was her life which was now so different. She also felt it wasn't fair for her to inflict that on Lucy. She was hopefully due to become a princess and either live in LA or Dubai. And that she was a woman in her own right. She recalled her own father placing restrictions when she was younger, and she didn't want to replicate it.

Split went the first log. There was nothing more satisfying than splitting the first one, and knowing it would bring the house to life and keep it warm brought a smile to her face.

She bundled the logs, took them inside, and then sliced some bread for toast. She could hear Lucy using the hairdryer in the bathroom and knew she would be down shortly.

Her homemade jam took pride of place on the table, and a little gift for Christmas, beside the cup and saucer. It was a heart she had hand-whittled from a piece of birch wood too small for the burner.

'Morning, Mama.'

'Good morning, darling. Did you sleep well?'

Lucy already had her coat on. 'Not really. It was cold. The hot-water bottle was fine, but I had to huddle up in the blankets.'

Charlotte smiled philosophically. 'That's the bit I like.'

'Mmm,' Lucy said, rolling her eyes sarcastically.

'Do you like my tree? Have you noticed what's on top?'

Lucy peered around the corner. 'Ah! The angel. I can't believe you still have that.'

'Of course I do. It's looking a little weathered now, but I'll keep it going as long as I can.'

Lucy took a bite of toast. 'Daddy has one so high, it took ten men to carry it into the house.'

Charlotte took a deep breath and smiled. 'Well, this one took one very determined woman the best part of a day.'

Lucy scrunched up her face. She didn't understand.

'The taxi is here,' Charlotte said, handing Lucy the small gift. 'Save it for Christmas Day.'

Lucy nodded and tiptoed out to the car in her stilettos.

'Bye, Mama.'

'Bye, Lucy. Let me know you get there safely.'

The car drove away, and Charlotte didn't move from the spot. Her bare feet in the snow were no comparison to the internal pain of waving goodbye to her treasured daughter once again.

'Goodbye, my love,' she said as the snow began to fall.

33

CRACKERS

'I love crackers,' Mr Frogatt said, laughing as he pulled the Christmas cracker with Charlotte. After the bang, the contents shot out onto the small table.

Mr Frogatt cleared his throat. 'Why doesn't Father Christmas have any children?' he said, reading from the tiny piece of paper ejected from the cracker.

'We don't know. Why doesn't Father Christmas have any children?' Both Charlotte and Mrs Frogatt simultaneously laughed.

'Because he only comes once a year!'

Mrs Frogatt looked stunned.

'I, erm... got the naughty ones!' Charlotte said, biting her lip.

Then all three of them burst out laughing.

'Thanks for inviting us, Charlotte,' Mrs Frogatt said. 'I think we all need a good one this year.'

'Look!' Charlotte said, placing a little red plastic fish on Mrs Frogatt's hand. They all watched it. Slowly it began to move; firstly the head lifted and then the tail, until the whole thing curled up in her palm.

'Wait, wait,' Charlotte said, reading the instructions. 'Here we are. Curls up entirely. Means you're passionate.'

Mrs Frogatt looked at Mr Frogatt. 'Looks like it's your lucky day.'

Mr Frogatt's eyes nearly popped out, and again they all started laughing.

'Let's do it to you, Charlotte,' Mrs Frogatt said, placing the flat fish on her hand.

They all waited with great anticipation, and then it started to move.

'The tail's moving,' Mrs Frogatt said. 'That means... you're independent.'

Charlotte shrugged. 'Yep!'

'Wait. The head's moving as well.'

'What does that mean?' Mr Frogatt said enthusiastically.

They all laughed again at his inquisitiveness.

Mrs Frogatt scoured the little instruction sheet. 'It says... you're in love.'

Charlotte sighed.

'Jeez, that just about sums up my life. No clear vision. Independent and in love. Let's do it on you, Mr Frogatt.'

He started to blush. 'No. No. If it comes up passionate, we'll never get to the dinner,' he said, offering his cracker to Mrs Frogatt.

After the bang, a miniature set of handcuffs shot out in front of them. Mr Frogatt instantly stood up and grabbed Mrs Frogatt's hand. 'Right, come on, love,' he said, gesturing to the bedroom.

Charlotte's cheeks ached with laughter, and so did the Frogatts. They laughed and laughed, donned their paper party hats and finished off the rest of the risqué jokes, and Mr Frogatt uncorked a bottle of champagne he had brought and was saving for a special occasion.

Charlotte gathered the cracker debris and, still chuckling, asked if they would like some melon to start, and they eagerly agreed.

'I might be a few moments, as I want to check the turkey,' she said.

There was silence. The jovial air turned stilted. 'You haven't forgotten he's vegetarian, have you?' Mrs Frogatt said openly.

Charlotte stopped in her tracks. 'Have... I... forgotten... you're... vegetar... i... an? Yes!' Charlotte cringed. 'I totally forgot. I've never even cooked a whole turkey before, either. Oh, my lord. I'm so sorry.'

She scuttled out into the kitchen but could hear them talking.

'You shouldn't have said anything. I could have broken my twenty-year run.'

'You owe it to the animals, Ogden. We'll get around this,' Mrs Frogatt said, placing her hand on his knee and starting to cough.

'Are you okay, my love?'

'I'm weak today, Oggy, but I don't want to ruin Charlotte's day.'

She secretly took her tablets, and then, suddenly, Charlotte returned.

'Okay. I'm so sorry. I can do pasta twirls, sprouts, carrots and roast potatoes. Will that be okay?'

She looked in earnest at his stern face and then at Mrs Frogatt and then back again. Mr Frogatt burst out laughing.

'This is going to be the best Christmas ever,' he said before blowing on a kazoo from a cracker.

'I've never seen him like this,' Mrs Frogatt said to Charlotte, who had a face like a startled rabbit.

'Neither have I. Pasta it is, then. With cranberry sauce?'

'Yes, please,' the Frogatts said in harmony.

As a matter of principle, Charlotte had pasta too, the only difference was she had gravy, and the Frogatts continued with joyful chat and merriment. Then, Mrs Frogatt produced a tin foil parcel from her bag and placed it on the table. Charlotte watched intently as Mrs Frogatt unwrapped it and presented her homemade Christmas cake. A dark, rich fruitcake with white sugar icing and a couple of snowmen stood either side of a reindeer on the top.

Charlotte smiled. 'Is this the moment I get the cheese?' she asked with doubt in her voice.

They both nodded, and Mr Frogatt cut the cake into slices. Charlotte returned with the cheese Jim had so kindly given her, and Mr Frogatt cut that into slices too.

'I thought this was a joke. Like some kind of Yorkshire initiation.'

'It looks like good cheese.'

'A very kind offering from Jim.'

'Ah, yes. He does make a good Wensleydale, does Jim,' Mr Frogatt said, placing a piece of cheese on some cake and handing it to Charlotte.

'He made it himself?' she asked.

Mr Frogatt nodded. 'His cheese is held in very high regard.'

'Are you sure this isn't a wind-up?' Charlotte said, taking the food to her lips.

Mr and Mrs Frogatt watched with great pleasure as if they already knew the outcome.

Charlotte chewed.

Mr and Mrs Frogatt watched.

'It's lovely!'

The Frogatts smiled and started tucking into theirs.

'It's really lovely. The original salted caramel, I guess. Why haven't I had this before?'

'You weren't an honorary Yorkshire lass before,' Mr Frogatt said, holding up his glass of champagne.

'Cheers.'

And that was it. She did feel like an honorary Yorkshire lass, and she felt proud.

'Peter used to call me lass,' she said, clinking her glass and smiling from ear to ear.

Suddenly, there was a knock at the door. Charlotte stopped smiling. 'Who could that be?'

She opened the front door and was surprised by a huge bunch of flowers and a panettone the size of a small car.

'Mr Hawkins. What a surprise.'

'Please. Call me Hunter. Merry Christmas.'

Charlotte shuddered. 'Merry Christmas.'

'I was just passing and thought I'd just update you on the progress of the owl.'

Charlotte nodded.

'And with flowers and more cake? It's a long way to walk from the next valley, but that's a very kind gesture... Hunter.'

He thrust the flowers into her hand and peered inside. 'I hope I wasn't disturbing anything?'

'I have the Frogatts here.'

He carried on looking in and thrust the panettone her way too.

'I see.'

Charlotte struggled to keep hold of everything and passed

the panettone back to him. 'Help me bring them in and say hello to the Frogatts.'

Hunter barged his way in, and Charlotte followed.

'And how *is* the owl?'

'Veterinary. Mrs Frogatt. Merry Christmas. I won't stay long, just passing and thought I'd drop off a couple of things,' he said in his gruff voice.

Mr Frogatt smiled. 'Merry Christmas to you too, Hunter. How is the owl?'

'Owl? Oh... yes, it will be due for release when the weather improves. You did a good job there,' he said, searching with his eyes for Charlotte.

'Drink?' Mr Frogatt said, already pouring some champagne.

'Thank you,' he said, taking the glass and holding it up.

Charlotte came in from the kitchen.

'Oh yes, cheers.'

She clinked glasses and took a sip. Surprisingly, there was another knock at the door.

'Excuse me,' she said, wondering who on earth this might be.

'Jim!'

'Merry Christmas, Charlotte.'

'Merry Christmas, Jim.'

Jim presented her with a bottle of Ruby Port. 'I was just passing and...'

She stole the words right out of his mouth. 'And thought some port might go well with the cheese?'

Jim wasn't listening. He could hear the clinking of glasses in the house and peered through the window.

'Have you had a good day? I thought you said you were

going to the Frogatts? It's just I passed, and there was no sign of life.'

At that moment, Hunter came along the hall.

'Is everything all right?'

Jim's shoulders collapsed, and his face turned almost as white as snow.

'I see,' he said with deep, deep disappointment in his voice. 'I see!'

Charlotte looked to see Hunter strutting like a peacock in the hall.

'This isn't what it looks like, Jim.'

'I understand. I'm no fool,' he said, starting his walk to the gate.

Charlotte shouted after him. 'Come and join us?'

'Merry Christmas, Charlotte, merry Christmas.'

34

WEDDING BELLS

A March wedding inspired such optimism in the air. Longer days and brighter ones too, and daffodils in all the buttonholes brought out smiles on even the most sombre faces. Of course, it was meant to be her spring wedding, but she didn't want to spoil the girls special day with her melancholy.

The hen do was a whole spa weekend, and Charlotte, Jojo and Sam reminisced and laughed about all their calamitous dating histories and past relationships. Jojo and Sam steered clear of mentioning Peter, but Charlotte was aware of that. It was their day. They did not know Peter had suggested a spring wedding for them, so Charlotte buried her feelings and brought out her best smile. She did tell them about the unfortunate Christmas debacle with Hunter and Jim, and they howled in the jacuzzi, which was twice as loud for the people outside it, and received hard stares.

Charlotte explained that she had gone up to Jim's on New Year's Eve, taken the port and cheese, and put the record straight. They spent the evening together at his and welcomed the new year, wishing each other all the best. Charlotte didn't want to string him along but could see that he wanted more.

'I just said that Peter was the love of my life, and I wasn't over his death yet and couldn't see a time when I would.'

'Did he understand?' Jojo said, looking concerned.

'I don't think so. He's a very lonely man. He has his new dog and, of course, all the animals, but I can see he would like a wife.'

'We could have made the wedding a threesome, you know?' Sam said, sipping at a champagne flute.

'What about Scavenger?' Jojo said.

'You mean Hunter?'

'Yes. You know who I mean.'

Charlotte took a sip from her glass. 'He fancies himself, and he thinks I fancy him.'

Sam took two fingers to her mouth and pretended to gag.

'Exactly,' Charlotte said. 'Why can't men see that it's such a turnoff?'

'Because they are the least confident ones, really. And everyone knows it's just a front,' Jojo said.

Charlotte raised her glass. 'Well, here's to you two and your fabulous men.'

'Cheers.'

It was a little strange seeing two grooms waiting at the altar. It could have been a scene from a hilarious film, and what was even more strange was the sight of two brides in white coming down the central aisle. There was a little toing and froing among the main family members as to who sat where, but everyone seemed amicable, and the girls had chosen a big enough church to accommodate.

For Charlotte, it was a nice change of scenery to be out of

the house and join in the celebrations. There were some other girls from school she hadn't seen since they left, and Charlotte enjoyed listening to all their potted histories.

Seeing Sam and Jojo so happy filled Charlotte with joy, but there were times in the day when she was struck with brutal anxiety and pain that she never quite made it. She didn't show it, or at least hoped she didn't.

It was in the evening, she felt most alone. She danced with the girls, and the odd grandad asked her for a dance. Still, she later sided off into a quiet conservatory of the hotel for a moment of contemplation. She didn't want to appear rude and just disappear to her room. Instead, took a double Irish cream and sat alone.

She looked out into the night sky and sent her thoughts to Peter.

Wishing he was there with her, but also that the night could be a turning point.

She wanted a sign from him that it was okay for her to move on. It felt right that if she had a happy future, she had to finally put things to bed and get on with her life. Seeing her two friends so happy was a testament to that, and although he would never be forgotten, she had to clear a new space in her heart for someone, if anyone, who might wish to fill the gap.

She gazed up into the star-strewn night and wept. It was then it happened. A shooting star shot across the sky. Not fading quickly like she had seen before but holding out and bright. Brighter than any other star. She followed it as it went from right to left and then eventually disappeared.

'Thanks, Peter. I love you. Please be at peace, and thank you from the bottom of my heart for all the joy you brought me. I will be forever grateful.'

'Hey! Are you okay?' Sam asked. 'I was looking for you. Don't want you to be alone like this.'

'I'm fine, Sam. Thanks for looking out for me. It's been such a beautiful day, and, in a way, you've helped me to see what might lie beyond for me. I just took two minutes out to talk to Peter, and I'm feeling good.'

35

BEST IN CLASS

I ntegrating into village life was steady progress. Gaining the trust of hard-working Yorkshire folk was not to be underestimated, but she found out that a Yorkshire person's word is their word. A spit and a handshake were a done deal. They were honest people, by and large. Yes, some of them had inflated egos, but generally, people with good lives, some more tragic than others, but all fiercely loyal once you had proved to them you were of the same values. It was what she loved about Peter and what she had now grown to admire in the people around her.

Charlotte cycled into the village. The air was now warm, and the sun was high in the sky. Winter had long been cast aside, and preparations for the summer fete were well underway.

Charlotte met with Margaret for some insider knowledge of what to expect from the food and baking competition and maybe what was an easy class to slot into for her first time. Longest marrow or giant leek was not the prize to be going for, Margaret stated. Instead, suggested just simply going for the biscuit category or maybe the female wood whittling section, as it was greatly underrepresented.

'The main categories are very competitive. Cheesecake is always a difficult one. The vicar's wife has that one sewn up most years, and the Victoria sponge, in my view, is a no-go.'

'Why?'

'Lady Margot Mountjoy. That's why. She expects to win, and she spares no prisoners. Some say she buys in, and they might be right, but it's not worth the battle.'

Charlotte thought about where her skills lay strongest.

'I do need a decision, though, as I have to post all the entries to the organiser by midnight tonight,' Margaret said in her organised and forthright voice.

'Victoria sponge.'

Margaret did a double take and immediately put her teacup on the saucer.

'I thought wood whittling might be the best for your first go.'

'I used to bake sponge cakes and muffins with my daughter when she was younger. I'd at least like to have a bash at it.'

Margaret smiled. 'I admire your thinking. As I said, Lady Mountjoy won't take too kindly. Is that your final decision?'

Charlotte put her teacup down. 'Can I do jam too?'

Margaret coughed and nearly choked. 'I didn't even mention the jam section. It's the most sought-after title and the stiffest competition. I, of course, have a three-year gold star for my damson medley.'

Charlotte started to blush.

'Oh, I am sorry. I didn't mean to be rude. I had no idea. I wouldn't want to step on your toes. Not that mine will be anything worthy of even a prize. It's just I have some already made from last year, and it would be an easy submission, and to be honest, I'm struggling to even give it away.'

On returning home, Charlotte found a cream, hand written letter on the doormat.

She knew instantly who it was from by the address.

Charlotte, Holm Cottage, Somewhere at the end of a muddy track, Yorkshire.

Mira. The sheer penurious nature gave it away.

Dear Charlotte,

Sorry I haven't been in touch and could not attend the wedding of the century. I was otherwise engaged in South Africa with my fabulous man on yet another diamond-buying trip. If only they were for me! Lol.

Sam and Jojo said you looked miserable at the wedding and that northern life was taking its toll on you. The weather alone, darling, can't be good for your chest.

I've taken it upon myself to offer a lifeline. A lifebuoy in your turbulent ocean.

I'm travelling so much now with Eugene my apartment is largely redundant. You don't have to thank me, but it is yours until you establish yourself back in London life. You maybe don't realise it, but it's where you belong, and I know you so well. I wouldn't be a true friend if I weren't able to be straight and honest with you.

Call me

Mira

A deep breath. In fact, two deep breaths were needed to quash any instant feelings of anger.

'A true friend,' Charlotte said to herself.

She took the letter into the kitchen and stood looking out of the window. The lush patchwork of fields and vibrant green trees took her gaze far beyond the garden gate. Mira had shown her true colours yet again, and Charlotte confirmed her decision that Mira would no longer be a friend. They'd gone back a long way, but Charlotte knew who her true friends were. People who genuinely loved and cared for her. The people of Yorkshire had accepted her for who she was. No pretence or social agenda, just genuine folk with hearts of gold. Some more hearty than others, yet all genuine in their quest for community.

Charlotte took the letter and tore it up into small pieces, and pushed them into the waste food, which was awaiting the compost bin.

'A true friend,' she said again. 'Peter knew who you were right from the start. Goodbye, Mira.'

She pushed the final piece into the rotting fruit and vegetable peelings with her finger and then washed her hands vigorously for three or four minutes.

She set about making the label for her jam entry at the summer fete and hand-drew a sketch of a plum tree with its trunk running up one edge and the branches drooping over to create a space in the middle.

Plum Jam, she wrote in fountain pen and finished it with a little fat plum. In all honesty, the plum looked like an ink splodge, but she knew what it was, and that was what was important.

She did have a jar or two of damson, but she didn't want to compete with Margaret. Anyway, she had a medley, whatever that was.

Charlotte felt proud of what she had and hoped it would further her acceptance within the village.

With sleeves rolled up and a huge smile on her face, she tied her hair up and loaded copious amounts of strawberries, which she had harvested at the *pick your own* farm, into her jam pot. This would be the filling for her Victoria sponge. Nothing bought in for her entry.

While it was boiling, she opened her cookbook to double-check the sponge recipe and weighed out the flour. The hot sun through the window illuminated her face, and with a slightly floury hand, she switched on the radio. She instantly recognised the song and started to sing.

I'm Feeling Good blared out.

Now for the butter and sugar.

The big day had arrived, and storm clouds threatened to put a damp squib on the day. It was too good to think an English summer fete would not be accompanied by some form of rain. The forecast was to improve as the day went on. As Charlotte cycled past the event field on her way into the village, she witnessed 4x4s, pickups, trailers, and burley men busily erecting marquees and gazebos.

'How thrilling,' she said out loud and took both hands off the handlebars and clapped with excitement.

She needed a cake tin to safely transport her entry and wasn't prepared to risk just a plate, and some cling wrap.

'You going to the fete?' Bob said, handing her a tin.

'Sure am, Bob. I've been looking forward to it for weeks.'

'Is this the right size?' he asked, removing the lid. 'I've had a run on these this week.'

'I think it's perfect. Are you presenting anything at the show?'

'My wife's done a floral display, and I'm organising the horseshoe toss and the wellie wanging.'

'Wellie wanging? That sounds fun.'

'Yep. See how far you can chuck your wellie. I'm organising this year because I've won the last five years. Give the younger ones a chance this year.'

'Will I be able to do it?'

'Absolutely. Just turn up. It's a pound for three wangs, and all the money goes to the youth club.'

'I hear there's a dog show and a dry-stone walling completion.'

'Yes. All the old favourites. Horse-drawn ploughing, hay bale toss, three-legged race and some shin-kicking.'

'Did you just say shin-kicking?'

'Proper hobnail boots and as much damage to your opponent's shins as you can give. Or take! Will you be entering?'

Charlotte's eyes began watering. 'I most certainly won't be. Sounds barbaric.'

'Traditions die hard around here,' Bob said proudly.

'I'll stick to my Victoria sponge and some wanging, if that's okay?'

They both laughed.

'You know Lady Mountjoy always wins the Victoria sponge? She sent her people down for a new tin and some posh doilies this week.'

Charlotte paused. 'Mmm. A doily. Great idea. Do you have any left?'

By 11.30, the clouds were dispersing, and the ground was beginning to steam as the sun offered optimism among the marquees and main roped-off arena. Charlotte dodged hay bales being placed around the edge for seating and carefully carried her entries close to her chest. A trip now would be a catastrophe.

She found her place at the display table. A simple folded card said, *Miss Charlotte*.

She laughed.

She hadn't been called that for many a year, and seeing it seemed strange. Taking a pen from her bag, she crossed it out and replaced it with *Charlie*.

She placed the jam jar on the table and polished it with her sleeve. Next came the cake. A white plate was waiting. Most other entries were already in position, and not another doily in sight. Charlotte instantly noticed the card, *Lady Mountjoy*. She had yet to deliver, so she couldn't compare. Charlotte placed her doily and cake on the plate, carefully positioned it, and rotated it into the best light. A final dusting of icing sugar, and that was it. No more fiddling. It was what it was, and she could do no more.

Suddenly Charlotte heard a kerfuffle outside, and then a huge mother-of-the-bride style hat with peacock feathers walked in, and underneath, Lady Mountjoy, flanked by two very stressed-looking maids.

'I want my usual place,' she said, pointing at the table and forcing her staff to clear the prominent position in the centre of the table.

One maid polished the plate while the other took a doily from a hermetically sealed bag and placed it on the plate. It was then Lady Mountjoy's eyes fell upon Charlotte's cake. Her fake eyelashes were still, like a praying mantis about to make its kill, and then slowly moved to Charlotte's feet and upwards to her face.

'A doily?' she said with disgust.

Charlotte could see her lip quivering and her cheek trying

to follow suit but was restricted by the Botox.

Then a hand appeared. 'Oh! It's you.'

Charlotte politely shook her hand. 'Charlie. I'm in Holm Cottage.'

'Oh yes, the single lady down by Mr Bickerdyke's land.'

'We met at the biscuit-making event at the WI,' Charlotte replied.

Lady Mountjoy's face immediately looked like it had smelled a bad smell, and she started shaking her head.

'I don't remember. Was it explained to you that a doily is not permitted?'

Charlotte smiled politely.

'No. But it seems unfair that you are permitted, but no one else is. Surely it should be a level playing field?'

Lady Mountjoy's other cheek started to twitch.

'It is purely down to the moistness of my cakes. A bare plate would not be able to soak it up.'

Charlotte nodded. 'Not light and fluffy, then?'

Lady Mountjoy immediately started fussing and gesticulating to her staff.

'I'll be mentioning this to the judges.'

Charlotte nodded. 'Please do, and lovely to meet you again, Lady Mountjoy.'

Before she could finish, she was over at her cake issuing orders to make her folded card obvious, and her maid placed a single strawberry with the leaf still attached on the plate beside the cake.

'Are strawberries permitted?' Charlotte muttered to herself.

'And now the dog agility competition,' the commanding voice on the loudspeaker announced. Charlotte calmly exited the marquee and settled herself on a hay bale to watch the dogs negotiate seesaws and jump through flaming hoops.

Later, she bumped into the Frogatts. Mr Frogatt was pushing Mrs Frogatt in a wheelchair and was barely visible due to her holding a huge fluffy squirrel. 'Let's just say the coconut shy didn't know what hit it,' Mr Frogatt proudly boasted, and Mrs Frogatt beamed as she passed over the squirrel and tightly embraced Charlotte's hand.

'Are you okay, Mrs Frogatt? I hope you don't mind me saying, but...' Charlotte looked at the wheelchair.

'I've not been well for a while, Charlotte. Didn't want to go on about it, especially when there are people far worse off than me,' she said, squeezing Charlotte's hand tighter.

'She needs a bone marrow transplant. It's cancer,' Mr Frogatt blurted out. 'Right, I've said it. We couldn't keep hiding it. It's driving me mad, everyone asking, and us trying to carry on as normal. She's dying, Charlotte, simple as that.'

His voice faltered, and he was on the edge of tears.

'I had no idea. I'm so, so sorry to hear that. Why didn't you tell me sooner? Is there anything I can do?'

Mrs Frogatt took Charlotte's hand in both of hers.

'It's my fault. I told him not to tell anyone. People have enough on their plates without worrying about me. I'm waiting for a transplant, and I have good and bad days.'

'What's the delay?'

'The waiting list, that's all. I'd go private if I could, but the costs are ridiculous. Anyway, it's not stopping me from having a lovely day today, and I'm on a good day. Did I hear you say something about wellie wanging?'

'Yes! Do you think you're fit enough?'

'I'll give it everything I have, anyway, I know Oggy will be secretly chomping at the bit for a go.'

'Is that right?' Charlotte said with the excitement of a child.

'No,' he said. 'But if my throwing arm is still on form,

they'd better watch out in Harrogate.' They all burst out laughing, and Mrs Frogatt's roll of her eyes said it all.

Mr Frogatt took Charlotte by the hand. 'I'm sorry, Charlotte. I was sworn to secrecy. It's just been building inside me. I shouldn't have blurted it out like that.'

'You don't have to apologise to me, Ogden. I'm just upset hearing the news.'

'Well, it's frustrating having to wait. I want her fit and healthy.'

Charlotte huddled the three of them together. 'If it wasn't for you two, I don't know where I'd be right now. Let's enjoy the day, and we'll get through this together.'

'Hi, Bob. Can we have three goes, please?' Charlotte said, handing over the cash.

'Hello, Veterinary. Mrs Frogatt,' Bob said, smiling and handing them each a wellington boot. 'Remember, you get three throws each, and you're aiming to beat the red stick over there.' Bob pointed to a wooden post painted red with a sun hat on top.

'It's miles away,' Charlotte said, squinting at the post.

Mrs Frogatt threw first from her chair and let go a little late, seeing it career off the side of the pitch and land on the roof of the children's face painting tent.

Charlotte threw next, and the wellie slipped out of her hand and flopped onto the floor.

'It's harder than you think.'

'Come on. Let the dog see the rabbit.' Mr Frogatt was on form as he threw his high, but it fell way short of the mark.

'Can we have a run-up?' Charlotte said, jogging up and down on the spot.

'Absolutely,' Bob said. 'As long as you don't cross the line.'

He gestured to the rope on the floor.

Charlotte gave Mrs Frogatt a slight push to the line and, this time, kept her wellie on the pitch.

Charlotte gave an enthusiastic run-up and managed, this time, to achieve some distance, and Mr Frogatt tried a low but fast underarm.

'Hey, that's cheating!' Charlotte cried.

'Don't cross the line he said. Nothing else.'

Mrs Frogatt and Charlotte looked at each other. 'Right. That's a game changer,' Charlotte said, winking at Mrs Frogatt.

'Sure is,' Mrs Frogatt said, almost skimming her final shot across the grass and then somersaulted a little further. 'I can't believe anyone really threw it as far as the post?' Mrs Frogatt declared.

'Bet Bob placed it there as a joke.'

Charlotte laughed as she took her final run-up and then released with a squeal.

'Not bad,' Bob said. 'Better luck next time.'

'Okay, this is it.' Mr Frogatt wiped his hand on his trousers before gripping the wellie tight. He ran, skipped, hopped, and then threw the throw of his life before collapsing on the ground, complaining of cramp in his wrist.

They all laughed and shook their heads. 'Let's have a look at the leaderboard and find out who threw that huge distance,' Charlotte said, still shaking her head.

'Hunter! Who else. It had to be Hunter.'

It wasn't long before the prizes were due to be announced in the crafts and produce classes. The marquee's doors were still tightly closed while the judges made their final appraisals. Still, people were eagerly gathering outside in anticipation. Then, suddenly the doors flung open, and the loudspeaker announced the judging was over.

Charlotte looked at Mrs Frogatt.

'Good luck with your flowers.'

'Good luck with your cake.'

They both nodded and went their seperate ways. Firstly, Charlotte headed for the jam section. There was a notice right by her jar.

'Best in Class. Newcomer,' it said.

No way, she thought, picked up her gold rosette, and proudly pinned it to her blouse. She bumped into Margaret, who promptly revealed her double gold rosette which was twice the size of Charlotte's.

'Best in Show.'

'Oh Margaret, you must be so pleased.'

'To be honest, Charlotte, I am. I knew it was a good one this year, and to scoop the overall prize was a dream come true. How did you get on?'

Charlotte thrust her chest towards Margaret and said nothing.

'I'm so pleased for you. Gold in the newcomer's class. That's superb.'

Charlotte scrunched her lips. 'Well, there was only me and a prune surprise!'

They doubled over laughing. 'I'd better watch out next year.'

Charlotte swiftly moved on to the bustling cake section. Without seeing the cakes, she had already guessed the outcome. Lady Mountjoy was surrounded by photographers from the local press, a tv crew and many other nosey onlookers. She could see her gold rosette pinned prominently to her bosom.

While everyone was distracted, Charlotte searched for her cake. There was no certificate this time. Instead, a big dirty thumbprint on one side, causing the whole cake to subside, and no doily either!

Charlotte's face dropped. Sabotage?

'It looks pretty good to me. I could do with a bit of cake,' a familiar male voice said behind her. Charlotte rolled her eyes. Here we go again. She didn't even bother to look around. Jim, Hunter? Which one was it to be?

'I've missed you.' The voice said.

Charlotte paused. Okay, yes. Right on cue, an apparition of Peter, just when she needed a confidence boost. 'Yeh, yeh. Sabotage, I call it,' she said, slowly turning.

'It's been a long time.'

Charlotte knew the drill. She'd hoped the apparitions would start to fade and finally leave her in peace.

'Yes, it's been a while,' she said half-heartedly.

She then noticed when he threw his bag on the floor, it made a sound, and not only that, she could also smell him, and he was thinner than she remembered. She pushed her arm out and prodded him with her finger. The physical touch of his shirt and the resistance from his skin made her quiver.

Charlotte froze, and her heart stopped. She knew her brain had this weird way of showing her that she was doing okay and that, occasionally, it would throw a spanner in the works to test her. This was the best so far. To smell him so close was good. But she was tired of the testing. It was time to forget and move on.

'Do I get a hug then?' he asked, holding his arms out.

'Is it really you, Peter? Tell me it's you?'

Peter wrapped his arms around her and pulled her in tight. His strong arms were something she had thought she would never feel again.

'It's me. I'm home. I've missed you so very much.'

'Is it you, Peter? Are you real?'

'Yes, of course, it's me.'

'Well, kiss me.'

Peter squeezed her tight. The strength of his arms around her waist made her gasp. He physically lifted her off the ground and then placed his lips on hers in a way that only Peter could. To feel, smell, and taste him was a complete shock and sheer ecstasy.

Charlotte relished the moment and wriggled. She pushed him away and felt her feet on the floor.

'They told me you were dead. Where the hell have you been?'

'They imprisoned me. Henry Winterbourne's cronies. Or should I say, Trenton Barraclough!'

'Trenton Barraclough. Who's he?'

'The imposter. I have news. Good news.'

'Why did it take you so long? And what about the shark?'

'What shark?'

'I don't know. I don't know what to believe anymore.'

'Well, I'm here, and I'm real. Did you say I could have some of your cake?'

Charlotte looked at him. She examined every inch of him. She explored his face, his ears, eyes and even his teeth. She sure as hell wasn't going to get her hopes up unnecessarily.

'It's so good to see you, Peter. I can't believe it's you. I'm going to prod you again.'

'I love you,' he said, allowing her to stick her finger into his chest.

'Take me home, Peter. Take me home and explain everything.'

36

THE CAGE

A warm breeze gently blew across their naked bodies. The windows open, and the sound of birdsong outside gave a calm and peaceful feel. Charlotte could do nothing other than look at his sleeping body next to her. It still wasn't a reality, and it seemed odd to have another human in her bed again. Although his muscles were still defined, she could tell he was malnourished. What on earth had happened to him? Why couldn't he make contact? What news did he have? She had so many questions, but she wanted him to rest.

She took a warm shower and spent some time pampering her body. Time she had not devoted much of over the last couple of years. She looked at herself in the mirror and was shocked at how many greying hairs she had, and there were wrinkles that were previously smooth skin. She'd neglected herself, and what was obvious, she had been afraid to look herself directly in the eye. Maybe she was scared of the reality of life; maybe just scared of herself?

In the kitchen, she assembled a tray of coffee, crumpets, toast, cereal, honey and her prized jam. Did it look too much?

She felt the distinct urge to feed him and nurture him. Anyway. She was starving too.

On entering the bedroom, he was awake and sat up, looking out of the window.

'I made some breakfast.'

'You're amazing.'

'Look, I don't want to pressure you, but I think you owe me a few answers.'

Peter nodded his head. 'The house looks more modern and homely, somehow.'

'Yes, new windowsill, paint, screwy things and total vermin control. You're looking at bloody Wonder Woman here, but for heaven's sake, what the hell happened to you? Start at the beginning!'

'Okay, fair enough. Look, it's good news.'

'And?' she asked.

'Henry Winterbourne the 4th isn't who he says he is. His real name is Trenton Barraclough. He was born in Essex, England, but raised in Hong Kong. A businessman who had dealings with your father. By all accounts, your father ripped him off. I'm not sure of the exact details, but he wanted to seek revenge.'

'So, Daddy never had a son then?'

'Well, not exactly. I'm sorry to say that your father was not a faithful man, and he fathered a son to a woman out there.'

Charlotte listened intently.

'That son, your half-brother, was named Henry Junior, but he died before his first birthday. There was no official record of his death, and no death certificate was ever found. However, I have anecdotal evidence from a relative that one did exist. Records around that time were extremely sketchy. A flood at the administration destroyed many thousands of documents, and record-keeping, in general, wasn't as thorough as we would expect either.'

'So just a birth certificate existed?'

'Yes, but that was held by the mother.'

'So, who was his mother?'

'A woman called Rai Chi. Your father looked after her secretly for years until his death. She died five years ago, and the birth certificate and some other documents were taken by her sister, who I managed to find. I hid the papers in a cavity in an old acer tree in the hills.'

'Go on?'

'It seems that Trenton somehow found out about the son who died and created a false ID using the dead baby's name. And because there was no death certificate, no one questioned it.'

'So what about the evidence presented in court?'

'Well, the birth certificate was real, but everything else was fake.'

'The letter of wishes?' she asked.

'Fake! I found out that your beloved Mr Scrivener is as bent as a nine-bob note.'

Charlotte shook her head. 'What do you mean?'

'He was in on it all along. I suspect, disgruntled that you or your father hadn't paid him off years ago for his loyal service, he couldn't refuse the offer when Trenton approached him to pull off the scam. You said nothing was read out when the will was declared? Well, it didn't exist. Mr Scrivener forged your father's signature and, of course, he knew your father inside out, so using his language was easy for him. It fooled the court and you.'

Charlotte took a long, slow, deep breath. 'But you're missing the DNA?'

Peter bit off a piece of toast. 'Fake! Your father's DNA was on record, and all he had to do was re-submit the sample to the lab and, together with the birth certificate, bingo!'

Charlotte couldn't believe what she was hearing. How could she have been so naïve and stupid?

She took another breath and a sip of tea. Peter chomped on the remaining toast.

'Nice jam.'

'Funny. Get on with it. That's great news, but none of this explains what happened to you.'

'Well, when Trenton found out I was sniffing around in Hong Kong, he knew I might discover the truth. He was building an empire out there and selling off everything that was once yours to fund casinos and hotels and the like. Money laundering essentially.'

Peter paused and took a large gulp of tea, and rammed another slice of toast into his mouth.

'His cronies put me in a cage.'

'A cage?'

Peter closed his eyes and started rocking back and forth. 'A steel cage in the foundation of the new hotel they were building, with just rice and water and the occasional melon to eat. As soon as the foundations were completely dug, they would be filled with concrete with me inside them.'

Charlotte put her hand on his. 'Are you kidding me?'

'No. There was no way of contacting you. There was nothing I could do.'

'But how did you become free?'

'They let me out for ten minutes a day. You know to go to the toilet. In the day, there were too many guards and people. I thought many times about making a run, but instead, I waited until night. There was only one guard after 11pm. I managed to secrete a wooden slither from the toilet hut in my trousers, and I knew the guard would be along to give me water. He always had bare feet and would walk on top of the cage.'

Charlotte's eyes and ears were transfixed.

'He walked on the cage, and I stuck the wood straight through his foot. He fell. I grabbed his head through the bars and took the key.'

'What happened to the guard?'

Peter paused. 'I did what I had to do.'

'You killed him?'

Peter took another gulp of tea. 'I ran as fast as I could, retrieved the documents from the tree and headed straight for the consulate. They got me out on a military plane, and the rest is history.'

Charlotte was speechless. She wanted to say so much, but nothing came out. All the thoughts competing with each other prevented it.

'Did you do the windowsill?'

'Peter. Stick to the agenda. What about the shark attack and your papers?'

'They loaded another man with my passport and threw him into the sea. Well, that's what the police told me.'

'So, the police are involved?'

'They're on the case.'

'And the passport was readable?'

'Conveniently concealed in a plastic bag!'

'So, what happens next?'

'The police are on to it; as I say, we just need one more piece of evidence, and I think your father may have hidden it at Loxley.'

'What is it?'

'The death certificate. It must have existed, and it's strange the mother didn't have it. It's a long shot, but we need the physical copy as records in Hong Kong at that time, as I said, are patchy.'

'But surely Mr Trenton will have found it by now?'

'Only if he knows about the secret passage and the office itself. I'm sure your father would have hidden it there.'

'How are we going to find out?'

Peter crunched on another slice of toast and nodded with approval. 'We're going to break in.'

Charlotte's eyes nearly popped out. 'You're not going to do your head through the bars manoeuvre, are you?'

'Hopefully not, but it does mean if we can locate the certificate, you might be able to get everything that is rightfully yours. You can live at Loxley again.'

'Why don't we just let the police deal with it?'

'They haven't made their move yet, and I'm worried if Trenton gets wind of it, he might do something stupid, like torch the whole place.'

'Not Loxley?'

'We have to get there first, or we risk losing everything.'

She felt his hand on her cheek and then pushed her hair up around the back of her ear. 'You are more beautiful than I ever remembered. I've missed you.'

Charlotte sighed and shook her head while looking at his masculine jaw.

'Come back to bed.'

'You are the most courageous man.'

'Stupid, yes. But courageous, I'm not so sure?' He brought her face close to his with his hand. 'I'm not going to let you out of my sight again,' he said, kissing her, firstly on her cheek, then again on her lips.

'Oh Peter, I've missed you.'

Removing her dressing gown, she slipped under the duvet, and her naked body found the warmth of his. Watching him place the breakfast tray on the windowsill, she drew comfort from his broad shoulders and his strong back. His skin was smooth. Not one hair on his back, in contrast to his chest.

As he turned, he brought the duvet over them. Charlotte felt safe as he brought the whole length of his body up against hers. He was always warm. Even when she thought she'd lost him, she could sometimes imagine his warmth beside her.

His hand caressed her face again, tracing her jaw, cheekbones and nose. His finger gently mapped out her face, and then her heart instantly raced as he pushed it provocatively into her mouth. Sucking it, she felt a tingling in her toes, which enlightened her senses.

His kisses followed. Playfully teasing her lips and then her neck. Nibbling her ear was her switch, and he knew it. The tingling became warmer and more like a wave than a tingle. A small wave at first, lapping up gently, like the blissful Mediterranean Sea kissing the sandy beach. Then, waves of greater strength swirled and built.

His hand was now all over her body. Exploring her, teasing, and rubbing, making the waves larger and stronger. His masculine scent consumed her as he brought his body above her and parted her legs with his knee. Impossible to resist and defining his biceps with her hand, she felt the weight of his body on hers. She'd missed that, and she craved him.

The waves, now swelling as he thrust himself confidently. Swelling deep and then crashing, like a rip tide, in and out, riding the wave and each one stronger and higher.

Lost within his eyes, the swirling continued. Each wave, now encircled by another, came one after the other, then another and another. She held strong onto his arm. The strength of his muscles enabled her to hold tight and ride the raging tide. The storm was building. Each wave now indistinguishable from the next. A whirlpool of desire and emotion, spinning out of control and the warm ocean consuming her mind and body.

Storm clouds on the horizon, and the constant buffeting of waves crashing and withdrawing, before rolling in and flooding every fibre of her soul. She was lost at sea, a shipwreck in blissful peril, unable to see the shore, yet heady with freedom as she was tossed around in uncontrollable ecstasy.

Again and again, the powerful currents ebbed and flowed until she could hold back no more. Vulnerable and on the edge of drowning in its deep blue trance, she gave in to its power, opening the floodgates for everything to rush in and consume her.

Her body was like driftwood in a mighty ocean of intense freedom, and her heart beat to the sound of the sky. She was floating. Floating on the purple velvet of his desire and consumed by his release of power and control.

Love! This was not love. This was life!

37

THE THREE MUSKETEERS

'This is the most exciting thing to happen to me in a long while. It's like we're the three musketeers,' Mrs Hathersage said, switching on her head torch as she crept through the undergrowth. 'I knew all along he was a nasty man.'

Peter gathered everyone together. 'Okay. Mrs Hathersage, hold in that anger. We need you to be as calm and natural as possible. What did you say to him when you called?'

She looked at him, blinding him with the powerful torch beam.

'I said I had left a few personal things behind. There were so many cases and boxes when I left that I got in a bit of a muddle. He has no real idea of what goes on downstairs.'

'Great, so you go in as you would and distract him. We need twenty minutes, ideally.'

'Roger that,' she said with a grin.

Peter nodded. 'I just want to remind you that this is a very serious business. If we get caught, we could all end up in cages. He's an evil man, and I don't want you two in any danger.'

They huddled closer together in the trees. They could see the house emblazoned with lights and hoped they could get closer and remain undetected.

Suddenly, Peter looked puzzled. 'Wouldn't you normally arrive in a car?'

'Yes. But I'll say I got a taxi, and I wanted to walk up the drive and admire the spender of the house one last time.'

'Genius.'

'Charlotte?'

'Yes.'

'Once she's inside, we go for the back door. There's a staff shift change on the hour, and there should be a window of opportunity to sneak in, up the back stairs and to the secret passage as quickly and quietly as possible. Okay?'

'Roger.'

'Jeez! Will you two take this seriously?'

'It just seems silly, sneaking into what was my house for over forty years.'

'Well, it's not your house now, and if you want it back, this plan has to work.'

Charlotte and Mrs Hathersage both nodded and joined hands in unity in front of them. Peter placed his hand around both of them. 'Okay. Are we ready for action?'

'Yes!'

They kept to the shadows of the trees as much as possible and only used their torches when negotiating bridges and the haw-haw. Peter had to grapple Mrs Hathersage up on his shoulder, but once they were on the lawn, it was a no-torch zone.

'There could be dogs. We don't know that, so keep as quiet as possible.'

'I'm sure I remember him saying he was allergic?' Mrs Hathersage said, hiding behind a rhododendron bush.

'Well, let's hope so. Okay. We give it two minutes, then, Mrs Hathersage, you make your entrance. Five minutes later, it's the staff change, and we go for it. Everyone happy?'

'Yes!'

Mrs Hathersage straightened her pinafore and handed her torch to Peter.

'Good luck. Any problems, you can use the internal staff coms system and buzz through to the office. One buzz to tell us you're leaving the building and two buzzes if he suspects something and we need to hightail it out of there. Okay?'

Mrs Hathersage gave a thumbs up and started her walk to the front door.

Peter and Charlotte looked at each other and then watched her silhouette walk to the door.

An anxious wait... and she was in.

'Okay, gorgeous. It's showtime.'

The pair maintained their cover and circumnavigated the house to the rear. Right on cue, the staff started to depart. They always left a little earlier than they should, leaving a timely gap and their opportunity to slip in unnoticed.

Peter and Charlotte hid behind a topiary hedge, and Peter monitored the door.

'Shit! There's a chef having a fag by the door. He's in full uniform and doesn't look like he's going anywhere.'

Charlotte grabbed his hand.

'Come on, I know where we can bypass the door.'

She led him across a gravel drive and along the edge of the house to an open window into the kitchen. Charlotte whispered as she showed Peter the route up onto the wall.

'I used to sneak in here as a child and steal biscuits from the kitchen.'

Once in, they craftily worked their way to a storage area and then some steps up to the first floor. The house was quiet inside as the two of them tiptoed along a vast hallway and up another flight of stairs. Charlotte put her arm out to stop Peter.

'There are several squeaky floorboards halfway along this corridor. Follow me, get a good run-up, and we'll jump them. The carpet is thick, but land on your toes.'

He acknowledged and watched her go, then followed, hoping that his timing was as good as hers.

A little further, and Charlotte stopped. Hands on hips, and slightly out of breath, she gestured to the candlestick on the wall with her eyes.

'Ready?'

'Ready,' he said, watching her pull it towards her and then releasing the secret panelled door before them. Charlotte entered first, ducking her head and then using her torch in the narrow passageway. Peter followed and then observed her open the door to her father's secret office.

Peter switched on the light. There were no windows, so there was no chance that anyone would be alerted.

'Okay. There must be a secret safe or cupboard somewhere. Do you know of any?'

Charlotte scrunched her lips and shook her head.

'Shame. You scour the bookshelves, and I'll tackle the desk.'

They set to work, but nothing materialised. Charlotte checked behind the paintings and photographs. Nothing. Then feeling with her hands along the solid oak wood floor. She was convinced there might be a loose panel and a knot hole to place your finger, but nothing after much searching.

Peter opened the bottom two drawers and removed everything. There were papers, but mostly business-related, old newspapers and handwritten ledgers.

'There has to be something somewhere, but we're running out of time,' Peter stated with frustration.

He ran his hands around the desk. Nothing underneath and no apparent false back on it either.

Charlotte opened the top drawer and stared. It was there. Her father's hunting knife. The handle was carved from a deer antler from the estate, laying beside the family crest-embossed leather sheath. Charlotte became mesmerised by the glinting blade.

Peter looked at her. 'There's no time to be distracted.'

She looked at him and took a breath. 'I know. Sorry. So many memories.'

Peter took her hand. 'Be strong!'

She squeezed his hand and smiled.

'Hold on. What's this? The legs on this desk are not symmetrical. This one is fatter. I mean, deeper. Pass me the knife.'

Charlotte handed him the knife, and Peter pushed it into what looked like an ear of a carved mouse, running up the leg.

There was a pop, and the leg opened to reveal a secret compartment. Peter and Charlotte looked at each other.

'The knife was the key after all,' she said.

At that point, they were distracted by the intercom, which buzzed once.

'She's leaving,' they both said simultaneously. Then, worryingly, it buzzed again.

'Shit!' Peter said, thrusting his hand into the compartment.

Charlotte waited impatiently. 'Come on, Peter, we have to get out of here.'

Peter produced a leather wallet about the size of an A5 diary. He flipped open the metal clasp. A photo dropped out. It was a picture of her father holding a baby in his arms. Charlotte looked at Peter. 'What else is there?'

He pulled out some papers, rifled through them and stopped. 'It's here. The death certificate. We've found it. Come on, let's get out of here.'

Charlotte made a move for the door and held back. She picked up the knife from the floor and carefully placed it back into the drawer.

Peter looked at her.

'Sorry. Old habits!' she said, wincing.

Peter acknowledged with a smile and then grabbed her hand. 'We have to work out how to get out, and he could be anywhere.'

They ran and jumped the floorboards hand in hand. Charlotte was scared inside but also felt an incredible connection with Peter. He was her hero, and he had come to save her. She trusted him with all her life.

They slowed right down and peered into the kitchen. It was busy with life as dinner was obviously well on its way.

'There's another route,' Charlotte said.

'Where?'

She gave Peter a look he'd never seen before. 'Out of the goddamn front door.'

Peter smiled a huge smile. 'I love you so much. Come on.'

They ran so fast, their legs couldn't keep up. Hand in hand, they raced to the entrance hall, not daring to stop or look around. Peter lifted the enormous iron latch, kicked open the door and then jumped the eleven steps in one go onto the gravel drive. Charlotte skipped down each one and met him at the bottom.

'Come on, head for the trees,' he said, holding out his hand.

She gladly took it, and they ran and ran. Together they descended the haw-haw wall and then into the trees and headed for their place of original entry.

'Did you get it?' A voice said from behind some wild privet.

'Mrs Hathersage. Are you okay?' Charlotte asked, relieved they had caught up with her.

'Yes, I'm fine. Did you find anything?'

'We're pretty sure we have. It wasn't easy to find, and you really spooked us with the two buzzes. What happened? Did he smell a rat?'

Mrs Hathersage looked puzzled. 'No, dear. I pressed the button but then wasn't sure I had pressed it hard enough, so I pressed it again to make sure.'

Peter looked at Charlotte. Mrs Hathersage looked at Peter. Charlotte looked at Mrs Hathersage, and then they all started laughing, and Peter put his hand on both ladies' shoulders.

'I don't know about the three musketeers, more the like the three blind mice.'

They scuttled off to a side lane as the blue flashing lights of a police car lit up the night sky and then hurried past and on towards the house.

Peter placed his arms around the two of them. 'I don't think that will be his last visit from the cops.'

38

HOLM

They drove into the night to reach the cottage. Mrs Hathersage nodded off to sleep in the back and Peter concentrated on the road in silence. Charlotte admired his composure and also sat in silence, looking out into the night. Once home, Charlotte put on some tea. It was late, but they were all eager to scrutinise the contents of the stash in the proper light and work out their next move. Peter lit the fire, and they locked all the doors.

Charlotte looked agitated. 'Do you think we'll be all right? I mean, I couldn't bear the thought of living in a cage.'

Peter put his arms around her and winked at Mrs Hathersage, who was placing a wool blanket over her knees.

'Of course. Who the hell knows where or who we are? You're a Yorkshire jam medallist. You're an old relative come to visit, and as far as anyone is concerned, I don't exist.'

There was silence as they once again took turns looking at each other for reassurance.

'Let's have a proper look at the paperwork,' Peter said, opening the folio. 'When we've finished, I'm going to hide it in a box and conceal it in the cellar. It will be well hidden there, and no one will find it. But at least we are all in the know. Okay?'

They all looked at the pristine photograph in front of them. Charlotte's dad proudly held a baby and stood in front of a magnificent acer tree.

'It's Acer sino-oblongum, the south China maple,' Peter said, holding the photo close to his eyes. Charlotte and Mrs Hathersage looked blank.

'It's a species only found in China's Guangdong Province and Hong Kong. Well, at least then,' Peter said, scrutinising the leaf shape and bright red seed wings with a squint.

'There's a date on the back. 1968,' Charlotte replied.

Peter nodded. 'That's about the right time.'

Mrs Hathersage pulled her chair closer to the fire. 'What else is in there?'

Peter held a piece of paper in the air. 'This!'

They all looked. 'The death certificate. Master Henry Joseph, Tito...' They all looked at each other again and raised their eyebrows. 'Winterbourne. 1968 DOB. Date of death 1969. Kowloon City, Hong Kong.'

Charlotte took a breath that not only filled her lungs but nearly lifted her off her feet.

'Bingo.'

Peter pushed it back into the wallet. 'Okay. It's going down the cellar, and first thing tomorrow, I take it to the police. Everyone fine with that?'

Everyone agreed, and Peter disappeared downstairs. Charlotte and Mrs Hathersage clutched at their tea mugs and huddled by the fire.

'There's an electric blanket on your bed, Mrs Hathersage. Give it a few minutes, and it'll be toasty in there.'

Peter returned and acknowledged the stash was hidden behind the boiler, and he was heading for a bath.

Charlotte left Mrs Hathersage to head to her bed and took a mug of tea up for both of them. On reaching the top of the steps, she immediately noticed the bathroom door closed and steam billowing from the gap beneath. She edged closer to the door and could hear him humming to himself.

'I have tea here, Peter,' she said, giving two gentle taps on the wooden slatted door.

She entered, and amongst the steam, his huge smile met her straightaway and then his outstretched arm to receive his brew.

Charlotte perched on the loo and watched him almost drink the tea in one gulp. His thick black hair was wet, and she focused on how long and unkempt it was. He was greying more than ever. It made him look more distinguished. Not like a county judge or a bank manager but of someone with life experience and even more manly, if that was at all possible.

He looked at her, still smiling. His eyes, a much richer blue than she remembered. He'd lost the bright, sparky, naïve azure tone she had first been attracted to and assumed a much deeper ocean blue of someone who had witnessed things no one else should ever see. Calm, confident, yet with ripples of pain.

She watched him wash the soap off his masculine shoulders. His arm muscles were easily one of the sexiest things about him. She wanted to touch him but instead enjoyed the visual thrill of imagining him supporting himself above her.

As the soap disappeared, she noticed cuts to his chest. They were healing but still raw in places. He didn't acknowledge them as his hands splashed the warm bath water over his body.

They were long. Some almost stretched from one shoulder to the other, and then some on his back. Red and angry-looking.

'What did they do to you?'

Peter turned his head. His face serious, his eyes focused on hers, then tilting down to the floor and his chest rising with his quickening breath.

'I have some cream for those cuts. I'll get you fit and well again,' she said, leaning over and taking his chin in her hand. 'Don't ever leave my side again. Do you hear?'

He nodded and kissed her hand while focusing his eyes on her once again.

'We're going to get back what is rightfully yours. Don't worry about me. These are nothing,' he said, glancing at the scars. 'You deserve better than this cold, draughty hovel. We'll make sure justice is done. We have what we need now. Loxley will be yours again.'

Suddenly, the bathroom was illuminated with a vehicle's headlights from outside. Charlotte and Peter looked at each other. Peter rose from the bath, his commanding torso dripping with water.

'Make sure Mrs Hathersage is safe. Don't wake her unnecessarily but lock yourself in the room with her and keep quiet.'

'Are we in danger?'

Peter's face was now serious, and his eyes were alert and wide open like an eagle. He stood and placed his hand on her shoulder.

'We'll be fine. Trust me.'

He slipped on his jeans and t-shirt and headed for the landing. He peered through the window as secretly as possible.

'It's a black Range Rover. Know anyone with one of those?'

Charlotte hesitated. 'I do. But somehow, I don't think it's Lady Mountjoy coming to confess her cake sabotage.'

'What?' Peter replied, shrugging.

'Forget it. What do we do?'

'As I said. Lock yourself in with Mrs H and let me deal with this.'

'Okay. I trust you.'

~

Peter crept down the stairs, locked the back door, and positioned himself by the tiny window in the hall to observe the vehicle and remain concealed in the dark. He used the camera on his phone to get a closer look at the Range Rover, which had its lights on full beam and pointing directly at the house.

'Don't even try it,' Peter said, putting his phone in his pocket and clenching his fist.

Peter noticed the door handle slowly move downwards. His heart began to race. How many were there? he thought.

Charlotte and Mrs Hathersage were his main priority, but he knew whoever it was, they were probably not the kind of people to play fair.

The door handle went again, and at the same time, torchlight at the rear door. There were two of them.

He could maintain vigilance on both doors from his position but knew he could only defend one. A loud knock on the front door alerted Peter. Without warning, the back door flung open, and a tall, broad-shouldered man in a balaclava assertively entered the kitchen and turned on the light.

'We know you are in here. Just do as we say, and nobody gets hurt,' the man shouted.

Peter launched at him. The man produced a steel bar and swiped at Peter, hitting him across the chest. Peter flung himself against the wall, his chest in great pain. He pushed himself away and managed a clean punch on the man's jaw with his fist. The man staggered back, and then the second man came through the door.

Peter's eyes flicked between them. Being outnumbered was not a position he wanted to be in.

The second man lunged and grabbed him by the collar. Peter aggressively raised his knee into the man's groin. He doubled over, and Peter gave a punch, which caused the man to collapse on the floor.

The steel bar struck Peter again, this time by surprise across his back. Peter's lungs deflated and were unable to recover. His desperate attempts to breathe were fruitless as he lay on the floor, fighting for survival. He kicked frantically in desperation and knocked the first man off his feet as the steel bar hit the ground just inches from Peter's head.

In agony, he forced a breath and managed to kneel. His vision blurred. He didn't see the hand of the second man grab him by the throat, which picked him up and thrust him against the wall.

'No need to take this any further,' the man said through gritted teeth. 'Just calm down and take a little trip with us, and everything will be okay.'

Peter took the opportunity to gather his breath, despite a hand gripping his throat. 'What do you want?' he said, gasping.

The man laughed. 'Those concrete boots. Made to measure, I've been told? It's all over, Peter. Just come quietly.'

Peter shook his head, gritted his teeth, and looked the man straight in the eye.

'I never found them comfortable,' he said and, with all his force, released the man's hands from around his neck, struck him with his elbow and again with his knee right between the legs. He could see the other man gaining his feet and securing the steel bar in his hand but ran at the first man, making him fall against the bannister. His torso smashed through the wooden spindles and wedged himself. Peter lashed out with his foot against the bar-wielding man, who didn't falter. He came lunging forward, raised the bar aggressively above his shoulders and, with one savage blow, came towards Peter's head.

Peter ducked, sidestepped him and watched in complete amazement as the momentum of the bar, hurtling down, crashed into the first man, knocking him out cold. Peter took a deep breath and lunged for the second man, pushing him against the wall. Eye to eye, Peter attempted to grab the bar. The man forced him back. His neck thick like a wrestler and his arms bulging, Peter stood little chance against him. Being forced backwards, Peter couldn't stop him. He stumbled on the fragments of the bannister on the floor. Then felt his back crash against the wall. The steel bar forced its way towards Peter's neck.

Peter tried everything he had to resist but couldn't. He could see the veins on the man's forehead bulging, and he grunted as he brought the bar to Peter's neck and began to push it, restricting Peter's breath. Peter tried again to hold him off, but straining to breathe made him weak. He mustered all his strength and pushed against the bar. He managed to gain some respite and capitalised on the available air. Then the man's overwhelming brute strength, forced the bar again into Peter's throat. He gasped for air but couldn't. The bar throttling him, he dug deep but had nothing left to give. Peter's eyes began to blur. His lungs were empty, and his head felt dizzy. He choked and desperately wanted to take a breath. He could feel his legs weakening and his ability to defend himself useless. His feet now completely off the floor, the man took pleasure in hanging Peter by the steel bar and wringing the life out of him.

Peter's world went silent. His eyes could no longer visualise reality, and he felt his legs slam into the ground as if falling a thousand feet. His knees gave way, and he fell to the floor. That was it. He could do nothing more.

Seconds later, the man's full weight fell on him, pushing him further into the ground. His lungs grabbed at the air around him and briefly inflated his chest. Finally, he flailed his arms and levered the man's dead weight off him and sat with his back against the wall, gasping and coughing as his lungs fired up like an old spitfire.

His eyes began to fill with colour, and as they slowly began to focus, he could see Charlotte on the stairs wielding a log-splitting axe.

'It's amazing what a bit of log chopping can do for you, isn't it?' she said, tossing the implement to the floor and then rushing over to Peter and kissing him.

Blue flashing lights filled the house as Peter fought to regain his breath. He was exhausted and couldn't move.

'Are you okay?' he cried. 'Charlotte. Are you okay?'

'I'm fine, don't worry about me. Help is here, Peter. Help is here.'

'And Mrs Hathersage?'

'She's fine, Peter. We're all fine.'

'Did you kill him?'

'I used the handle, Peter. I'm not stupid!'

39

A LIFE WORTH LIVING

The one thing Charlotte detested about hospitals was the smell. The sterile and municipal sweet air filled her with dread.

To see Peter lying there, bandaged, and connected to a beeping machine, tangled her stomach and mind in equal measure. He was asleep, his face peaceful, but she knew he was hurting. Three broken ribs and concussion, the doctor had told her, and although they were keeping him in for observation, it was suggested he should make a full recovery. The nurse had given her a pillow, so she could doze off in the high-backed chair beside his bed. She wanted to be there for him when he woke, so she kept vigil and resisted. She had injured her arm as she gave the final blow, but it was a minor injury in comparison, and she didn't mention it.

The police had taken all the necessary documentation and grilled them both while at the house. They were kind, efficient, and just doing their job, but Charlotte felt she had been stripped bare. Devastation wasn't the right word. More, invaded, raped of her dignity and confused. She'd accepted the loss of her inheritance with courage and honour, but knowing now what a tyrant this imposter was made her shudder and question her own judgement.

One thing which was never in doubt was Peter's commitment to her. He was a stickler for fairness and justice and wouldn't forget this. Part of her just wanted to shut the door on the whole escapade and let it lie, but she was determined not to let him down. She owed him everything.

Watching his face, she noticed his eyelashes flickering, and then his face began to stir. Taking a small towel, she dipped it in warm water and dabbed his brow. With his eyes still closed, his face showed appreciation with a smile, even though his lips didn't move.

'I'm here, Peter. Just take it easy.'

His eyelashes flickered again, and then his eyes gradually opened. She could tell he was still dazed. His eyes glazed as if focusing on nothing.

His hand moved as if trying to grasp at something. 'What is it, Peter?'

He remained silent but continued searching with his hand. Charlotte took hold of it and felt him squeeze tight. His eyes closed as he maintained his grip. She knew what it meant. She knew he would never let her out of his sight again, and she knew their bond was greater than ever before.

He coughed and turned to look at her. Opening his eyes, she watched his pupils focus on her, and life returned to his face. 'We will have justice, Charlotte. You deserve better than this shambles of a situation. We will get what is rightfully yours, and I won't rest until that man is in prison and you are rightfully where you belong. At Loxley and the head once again of the Winterbourne household. I give you my word.'

Charlotte offered a glass of water to his lips. 'One day at a time, Peter. One day at a time. Let's get you fit and back on your feet first.'

~

For a couple of weeks following his release from the hospital, Charlotte watchfully nursed Peter. She was still a little nervous that some other thugs might force themselves into the house, but the police supplied a panic button to put her at ease. It didn't stop her from looking out the window whenever she heard a noise. The village rallied, and the cottage became a hive of activity. Food parcels, homemade this and that, and offers of vigilante reprisals were all flooding in. It was the subject of much gossip in the area, but Charlotte didn't tell more than she wanted. It was passed off as a bungled burglary, and Charlotte was happy not to have to divulge her entire back history and the fact she was the rightful heir to a multi-million-pound dynasty and all the trappings.

They were kind people, and she had been accepted within the community, but she certainly didn't want Jim and Hunter Hawkins in balaclavas brandishing cricket bats, causing more upset. Accepting soup, bread, and cheese was enough to make Charlotte feel incredibly grateful and humble. She would tell them the truth one day. She owed it to them, but not just yet.

While Peter was sleeping, Charlotte called Mr Shorofski, her shrink in London, to whom she had not spoken to for some years.

He was the sort of man who could say nothing, but with great meaning. A man who could extract thoughts from your mind you didn't know you had and reduce you to tears before walking out and feeling invincible. She respected him, and he had indeed helped her hugely in the past.

His soft tones greeted her.

'Hello, Mr Shorofski. Thank you for taking the time to talk with me. I'm once again feeling guilty. You don't even have to say anything. I know that's the story of my life, but this time I can't seem to shake it.'

'Go on,' he said as if instantly understanding.

'Well, I have put Peter through the most horrendous situation, and it made me realise how selfish I am. How ignorant I am, and I so badly want to change that.'

'Mmm,' he said and paused.

She could hear in her mind's eye he was scratching his chin and crossing his legs in his leather swivel chair.

'And what do you think I can do for you?'

This instantly threw Charlotte. 'Well, I was hoping you could at least disagree with me or offer some hypnotherapy or something?'

Mr Shorofski paused again. 'If you came to me with a problem and didn't know what it was, we would have to delve deep and explore what made you feel like that. Instead, you have told me that you are selfish and ignorant and that your guilt is justified.'

Charlotte gripped the phone tightly and started to well up. 'Well, I didn't expect you to just agree with me.'

'I'm not agreeing with you.'

'Oh!'

'It seems you are fully aware of what the issue is, and that's the most empowering thing anyone could want. If one were in some form of denial or wallowing in depressive self-pity, then it may be a different story. But, in reality, I'm the last person you need to be speaking to.'

'Oh! I see. Well, actually, I don't see. I'm confused now.'

'You're being true to yourself, Charlotte. That's the most

powerful thing anyone could wish for. I can't give that to anyone. It comes from inside and often a dark place, where the key is not always easy to find. Be true to yourself, and you will heal. Be true to the people around you, and they will heal. Be true to your life, and it will be a life worth living. I won't be charging for this call.'

Charlotte remained silent. Her head spun, and her heart thumped.

'Was there anything else?' he asked calmly.

'There's... nothing else.'

40

SEXIEST WOMAN IN WELLINGTONS

'It's a letter!'

'I can see it's a letter. Are you going to open it?' Peter asked, not wanting to sound too pushy.

'I'm not sure I want to.' Charlotte stared at the brown envelope on the welcome mat by the front door. 'It's from them.'

Peter nodded and held her hand. 'Probably. They said it would come.'

Charlotte looked at him with forlorn eyes. 'It all seems unreal, like we're living in an abstract artist's painting. Can we take a walk first? For some reason, I'm scared to open it.'

Peter squeezed her hand and passed her wellington boots.

Charlotte placed the letter between the salt and pepper pots on the kitchen table and encouraged Peter into the rear garden. She passed the wooden chopping block and pivoted her hand on the axe protruding from it.

'Come on,' she said, grabbing his hand. 'There's something we need to deal with.'

'Where are we going?'

'To the view beyond. Where else?'

Peter shook his head. 'You're crazy. You know that? You're a mad woman.'

Charlotte looked back at him. 'I know exactly what I'm doing, Peter. It's where you came to me. It's where I came to me, and it's where I saw the future.'

'Yep! As I said. Completely bonkers,' he said, rolling his eyes and laughing.

Charlotte raced Peter through the back gate and into the field. The air was cooler than of late, and the sun was lower in the sky. The blackberries would be ripe soon.

'Will you help to gather them for my jam?'

Peter nodded.

'I noticed that the hedgerows change dramatically through the seasons. They are barren through the winter, and then white snowdrops give way to the blowsy daffodils, which in turn reluctantly hand over to the splendour of the bluebells and, in turn, the fronds of bracken and nettle.'

'Why are the bluebells in the hedgerows? I thought they were woodland flowers,' Charlotte said, spinning around joyfully.

'They are woodland flowers. They thrive under the trees, but the hedgerows are what is left of the original woodland, which has been cleared to make the field. It was the old woodland edge.'

'I never knew that,' she said, skipping along. 'I thought they were all planted by farmers.'

'Some are, but you won't find bluebells in those. They are an indicator of ancient woodland. Woodland and trees which have occupied that site for thousands of years.'

'Sexy man,' she said, blowing him a kiss.

'Where are we going?'

'To the view beyond. I told you.'

'I've never been down here before.'

'Yes, you have. It was you who showed me the view beyond. I reached out to you. Anyway. You're buried there,' she said with a more sombre tone.

'Are you sure it wasn't you who had a bump on the head?'

'Come on, I'll race you,' she said, picking up the pace.

Charlotte ran ahead, jumping over fallen branches. She leapt over the clints and grykes with Peter hot on her tail as she raced along the limestone pavement. Suddenly she stopped and put her arm out in front of Peter to prevent him from carrying on over the edge.

'It's over there.'

Peter admired the vast countryside before them. Harvested fields, hay bales dotted randomly, the river valley and the autumnal reds, yellows and browns taking hold of the chestnuts, birch and willow.

'Sit with me,' she said, laying out a blanket.

'What's that?' Peter gestured with his hand to the gap between the rocks.

'It's you and me,' she said, staring at the homemade wooden cross.

Peter looked blank and scrunched his eyebrows. Charlotte crawled over and plucked it from the ground.

'You know, you're the sexiest woman in wellingtons.'

Charlotte looked back at him and smiled. 'I've been perfecting the look and, honestly, nearly put forward my idea of bedroom meets boggy field to Vivienne Westwood.'

They laughed together as Charlotte brought the cross in front of them and took her seat. She began untying the string which bound the two pieces together. 'I truly thought you were gone forever. This is my place, where I came to be with you.'

She took the pieces of wood, separated them, and held the

beech stick high. 'This is me. I went to the hospital making this, so it really is a part of me.'

Peter looked concerned. 'What?'

Charlotte carried on. 'And this is you, my rock, my strength,' she said, bringing the oak stick up to meet the other. 'It's time for us to move on, Peter. You and me into the view beyond. Together.'

She stood and pulled his arm, so they went shoulder to shoulder, looking as far as the eye could see.

'It's been hard for you, hasn't it? I'm sorry for everything,' Peter said, taking the sticks into his hand and examining her craftsmanship.

Charlotte didn't know what to say.

'And you're right. There is a view beyond, and I can see both of us. Stronger for what we have been through and wiser too. I won't let you down again.'

'You haven't let me down, Peter. In fact, the opposite. You've shown me what is important in life. That happiness is achievable and that it comes when you least expect it. Thank you.'

'Take your stick, and this is what we will do. On the count of three, we throw them as hard as we can into the river. You and me, free, together on our next adventure to the open sea. Nothing to stop us, and without a care. This is it, Charlie, you and me into the view beyond. One... two... three.'

Both sticks flew through the air, tumbling their way towards the water. Peter's hit a rock and ricocheted into the air before splashing upstream into the water, and Charlotte's seemed to glide effortlessly before becoming trapped in a hawthorn tree. They looked at each other. Charlotte was so bitterly disappointed.

Peter pointed. 'Look.'

A robin swooped down and landed in the tree. Its song so loud and joyful, they could hear it as clear as day. Its red breast was obvious as it flitted around the tree, singing at the top of its voice.

'Mum,' he said with a lump in his throat. 'It's good to see you, Mum.'

Charlotte looked at him. 'You mean, the old woman?'

Peter shrugged and then pointed again.

The bird started flapping its wings, and Charlotte's stick dislodged from the tree and plopped into the river as Peter's stick came to meet it. A tricky start, but they were off, together into the unknown. There would be turbulence and waterfalls, but they were off, off to a better place.

Charlotte felt his arm around her, squeezing her tight. She smiled and shed a little tear. His other hand pushed her hair back off her face, and then she felt his kisses on her cheek and then her lips. He was a sublime kisser. Manly, yet delicate, purposeful, and sensual. She was in love. Utterly in love with him and besotted. She wanted him, and as he led her back to the blanket, she knew she was ready to give everything.

They sat on the blanket, and he continued with his kisses. The way he held her was exquisite. Powerful and in control, and she was happy for him to enjoy the freedom. Her hand could feel the hairs on his chest between his unbuttoned lumberjack shirt. She didn't want the thoughts of what he'd been through to come into her mind ever again, but it made her fancy him more. Knowing how courageous he was, how he'd defied death and fought those thugs in the house to protect her, was enough to make her squirm with joy. How could he be so masculine yet composed and delicate with her?

She was eager to find out.

41

THE LONG WALK HOME

'Open it.'

'I don't want to.'

'It'll be good news.'

Charlotte took the letter and stared at it. 'Good news for who, exactly?'

Peter shook his head. 'What are you talking about?'

'I know what it will say.'

'You don't know until you open it. This is about you getting everything back. Your family's dynasty, everything you rightfully own, everything you fought so hard to keep. Remember how passionate you were about making sure I wouldn't take it all from you? It nearly broke us up forever, and now you're saying you're scared of what it might say?'

Charlotte threw the letter on the table. 'I don't know what I'm thinking, Peter. I'm confused. There's been so much trouble over all of this.'

Peter put his arm around her. 'Think about Lucy and her inheritance, if nothing else.'

'I wish she was here, Peter. I miss her dearly.'

'Has she been in touch?'

Charlotte looked down at the floor and wiped a tear on her sleeve. 'No. I texted her, but she rarely replies. LA life is busy, with parties and the like. She's a woman now and even a princess for all I know.'

'She's still your daughter. She'll be excited that the family home will once again be restored to its rightful owner.'

Charlotte said nothing, just raised her eyes and gazed out into the view beyond the kitchen window. 'Look. A deer. I've seen him before, such a beautiful creature.' Charlotte pointed to the magnificent animal, now in full adult antler and head held high, looking proud.

'Open the letter, Charlotte, and let's get this sorted once and for all.'

The letter was short and to the point.

Dear Ms Winterbourne

Following the recent prosecution case in relation to your estate, I would like to arrange a meeting to run through the documentation so we can finalise the issue. May I suggest meeting at Loxley at your earliest convenience?

Mr Blakemore

Acting Solicitor

Charlotte carefully refolded the letter and placed it on the table.

'It seems we are going back to Loxley, but this time not through a kitchen window.'

Peter kissed her on the cheek. 'I couldn't be happier. This is the result we have been waiting for. You'll be back where you belong, and you can have your old life back.'

Charlotte continued to watch the deer as it moved around freely within the garden.

'Maybe we can resurrect the swing?'

Peter smiled and put the kettle on. 'One step at a time, hey?'

~

Charlotte looked up at the sign above the stone archway while Peter dealt with the taxi.

LOXLEY.

The carved lettering was still pristine, although the stonework appeared neglected and stained from the moss and honeydew from the overhanging trees. Peter took her by the hand, and they began their approach through the parkland to the house.

'Why didn't we get the taxi to the door?' Peter asked, walking quickly.

'I want to see everything. Remind myself what this place is. Remember, the last time we were here, we were sneaking around the shrubbery in the dark. I want to look at it with fresh eyes. It's been a long time.'

Peter quickened the pace. 'Sure. It's exciting, though. I bet you never thought you would get it all back. Let's hope he hasn't spent everything.'

Charlotte stopped dead. 'Peter! Will you stop going on and on about the money?'

'Sorry. I'm excited for you, that's all. When I was starving in that cage and the searing heat driving me crazy, the thing that kept me going was knowing I was going to find the truth and put you back where you belong. Be thankful for what has happened. It's been hard for both of us. I've beat myself up, knowing you've been struggling in that damp, run-down house and having to find work. Your pain is over now. Yes, Mrs Hathersage has retired, but we can find another amazing housekeeper. I'm sure most of the existing staff will be happy to see you again, especially if they've been badly treated.'

Charlotte's face crumpled. 'I do hope the staff haven't been treated badly. I'd never forgive myself.'

'Fingers crossed,' Peter said, hurrying her along and trying to remain optimistic.

Charlotte continued to drag her heels. 'Look, there's that elm tree you showed me. Ulmus, isn't it? The Latin.'

Peter huffed. 'Normally, I'd be quite excited at the elm, but if we don't get a march on, we'll never get there.'

Charlotte made a beeline for the tree. 'I want to say hello to it. Ask it how it has been doing. I want to get to know this place again and show it the respect I never gave it.'

Peter followed her to the tree. 'Jeez! There's a time and a place for all this. We haven't time to go on a grand tour, talking to all the trees. We have to meet the solicitor, and we are already late.'

Charlotte placed her hands on the trunk of the tree. 'You know your problem?'

'What?' Peter said, knowing it really was a worthy tree, but nevertheless feeling he needed to take some control.

'You need to chill out a bit. Not take life so seriously. Enjoy the moment.'

Peter stood staring at her and watched her examine the tree from its roots to its very top.

'There's some deadwood. What do you think, old age or root compaction?'

He took a deep breath and pinched his arm.

'What the hell is going on here? What have you turned into? There are Picassos, Constables, a bathtub so big you could get lost in it, a four-poster bed indented with Henry

VIII's belly, and you're talking root compaction! Will you hurry up?'

'You've lost your love for nature, Peter. I'll show you what's important in life,' she said with tongue firmly in cheek.

'Okay, okay. So now you're a comedienne too. I'll show you what's important in life,' he said, mocking her.

'I just look at the world differently now. I appreciate things I never noticed before. I used to become anxious, not eat and spend hours with my shrink, and the cycle was non-stop. My swing and oak tree was my sanctuary. I didn't know why. It just seemed right. I know there are bad memories, but that's where I broke the cycle. I've grown, Peter. Grown in ways I never thought possible. I'm happy with who I am for the first time in my life. I had to do all that myself, but you showed me how to do it. Remember climbing to the top of the oak tree?'

'Of course.'

'We talked about the five steps to well-being. One: be active. Two: learn something. Three: give something. Four: connect. And five: take notice.'

Peter shrugged. 'Well, that's just common sense.'

'Well, that might be for you, but I've had to learn that. I took so many things for granted as a child and a young woman.'

'So, what's your point?'

Charlotte laughed, looked at the twigs, pinecones and leaves on the ground, and then kicked a pinecone into the bracken.

'You! That's my point. I...'

She didn't have time to finish when she felt his strong arms pulling her tight into his chest and then his lips against hers. It felt sincere, honest and beautiful. A kiss that meant the world and made her feel secure and protected.

It lasted an exquisitely long time, but time didn't matter. It was his intention that was sublime. Safe in his arms and lost in his kiss, she was lightheaded, her feet as if floating and her heart pounding to the same beat as his.

'I love you, Charlie. You've given me a purpose, a life full of meaning. I've grown because of you. I'm stronger, wiser and proud to be at your side. You are my world, and my heart is yours to keep.'

Charlotte remained lost in his eyes, still floating on air. 'We can do this, can't we?' she said, looking for the final reassurance she needed.

'Yes,' he said with confidence. His eyes were determined and penetrating hers.

'It's you and me then. Come on, let's do this.' She grabbed his hand and, with vigour, marched back to the drive and headed for the house. 'I love you so very much, Peter. You trust me, don't you?'

He looked at her in disbelief. 'Yes, of course.'

'No matter what I say or how silly I might be?'

'Yes. You know that.'

'I've never felt so liberated. You set me free, Peter. You are my guardian angel, and I want to make you the happiest man alive.'

He nodded and squeezed her hand tight. 'You already do that.'

Approaching the front door, Charlotte felt a wave of anxiety start in her toes and then rapidly to her heart. She looked at Peter for reassurance. He smiled and maintained his tight grip.

On first inspection, the house looked as it had always done. Impressive and stately. The intricate stonework was untouched, and the turrets, gargoyles and topiary were all as she remembered. Then, suddenly, the front door creaked open, and a man wearing a grey pinstripe suit and immaculate black patent shoes appeared. He was followed by another man who appeared to be in an identical suit but was carrying a black leather briefcase.

'Ms Winterbourne?' the man with the patent shoes asked.

'Yes. Charlotte. And this is my partner, Peter.'

'My name is Samuel Beardmore, I'm one of the senior partners, and this is my colleague, Mr Daniel Wiseman. He will set out today's meeting and review the finer details. Please, come through.'

Charlotte and Peter shook hands with both men and followed them into the drawing room, where three seats had been positioned around the oval mahogany table. Charlotte scrutinised everything as she passed through the entrance hall and into the room. She tried not to show emotion but felt almost like her home had been soiled. Like an intruder had invaded her personal space and tainted the air. She noticed some paintings had been moved. All the family portraits had been removed, leaving patches of bare, unbleached walls. Her favourite wildflower canvases and pressed flower ensembles were gone. Instead, an array of ugly and brutal hunting scenes, stags and boar's heads and guns were back on display in a barbaric homage to cruelty and death.

Mr Wiseman stood by his seat, and Mr Beardmore promptly drafted in another chair for Peter. Charlotte took to her seat, and the gentlemen followed suit. Glasses of water were poured, and Mr Wiseman opened the briefcase and arranged the paperwork on the table in front of them.

He cleared his throat and took a sip of water.

'Ms Charlotte Winterbourne?'

'Yes.'

'In front of our witness today, Mr Beardmore, I have the documentation for you to sign, which will transfer everything listed hereafter into your legal ownership.'

Charlotte nodded.

'I will run through each element, and when you are happy, I will require a signature from yourself and the witness. Are you happy to proceed with everyone present?' Mr Wiseman looked at Peter as he rested his fountain pen beside the paperwork.

Charlotte responded without hesitation. 'Yes, absolutely.'

'There is some good news and some bad, I'm afraid.

Item one. Loxley, the house, estate, woodlands, lakes, and all outbuildings.

Item two. The London house, gardens, and outbuildings.

Item three. All contents of both properties, including artworks, sculptures, jewellery, silverware, antiques and fixtures and fittings.

Item four. All assets, bank accounts, investments, and portfolios. Totalling two hundred and eighty-one million pounds.'

Charlotte took a sip of water and maintained eye contact with Mr Wiseman.

'Now for the bad news. The Alpenblick Hotel in Austria and the Corsican villa have both been sold, and the police are still investigating the whereabouts of the proceeds. It may be the case that some capital has gone towards funding people and narcotics trafficking and may have been laundered offshore somewhere. More details will follow on this and information regarding missing vehicles, some paintings, including a Ruben and a Canaletto, and one or two smaller items not listed within the original catalogue. As I said, these will be dealt with separately, and we hope to return them to you as quickly as possible. Do you have any questions?'

Charlotte straightened her back. 'Have any of my father's things been removed?'

Mr Wiseman glanced over at Mr Beardmore. 'We believe that his office was targeted, but it's unclear to the nature of the disturbance.'

Charlotte took a deep breath. 'Can I take a look before we proceed any further?'

Peter and Charlotte approached her father's secret study. Charlotte pulled down on the wall-mounted candlestick, and the concealed wooden panel door opened to reveal the entrance.

Peter followed Charlotte along the dark passageway, up the steps and into the concealed room. The large, solid wood desk, which once took centre stage, was smashed to pieces. An axe lay among the debris of splintered wood and papers. Paintings, certificates and anything else which once adorned the walls were also mixed with the devastation. Charlotte looked at Peter and shook her head.

'It's worse than I thought.'

Peter put his hand on her shoulder. 'He had no respect.'

Charlotte attempted to sort through the mess with her foot, tossing timber aside to see what was beneath.

'There's nothing of value here now,' Peter said calmly. 'He will have taken anything worthy of sale. We can get this sorted. It looks worse than it is.'

Charlotte sat on her haunches and took a deep breath. 'You're right. In a strange way, it feels like closure. This was a museum to my father, and what was the point? I hated him. Why would I want to be constantly reminded of him?'

Peter took his time to reply. 'You were conditioned that way. The dynasty, the family crest and lineage. It's only what has gone before and what you are supposed to leave for the next generation.'

Charlotte's look of disgust made Peter feel uneasy. 'It's tradition and a responsibility of your status. Your duty.'

Charlotte's head remained down, her eyes glossing over at the pile of rubbish in front of her and a numbness replacing any sentimental attachment.

'At least you have most things back now, and you can pick up where we left off. You can carry on as expected. Clearing up this mess is a minor inconvenience,' he said with an optimistic smile.

Charlotte stood. Her back was straight, and her head held high. 'What this means, Peter, is that I can finally move on. I'm no longer trapped by my father. I am no longer imprisoned by his traditions and expectations. This has done me a favour. It's just scrap. Nothing but the smashed-up legacy of my father and no longer the museum of tyranny. I can move on now.'

'That's good to hear. This is your place now, and now everything is back where it belongs. You can begin to relax and enjoy once again the life you once knew.'

Charlotte laughed. 'Maybe I don't want to relax.'

42

THE SWING

Charlotte raced down the steps with great vigour.

'I want to go to the swing.'

'You have to be kidding me? What about signing the papers? The solicitors are waiting.'

'I've never been so serious in my whole life, Peter. Tell the solicitors to take a break, have some lunch, whatever. Two hours Peter, what're two hours?'

'Do you think you're being a bit precocious?'

'Yes.'

'Jeez, what's got into you? I thought we'd never go back to the swing.'

Charlotte produced her father's hunting knife and gold cigarette lighter, which she had found within the office debris. 'I'll show you what's got into me. Come on.'

'I'll catch you up. Two hours, I'll tell them.'

Peter eventually caught Charlotte up at the weir. She stood looking out over the lake, allowing the rushing cascade of water to add to her adrenalin. Stretching her arms out, she let the breeze blow through her hair and tried to inhale as much of the landscape before her.

'Can we do it?' she asked, sensing Peter was close.

'The weir? Of course we can.'

'Together, I mean?'

Without hesitation, Peter grabbed her hand and led her onto the top of the cascade. The stone's edge was like a dam wall preventing the rushing river from flowing freely over the edge. Instead, channelling the torrent through a gap and forming a waterfall, which tumbled aggressively into the vast lake beneath. To the eye, it wasn't possible to jump the gap. But both Charlotte and Peter had executed it perfectly before, although they were somewhat younger and more desperate in their missions.

Peter brought his face close to Charlotte's so their noses were touching. 'Together?' he said like a general leading his troops.

'Together,' she said, relishing his leadership.

The duo eyed up the gap. The torrent of water was so powerful, one mistake, and they would be drawn down and spat out onto the rocks below.

Charlotte felt him tighten his grip and then lurched forward. She followed with the knife and lighter within the tight grip of the other hand. They ran, the green algae making it impossible to establish a firm grip, but they remained committed. There was no turning back. Peter's feet left the ground, and then Charlotte's. The force of the water beneath them drew the wind and buffered them towards the edge. Charlotte closed her eyes and put her complete faith in her man. Her mind flashed back to when she was a girl, her father's story of the young poacher who had lost his life attempting the same jump.

A strange comfort filled her thoughts, knowing they could die together, and as the wind and the sound of the water disorientated her, she smiled and, perversely, enjoyed the moment of insecurity of their unknown fate.

She lost grip as Peter's arms began to flail. Her feeling of comfort was instantly replaced by dread as she kept her eyes shut and anticipated the inevitable. Her body twisted as she fell. The uneasy feeling of weightlessness and confusion made her panic. She opened her eyes and instantaneously landed on top of Peter.

Her hand grasped for anything tangible. Grass, the feeling of grass and soil in her grip, was not what she expected. Land, hard, solid land, and the sound of the water behind her meant she was safe. Peter's eyes were closed. She caught her breath and touched his face searching for any sign of life, then rested her head on his chest.

Thump, thump... his heartbeat was distinct and strong, resonating in her ear.

'You are a silly bitch,' she said to herself. 'A selfish, silly bitch.' She raised her head and looked at his face once more. 'I don't deserve you. I don't deserve you,' she said, beating her fist on his chest.

Peter's eyes opened. 'Are we in heaven?'

'No, Peter. We made it, thanks to you. I'll make everything up to you, my gorgeous, gorgeous man. I've been selfish, and you... You would do anything for anyone. I owe you everything, Peter. You saved me.'

Peter coughed and then laughed. 'It's only a little jump over a weir.'

Charlotte laughed and then started to cry. 'You idiot. You saved me full stop. You rescued me from my life and showed me a future.'

Peter wiped her tears with the back of his hand. 'Don't be daft, lass. You found me. Anyway, I'm only with you because you're a great weir jumper!'

Charlotte beat her fist on his chest once more. 'I hate you,' she said, whimpering.

'You would have used your other hand if that were the case,' he said, pushing the two of them up with his arms against the ground.

Charlotte looked at the knife and lighter. 'Let's finish this, Peter.' She took to her feet and headed up the grassy slope in search of the oak tree on the shore, which once was her sanctuary. Before long, she recognised the large expanse of exposed roots and then the stout trunk of the ancient tree. 'Another few years older, Peter, but it still looks the same.'

'It will be here long after we are gone,' he said, looking up into the vast spreading canopy.

Charlotte took hold of the rope which had once suspended her at her lowest moment. 'Lift me up on your shoulders,' she said, gesturing up into the tree.

'We are going to get rid of all this once and for all.'

Peter flung her up onto his shoulders effortlessly, and Charlotte sliced through the rope and let it fall to the ground.

Assembling the old rope and the now rotting wooden seat which once formed her swing, she took the lighter and watched the flame take hold of the rope. Immediately, the dry rope twisted and crackled as the flame grew larger. Peter placed a few twigs to further encourage it, and the pair watched silently.

The fire took hold, and smoke billowed into the air. Charlotte grabbed the seat and rested it on the fire. 'I don't want anyone to find this and perhaps do what I did. I want to forget about the past now.'

Peter kissed her on the cheek. 'It's a brave thing to do. I'm proud of you.'

Peter reached to his side and appeared to be searching in the stony soil.

'What about this?'

He produced the discarded plastic pregnancy test, which had been left at the scene unnoticed.

Charlotte took it in her hand and looked at the strip. The rain and elements had washed any evidence of its conclusion. 'This too, Peter. I would have loved to have a child with you. I can't think of anything else which would show my love for you.'

Peter nodded and smiled. 'I bet they would have been an incredible tree climber.'

Charlotte sighed a philosophical sigh. A sigh that said a thousand things and a sigh of melancholy joy left nothing but silence. She threw the test onto the fire and watched it shrivel in an acrid blue flame. 'I'm too old now, probably. We had our chance, and the timing was wrong. We had our chance.'

Peter put his arm around her and pulled her in tight. 'We had other things to deal with. It was probably for the best.'

Silence could say a million things, and as they watched the contents of the fire turn to cinders, it did just that. Nothing more needed to be said, and a feeling of closure filled their thoughts.

'Thank you, tree,' Charlotte said, gazing up through its sprawling canopy. 'Thank you.'

43

FREEDOM

Hand in hand, Peter and Charlotte walked back to the house. Through the walled garden, Charlotte brushed her hand over the fragrant lavender and smiled as she picked and assembled a small posy of flowers and a single white rose, which she held to her nose.

Mr Wiseman and Mr Beardmore were waiting impatiently in the drawing room. The paperwork was laid out on the table as before, and a fountain pen was in a wooden holder beside it.

'Thank you for waiting, gentlemen. I hope you appreciate I have had things to deal with before I sign.'

Mr Wiseman nodded and gestured for Charlotte to take her seat.

'Would you like for me to read out the contents again?' he asked, smiling.

'No. That won't be necessary,' she said, briefly closing her eyes and taking a deep breath. 'Firstly, I want to thank you both for your diligence and efficiency in resolving this case and holding everything responsibly in trust for this moment. I am... We are extremely grateful that justice has been done and the criminals have been prosecuted. This whole episode of our lives has been tough in many ways. I have lost family and not been allowed time to grieve properly, my daughter is now estranged, and friends I once considered close have abandoned me.

Some of the family assets have been lost forever, and I can see my father reeling at the very thought. He was proud of everything he and his forefathers had built. It shouldn't be allowed that an evil entity should be able to ruin it so easily. Loxley appears to be largely unscathed. My mother will be pleased her favourite seat by the walnut tree is as it was and beckoning for use once again.

In many ways, this house has become a museum to the family that was. Useless paintings stacked wall to wall. Priceless artefacts gather dust, and the smell of antiquity and opulence is less in keeping with this modern life.

I now have a partner who has shown incredible resilience, honesty and commitment to my welfare, and I know we will forge a life together with the things that really matter to us, and it is with great optimism I will not be signing this document.'

The three gentlemen exchanged uncomfortable glances and fidgeted in their seats. 'This isn't a time for games, Charlotte,' Peter said, offering some reassurance to the solicitors.

Charlotte looked at Peter and smiled. 'I don't want it, Peter. I'm serious. All this disgusting grandeur makes me feel sick at the thought of the pressure and responsibility of maintaining its future and for what?'

Mr Wiseman took the pen out of the holder and offered it to Charlotte. 'It's important you sign, Ms Winterbourne.'

Charlotte smiled and playfully took her gaze around the room. 'I'm not signing, and for the final time, I don't want it.'

Peter leaned forward. 'Do you know what you are doing?'

Charlotte stood, put both hands on the table and looked Peter straight in the eye. 'I know exactly what I'm doing, Peter. You have shown me the intricate wonder of a single chestnut leaf. The complex veins running beneath the surface, its strength, delicacy and purpose in close detail. You led me into the woods to sit as quietly as mice and listen to the thousands of sounds that I'd never heard before. Birdsong, loud and proud from such tiny creatures. The sound of the wind blowing through the leaves, and when you suggested we listen to an ant's noise as it climbs among the moss and lichens, I thought you were insane. But I listened, and I heard.

When I tasted wild garlic, bilberries and meadowsweet for the first time, my mind was opened. To smell the pear drops and pineapple when you crushed western red cedar between your fingers changed my thinking, and when we laid on our backs looking up into the vast sky, I understood our place within nature.

I'd never taken the time to appreciate what matters most in our lives, and you opened my senses to this reality.

I want to be in a rustic cottage with you, chopping logs and looking out into the view beyond.'

Peter smiled and shook his head. 'I love you. You are the most courageous, beautiful, craziest woman I've ever known.'

The solicitors sat motionless, not knowing what to do, and then Charlotte turned to them. 'This is no disrespect to you, gentlemen. I just need to do what is right for me. I will sign, but not in its current form. I want you to draw up something new. A document which benefits other people. Hard-working, generous people who already understand the value of life itself and would never ask for a penny. People who deserve it much more than me. Is that clear?'

Both men nodded.

'This place is Lucy's inheritance. I won't take that away from her. I don't need it and all its unhappy memories, good riddance,' she said, smiling.

The solicitors once again shared undeniable anguish in their eyes, and Mr Wiseman put the pen back in its holder.

'Peter,' Charlotte said again, leaning onto the table.

'Yes?'

'You deserve more than me. I have been self-centred, naive and blinkered to the real world. You are brave and strong, and your heart is true, I want you to have the London house. It's yours to do whatever you want with it. I never want you to work like a slave again. I want you to heal your wounds, rest your body and be fit and healthy to share the rest of your days with me at the cottage. Log chopping essential,' she said, grinning.

She turned back to the gentlemen. 'As for everything else, I want to give it all away to the people and causes I deem worthy. I'll send you the full details in a formal letter by the end of the week, so that you can draw up the new document. I wish it to be done anonymously, without linking to myself or Peter. If the proceeds of the Alpenblick and villa are ever recovered, I want the money to go to charities for helping with mental health, animal welfare and tree conservation. Again, I will list in detail the recipients within the same letter. Is that clear?'

Mr Wiseman looked like a very smart rabbit in the head-lights and was frozen to the spot. Mr Beardmore cleared his throat. 'We await your letter with anticipation, Ms Winterbourne.'

'Thank you. In that case, I will allow for both of you and your families to experience a holiday of a lifetime at my expense. I'm sure you haven't seen your wives and children nearly as much as you should have. Am I right?'

The men nodded, looked embarrassed and then thanked Charlotte. Then Mr Wiseman packed away the paperwork and pen and shook hands with Charlotte and Peter before leading the party out of the front door.

They watched the car disappear along the drive, over the humpback bridge and out of the gate. Charlotte walked in front of Peter.

'Thank you,' she said, looking out over the parkland. 'Thank you. And thank you and thank you.'

'What are you doing?' Peter enquired.

'I'm thanking all the trees. I should have done that a long time ago.'

'Thank you!' they both shouted as they ran among the trees.

44

A POSTCARD FROM HATTY

Peter picked up the card from the mat and looked at the picture on the front of the sun setting over sand dunes and joyfully coloured beach huts.

'It's a postcard from Mrs Hathersage.'

'Fabulous. What does it say?'

'It says: "Dear Charlotte and Peter. Thank you from the bottom of my heart. My dream of retiring to the sea is now a wonderful reality because of your heartfelt generosity. My house overlooks the bay, and I'm close to my sister, so easy to pop round for coffee and help when she needs it. She's not as nimble on her feet as I am, and sadly I fear she doesn't have long to live due to her illness. But I'm able to give her the love she deserves in her hours of need. I have a little dog now, too, Scamp. He loves walks along the beach and is great company in the evenings. My sincere thank you once again, and please pop by when you and Peter have a spare minute? Much love Hatty".'

Peter smiled as he looked over the photo again. 'I didn't know she was called Hatty. Hatty Hathersage! How lovely.'

'Yes, funny, isn't it? I never called her Hatty. This is the first time she has called me Charlotte instead of Miss Charlotte.'

'She knew then?'

'What?'

'That you helped her?'

'She's been in on the whole thing. I owed it to her. She was there for me since I can remember, and I beat myself up thinking she should have retired years ago, but I was too selfish to see it.'

'How much did you give her?'

'Enough, Peter. Enough to never have to worry.'

'Do you really think you'll be happy with me in this ramshackle house?'

'I couldn't wish for anything more. You're the man of the house, Peter. I have nothing and want for nothing. Look after me, protect me from any more evil, and I'll be the happiest woman that's ever lived.'

'You need never worry again. I'm here, and it's my duty to make sure you are safe. It's funny. All the things we have been through, you wouldn't wish on anyone else. In fact, we could write a book about everything that's happened. But seriously. All those things have made us stronger, and I've seen you change. Seen you grow from a struggling sapling, blowing every which way in the wind, to a mature, blossoming tree with so much beauty and resilience.'

'Less of the mature, if you please? Let's head off into the village on our bikes, pick up some food and head out for a picnic? I have the feeling it's going to be one of those days.'

'I'll race you,' Peter said, revving the handlebar like a motorbike.

They headed up the lane and saw the vicar colouring in the final red part of the roof thermometer. Charlotte looked at

Peter and raised an eyebrow. They carried on and waited at the crossroads as the blacked-out Range Rover of Lady Mountjoy pulled up before them.

'I do hope you'll be submitting an entry at the summer fate again, Charlotte?' she said while adjusting her headscarf in the mirror. Eye contact was not her forte, and neither were seatbelts.

'I can only wonder at how good your entries will be, Lady Mountjoy. But yes. I'll throw something together just to make the table look busy.'

She acknowledged by preening her excessively cantilevered eyelashes with the back of her finger, and then the electric window blocked out any further parle, and she was off.

'She doesn't know the fete is getting a bigger marquee this year, so we can space out the entries and less chance of subterfuge, perhaps?' Charlotte said, looking ever so smug.

As they pulled up outside the hardware shop, Bob was up a ladder mounting a brand-new sign above the door, and there was a new van parked out front too.

'Hello Charlotte, Peter, how's life?' Bob said with a screw clamped between his lips and both hands holding the sign in place.

Peter replied while steadying the ladder with his foot. 'We're really good, thanks. New sign?'

Bob fastened in the last screw. 'Yes, things are looking up for us at the moment. A new lease of life for the shop, and we're starting a delivery service too,' he said, gesturing with a nod towards the van.

Peter looked at Charlotte, who smiled. 'Put some fire-lighters and kindling on our delivery then, if you would?'

Peter put his arm around Charlotte. 'Things are looking up for Bob and the shop, as well as the church roof, then?'

Charlotte smiled and winked.

'Let's get some cheese and bread from the farm shop, and how about a bottle of local wine? There's a new vineyard in the next valley, apparently.' As Charlotte finished speaking, she spotted Jim leaving the gentleman's outfitters with a handful of bags. Charlotte waved, and Jim crossed the street. Peter shook hands, and Jim gave Charlotte a kiss on the cheek.

Jim was dressed in chinos, and a lovely checked shirt and a new jacket.

'You're looking very dapper, Jim,' Charlotte declared, noticing the label still hanging off the bottom of his jacket.

'Thank you, Charlotte. I took on your suggestion and spruced up my drab wardrobe. I hadn't realised how dated it was, and don't tell anyone, but I received a surprise anonymous cheque through my door with a note saying: spoil yourself, you deserve it! God knows who it's from? Maybe someone owed me for some sheep I'd forgotten about? But I've also decided to book myself on a singles holiday to Whitby. It's this coming weekend.'

Peter and Charlotte beamed like Cheshire cats. 'I'm certain you will find a lovely lady, Jim. Someone worthy of you, you're such a catch in your new clothes.'

'Thanks, Charlotte, someone's looking out for me somewhere.'

'Good luck,' they both said simultaneously as their smiles widened.

Cycling to the top of the hill was challenging but worth it. They parked their bikes and followed the way-marked route to Scardale Cove. Peter carried the picnic, and Charlotte led the way. On reaching the high point, the extent of the cove opened up beneath them. A sheer limestone rock face once would have had a waterfall cascading down hundreds of feet into the lush valley below. The river, now deep within the limestone fissures and exiting the cove at the bottom. Peter chose a perch with a superb view of the valley below and the river winding itself around rocky promontories and trees. Substantial stone bridges and farmsteads appeared tiny from their vantage point.

'It's beautiful here. So real,' he said as he unwrapped the food and laid it out on the bare limestone. 'You can come up here every day and see something different. My mum used to bring me up here, sometimes with Grandad. He knew all the different valley names, the rivers and, of course, the trees. See how some of them are deformed, almost leaning and with flat tops. That's the wind, constantly battering them. They grow on the lea side, where it is sheltered by itself. Ironic, really. I wish I could paint. I'd like to capture them somehow,' he said, using his fingers to frame the shot.

'I'll teach you. Next time, we'll bring paper and paints and do just that.'

Peter chuckled. 'You'll have your work cut out. I paint like a five-year-old.'

'We can create our very own Biennalle. Do you miss your Grandad?' she added.

'I miss all of them. Especially Mum. Although I have happy memories, I regret not knowing her when I was older. I would have loved for her to meet you.'

'Same here. Well, mixed feelings, really. Anyway, it's just us two now.'

'Well, you have Lucy.'

'No, I don't. I am her mother, but we see the world differently now. She has other priorities and everything to make her own decisions now.'

'But do you wish it were different?'

'Yes. Of course, but I'm resigned to the fact that Lucy has

her own life, and I've stopped beating myself up about being a dreadful mother. I did what I could.'

Peter handed her some chocolate. 'I'll never know. I always thought I'd love a daughter. Tomboyish, obviously. Someone I could teach about nature, climb trees and scrump apples.'

'Funny how life never pans out how you think it would,' she said, biting into the chocolate.

'You're so right. Makes things interesting though?'

'Life will never be boring with you, Peter.'

They released their brakes and lifted their legs, and the bikes gathered pace on the steep descent. 'Woohoo,' Charlotte cried. 'Remember on our date when we rode bikes in the park? We're free, Peter, we're free.'

At the junction, Charlotte ignored the sign to the village and instead took the right fork and along the track into the dell.

'Woohoo,' she shouted at the top of her voice.

'Why are we going this way?' Peter questioned as he pulled up alongside.

'I thought we'd run past the animal sanctuary. I hear they have a new owl enclosure.'

'Tu-whit tu-whoo,' he gleefully cried. 'Tu-whit tu-whoo.' As he took both hands off the handlebars and flapped his wings.

Charlotte giggled. 'You're mad, and I love it. Tu-whit tu-whoo.'

They careered further along the track and then slowed momentarily to witness a huge-scale construction project underway within the sanctuary. Numerous builders' vans, scaffolding and timber piles were being erected adjacent to the old owl enclosure.

'Where now? Lady Mountjoy's new spa and swimming pool?' Peter joked.

Charlotte scowled and then sped off. 'Tu-whit tu-whoo.'

'You're off your rocker.'

The road along the top side of the village was still partly cobbled. The raised stones made the bikes judder. Charlotte's teeth chattered uncontrollably as she slowed around the bend and dismounted.

'There's just one last place.'

Peter leant his bike alongside hers, up against the dry-stone wall, and they both looked up at the sold sign hanging from the house.

Charlotte led the way and tentatively knocked on the door.

There was no answer.

Peter peered through the window into the darkness. Charlotte knocked again. 'It looks like they're not home.' she said, looking up to the windows on the first floor for signs of life.

Peter noted the brass plaque by the door. 'Mr Ogden Frogatt. Veterinary.'

'Is the Land Rover there?' Charlotte questioned.

'Yes,' Peter answered as he spied the vehicle around the back. Then, through the side window, he noticed Mr Frogatt sitting motionless on an upright wooden chair in the dark.

'He's in here, but it doesn't look good,' he said, beckoning Charlotte.

'We need to break in, Peter. He looks dead.'

'He's sitting upright?'

Peter tapped on the window. 'His eyes moved, I'm sure of that,' Charlotte said optimistically.

Peter tapped again, but there was no response. 'I'm going in.'

He then walked back to the door and, with one forceful kick, smashed the lock and the door flung open. Charlotte dashed in to find Mr Frogatt with his head in his hands, sobbing.

'Mr Frogatt, are you okay? Mr Frogatt.'

He lifted his head slowly and looked at Charlotte. His eyes were red and glazed with tears. He was dressed in a suit and tie, which Charlotte thought unusual.

'Mr Frogatt, are you okay?'

He couldn't speak. His head moving slightly from side to side was his only communication.

'Where's Mrs Frogatt? What's happened?'

Charlotte noticed his breathing was rapid, she could see his chest rising, and he seemed to be hyperventilating.

'I'm going to call an ambulance. Do you think you might have had a heart attack?'

Mr Frogatt grabbed Charlotte's hand and pulled her close. He shook his head and maintained a tight grip on her hand.

Charlotte looked at Peter, who shrugged and scrunched his lips.

'I'll make some tea,' he said, disappearing into the kitchen.

Charlotte held on to his hand and pulled a chair beside him. 'We are here now, Ogden. Whatever it is, we can sort it. Where is Mrs Frogatt?'

Charlotte looked into his eyes. They were grey, light grey with what seemed like diamond flecks resonating with his tears. She had never seen him so close and felt a lifetime of compassion and love within them.

He calmed his breathing and squeezed Charlotte's hand even tighter. 'It's all happened at once. Mary is in the hospital.

They told me to go home and rest, but I had to see the solicitor about the house,' he paused. 'I can't believe things like this could happen to people like us.'

Charlotte smiled. 'Is she having the treatment?'

Mr Frogatt nodded. 'Yes, thanks to you. We are humble people, Charlotte. You didn't have to help us.'

'You helped me, Ogden. You didn't know it at the time, but I owe you a great deal, offering an incompetent, nervous wreck of a woman like me a job like you did. You accepted me like I was your own. I can never forget that.'

Mr Frogatt's eyes sparkled even more as he grasped her hand with both of his. 'But where did the money come from? You're not a bank robber, are you?'

Charlotte laughed. 'No. It's a long story, and one I will share with you when all this is sorted. In the meantime, I can assure you that the money is legitimate and a thank you for everything you and Mary have done for me.'

'Thank you, Charlotte, from the very bottom of our hearts. We had to move quickly on the stem cell transplant, or she wouldn't have survived. She's my everything. I couldn't cope without her.'

'So where is she now?'

'In the operating theatre. They said to come back, collect some of her things and return at 7pm.'

Peter arrived with tea and a few biscuits he had found in a jar. 'We'll take you to the hospital.'

Mr Frogatt shook his head. 'You've done enough. I'll be fine.'

'We insist,' Charlotte said, now holding both his hands in hers. 'We might need the Land Rover though. We only have two bikes!'

They all laughed.

'So, what's happening with the house?' Peter enquired.

'You didn't know this, but I'd re-mortgaged the house to fund some of Mary's previous treatment, which had failed. I should have been retired by now, but I had to keep everything together. So, with your help, we paid off the mortgage and bought that bungalow by the cricket pitch, so Mary can move around more easily.'

'Is that the house with the incredible view of the river?' Peter said with half a biscuit in his mouth.

'Yes. We used to pass that house on our walks and say how lovely it would be to live there. Never in our wildest thoughts did we think we would be living there one day. You saved us, Charlotte. It's like you were sent to us. I know that sounds daft, but it was Mary who said I should give you a chance, and she was right.'

Charlotte took a sip of tea. 'Well, it's not over yet. We have to hope everything is okay at the hospital. We should go. It's twenty to seven.'

All three exited the house, and Charlotte jumped into the driving seat of the Land Rover, with Peter next to her and Mr Frogatt in the rear. She backed the vehicle out of the drive and onto the road. Without hesitation, she found first gear, and they sped forward.

'Stop,' Peter shouted.

Charlotte slammed on the brakes.

'The old lady! You nearly hit the old lady,' Peter said, holding his head in his hands.

'Where?' Charlotte couldn't see anything. She leaned forward and looked out over the bonnet. Then, Charlotte jumped with shock as the wizened, warty face of the old woman suddenly appeared at the side window. Her beady eyes shone in the light of the streetlamp. Charlotte wound down the window.

'I'm so sorry. Are you okay?'

The woman stared into Charlotte's eyes. It was like being hypnotised, her jet-black pupils levering their way into Charlotte's brain, paralysing her. Then, the woman raised her arm, produced a single white rose, and handed it to her. Its pristine petals almost glowing in the dark. Charlotte pricked her finger on a thorn on the stem and watched the blood drip onto her leg. She put it to her lips to stop the bleeding, and as she looked back at the old woman, she was gone.

'Who is that woman?' Charlotte said, handing the rose to Peter.

'She's the hermit,' Mr Frogatt said.

'The hermit? Where does she live?'

Mr Frogatt put both hands in the air. 'No one knows. I've only ever seen her once before.'

45

SURPRISE

Peter placed a mug of tea on the windowsill, and beside it, the white rose into a glass vase. Perching on the edge of the bed, he watched Charlotte's peaceful face as she slept.

She was different somehow. Still as beautiful as the day they met, yet older and seemingly calmer than he'd seen before. Eyelashes thick and long and tiny wrinkles fanning out from the corner of her eyes. Her cheeks fuller, yet her jawline more slender. He couldn't explain it. She just looked happier and more content.

He traced her jaw and lips with his finger. Feeling in his mind, but not quite touching in the hope he didn't wake her. She deserved to sleep; moreover, he revelled in the opportunity to observe her exquisite serenity.

Her resting face almost smiling, and her breathing was peaceful. The steam from the mug rose and stirred in the cold morning air. The window was full of condensation, exposing finger-drawn pictures and words on each and every pane. Peter took a moment to study them.

From top left to bottom right, a house, drawn as if by a

child. Four windows and a door, and a chimney with billowing smoke. A face with a frowning smile and next to it the word *shame*. Peter sighed and cast his eye on the next row. The words *hope* and *lost*, and then at two stick figures leaping in the air, as if doing star jumps.

The condensation began to bead into tiny streams on the bottom row, where there were no words. Just an eye, then a tree and finally a pane with nothing in it. Peter placed his finger on the glass. Instantly, he could sense the cold but maintained contact and drew a love heart. It was for her. No words were needed. The heart said everything he wanted to. The single-line drawing allowed the morning sun to punch its way through and highlight Charlotte's face. She was sheer perfection, he thought.

She stirred as the dappled light danced on her eyes.

'Morning, beautiful.'

'You're up early.' she said, yawning.

'She's doing well, by the way, Mrs Frogatt. There's a long road of recovery ahead, but all the signs look promising. I took an earlier call from Ogden and offered to help them with the house move.'

'Will she still be in the hospital?'

'Probably. Best place if you ask me. Can't see her humping boxes and cleaning cupboards, so we'll take the strain. A couple of other guys, including Bob, also volunteered, and he's trying to get Max from the pub involved, so there will be beers on tap.'

'If I were a cynical person, I'd think it was just an excuse for a lad's booze up.'

'Never. What do you take us for?' he replied, grinning a cartoon-like grin. 'Here's some tea, and there's toast coming shortly. I want to make the most of the day and thought we could go on an adventure somewhere.'

Charlotte groaned and pulled the duvet up around her neck. 'Adventure? Why don't we have an adventure in bed?'

'I have a surprise for you.'

'What is it?'

Peter reached into his pocket and produced a set of car keys.

Charlotte looked puzzled.

'You forgot all about the car. It was compounded while I was in Hong Kong, and she's as immaculate as the day you handed her over.'

Charlotte gasped. 'The DB5?'

'Let's drive to Dorset and visit Mrs Hathersage. I fancy Lulworth Cove with the top down and the most beautiful woman by my side. Come on.'

Charlotte smiled and placed her hand on his. 'We can't.'

'What do you mean?'

Charlotte's smile dropped. 'I have a surprise for you. Pass me my bag.'

Charlotte opened her bag, and Peter followed her diligently with his eyes as she rummaged through lipsticks, lip gloss, mascara, hankies, hair bands, an electric bill, and several sweet wrappers... she looked at him and shrugged. A small shoe-horn, a plastic shower cap from a hotel, various colour swatch cards, a travel mug, and two pairs of wool mittens. She shrugged again and looked surprised. A conker, three identical foldable hairbrushes and some reading glasses. She put them on and then looked at him again.

'What is it?' he asked anxiously.

She opened her hand and revealed a white pregnancy test kit.

Charlotte dropped the bag and showed him the result.

Peter remained silent.

She looked at him closely, not knowing what his reaction would be. Her heart beating fast, she swam around and around within the azure blue waters of his eyes, passed the boy, beyond the man, and straight to his core. His pupils dilated like cave entrances to his soul. She climbed in, desperate to find the answer. Her insecurity looking for strength, her anxiety searching for warmth, and her heart was desperate for courage.

'It's positive.'

She could see he was trying to speak but couldn't.

'You're going to be a dad.'

Peter stood firm, his body rigid, just shaking his head and smiling.

'A dad?'

'Yes! The best dad in the whole world.'

He said nothing. He didn't need to. His eyes turned from deep lakes into seas, then oceans of emotional joy.

He wrapped his arms around her and squeezed her tight.

'It's our first scan today. I didn't know how to tell you. I was scared of how you might react.'

'What will the scan tell us?'

'Whether it's official. But I know it is. I can feel it. They'll search for a heartbeat and other signs.'

Peter placed his hand on her tummy. 'A dad?'

Peter pulled up at the door in the car. He'd hidden it up at the vicarage, so it would be a surprise. Lulworth Cove would have to be another day.

Charlotte was excited to see its gleaming body and stylish curves, especially with Peter again behind the wheel.

'Hello, handsome,' she said through the open window.

'Just wait there,' he said, jumping out of the car and dashing around to open the door for her. 'Peter, I can still open doors for myself.'

'You have precious cargo onboard,' he said, helping her into the seat like she was ninety years old.

'The car does suit you.'

'Well, thinking about it, we're probably going to need a car with more than two seats?'

Charlotte smiled and held his hand. 'Let's see what happens at the scan, shall we?'

With the top down and the wind in their hair, the car purred along the Yorkshire lanes into the next valley.

Charlotte opened the glove box in search of a tissue. She reached in and saw the two Oracle tarot cards stashed there since the day of her mother's funeral.

New Birth and Let Go of Your Past. She showed them to Peter, and they laughed out loud. 'It's all come true!' he said, looking up momentarily into the sky.

Charlotte nodded, looked at the cards one more time and then threw them up into the air, as if to cast off the past. The cards disappeared in the wind as the car raced along. 'What was the third card?' Peter asked. 'I thought you always pulled three cards?'

Charlotte nodded again. 'I do. But that one was dealt with on the day I drew them. We're free now, Peter,' she shouted with joy. 'We're freeee.'

The car continued to purr along the country roads, and their beaming smiles were a testament to their undeniable happiness.

Peter glanced over.

'What are you thinking?'

Charlotte hesitated before replying.

'I'm planning my Victoria sponge recipe for the summer fete.'

Peter shook his head and laughed. 'You're here to stay then?'

Charlotte looked at him with a smile she had never smiled before. At last, a deep feeling of belonging and security filled her conscious thinking and her subconscious. It was a whole-hearted and rounded sense of belonging, love and optimism.

'I've spent my whole life searching, Peter.'

'Searching?' he replied, keeping his eye on the road.

'Searching for who I am. You know I've had my issues, and I've never really felt at peace with myself. God only knows it's been tough, especially the last few years, but things feel different now. Like I belong. Like I've found my purpose.'

Peter indicated and pulled the car into an area off the road that had a view of the whole valley. The full length of the lime-stone escarpment drawing their eye along the meandering river flanked by oak, ash and alder. Fluffy white clouds and vapour trails of optimistic adventure broke the blue sky inter-mittently.

'Why are we stopping here? We'll be late for the scan.'

Peter walked around to Charlotte's door and offered his hand.

'This isn't a time to be showing me migrating ospreys, Peter!'

He led her to the edge of the rock and took a deep breath. 'Freedom,' he said, pointing up to the trails of white in the sky and an aeroplane glinting in the sun.

'You're right. We are free, Charlie. Free to be together, free to be a family.' He looked down at her stomach. 'But if we are going to do this life together...' He paused and began rummaging in his pocket.

'Then I need to ask you something.'

'What is it?'

'I was planning to do this at Lulworth Cove, but this will have to do.'

He took to his knee, and with the boyish naivety she had seen in him on their very first date, he held out his hand. Charlotte observed a black jewellery box on his palm. It was open, and on closer inspection, two exquisite wedding rings, side by side.

She felt her heart stop beating, then burst into action in her toes and fingertips. She felt tipsy and overwhelmed by the location. Her darling man knelt before her with matching rings, making her gasp for air.

'We didn't quite get around to it, did we? Will you marry me?'

Charlotte looked once again at the rings and then at Peter, who appeared to be in agony, awaiting her answer.

'Yes! Yes, I will.'

46

THE VIEW BEYOND

The thick air of complete silence filled the cramped, clinical room. The nurse manoeuvred the ultrasound scanner as Charlotte and Peter's eyes scrutinised the blurry black-and-white image on the screen.

Charlotte could see Peter stroking his chin and then tapping his fist against his mouth while shifting his eyes back and forth from the screen to the nurse. There didn't appear to be anything there. She could feel inside that everything was different. She just knew, but nothing materialised on the screen. Peter's anxious face made her feel uneasy. She was much older than many of the other girls in the waiting room. She knew the chances of a baby surviving were vastly reduced, but she wanted it for Peter. The glue would bind their union for the rest of their lives, and something Peter deserved more than anything. She clenched her fist and felt her engagement ring between her fingers. She smiled and wished for any sign.

'Is there anything?' she asked.

The nurse said nothing, just gave an ambivalent scrunch of her lips and tried a different position with the probe. Peter brushed his hands through his hair and sighed. Charlotte could feel the bed moving to the rhythm of Peter's leg anxiously tapping against the base.

There was a faint sound. A ripple. And then another. A crackle and then the faint trace of a beat. A tiny, watery beat. Charlotte looked at the nurse. Peter looked at Charlotte and then the nurse. Then all of them at the screen.

'There's a heartbeat, and I can see the head,' the nurse said confidently.

Charlotte could just make out the shape of the head and a nose. Then a hand. A tiny but almost perfectly formed hand.

'Look,' Peter said, pointing at the screen. 'Look!'

Charlotte felt a tingling in her toes as a warmth spread up and filled her entire body and mind.

'Is it a girl or a boy?' Peter asked, squeezing Charlotte's hand and rubbing her diamond with his thumb.

'It's really too early to tell,' the nurse said smiling. 'Maybe at the next scan we will know more if you want to know.'

Charlotte squeezed Peter's hand even more. 'It's a boy. I just know it. He's a boy. Look, he has your chin.'

Peter laughed and nodded enthusiastically while transfixed on the screen.

'And your big ears, by the look of it,' he said, laughing.

The nurse announced they could have a picture of the scan and to request it at the desk when they booked their second appointment. Peter took to his feet and thanked the nurse. 'Wait in reception,' he said. 'And I'll go and fetch the car. I don't want you having to walk in your condition.'

Charlotte laughed out loud. 'Peter, I'm fine. I'm not an invalid.'

Peter took her hand and looked at the engagement ring and then into her eyes. 'You two are the most precious things I could ever wish for. I'm the happiest man that's ever lived. You book us in for the next appointment and get the photo. I'll meet you at the door.'

'Okay, sir,' she said, saluting playfully. 'I love you, Peter.'

He turned. 'And I love you so very much.'

He disappeared, and Charlotte did as he said. The photo was just as they'd seen on the screen, and Charlotte examined every detail. She walked towards the door and could see Peter walking along the road. She walked to the top of the steps to get some fresh air and take another look at the photo in daylight.

Peter turned and waved.

'I know, I know, I'll wait here,' she said under her breath as she waved back.

Peter turned, and as he walked to the car, Charlotte froze to the spot and watched in disbelief as a massive lorry, travelling at speed, hit Peter head-on. She watched in horror as she saw him disappear under the articulated vehicle and then a commotion of people nearby who had also seen it.

Charlotte ran. Her legs nearly buckled at the shock of what she had just witnessed. She fought her way through the group of people, and there he was. Lying crumpled in the road. A large pool of blood trailed from his mouth.

She knelt beside him and held his head in her hands. His eyes opened. Charlotte could see his love for her. It was like he was passing on everything he had to her. His energy, his life and his soul.

'I love you, Peter,' she said as his eyes closed and his head became heavy in her hands.

'Thank you for everything.'

EPILOGUE

Crisp white bedsheets were Charlotte's absolute no-compromise. The smell of air-dried linen, with hints of garden lavender and rosemary, was one of life's joys.

She tucked in the bottom sheet and manhandled the duvet into position. Two pillows up against the oak bed head and a final cushion completed the simple yet comfortable look. Perching on the edge of the bed, she held the cushion close to her chest and buried her nose within it. The cover she had made from Peter's favourite shirt. Never washed and hand stitched, it held on to his unique smell and was still evocative of him as if he still had a presence within the house.

She'd woken with the larks, and the Saturday morning sun highlighted the condensation upon the inside of the window. Charlotte took in Peter's scent once more and sighed. She pointed her finger and traced the outline of the love heart, which became evident every morning, but today seemed somehow energised as the sun shone through it and warmed the room.

Peering through the outline, Charlotte looked out across

the back garden and out into the view beyond. A kaleidoscope of Yorkshire's natural beauty. She smiled again, held the cushion close to her chest and moved her gaze to the photograph of Peter by the bed. His brimming smile and sparkling eyes almost jumped out into the room itself. Tucked into the frame was the baby scan photo, which he never saw.

She dropped her smile and, with closed eyes, pictured once again Peter in front of her on one knee, presenting her the precious rings she toyed with in her hand.

Suddenly her ears tuned to the sound of footsteps along the hallway.

'Mum?'

Her smile returned instantly, and with proud eyes, she saw him enter the room.

'Yes?' she replied.

'I'm all packed.'

'Are you sure you have everything? Socks, pants, sun cream? Don't forget the sun cream,' she said, fussing.

'Mum, I'm thirteen, not three, and it's only scout camp to Giggleswick, not the Galapagos.'

She smiled and nodded. 'Let me look at you,' she said, adjusting his neckerchief.

'Thirteen. Where have the years gone? Look at you, all grown up.'

He stood to attention, his eyes revealing his delight at being grown up.

'Here. Take this,' she said, holding out a small pocket torch. 'It was your father's. You never know. Might come in handy if you ever need to save someone's life!'

ABOUT THE AUTHOR

J A Crawshaw was born in Yorkshire, England, in 1969. A lifelong environmentalist and tree lover, this story was greatly inspired by nature and its ability to influence our lives.

A passionate romantic, he is fascinated by life, the exciting possibilities and the people within it.

'I have a fire inside me to write which I can't hold back. I hope you enjoy my books and would love to hear your feedback, which will inspire me to carry on with my creative passion.'

If you enjoyed reading this book, please consider leaving an honest review on your favourite platform.

I would be eternally grateful. Good reviews will help the algorithms to recognise my work and help other readers to discover new books.

More information & your FREE book can be found at
www.jacrawshaw.com

instagram.com/j_a_crawshaw_author

goodreads.com/J_A_Crawshaw

tiktok.com/@j_a_crawshaw_author

facebook.com/jacrawshawbooks

ALSO BY J A CRAWSHAW

The Swing. 1st in series. The Life Changing Woman's Fiction Series.

The Void Between Words. My laid bare, gritty and humorous story of possibly the worlds most unlikely author. My dyslexic journey from non reader to author.

Poetry From The Heart. Abstract mind mumblings in poetry form.

For more information about all my books, events and insider knowledge on forthcoming events, visit my website

www.jacrawshaw.com

REVIEWS

We all value reviews, but seldom leave them.

Less than 1% of readers leave a review, so when I receive one, I'm thrilled. I mean, really thrilled, to the point, I leap around the room and become emotional.

I would be incredibly grateful and honoured to receive feedback on any store, platform or social media site.

Here are reasons why it's so important to me.

1. I can improve my writing, so you enjoy it more.

2. I know if I'm on the right track in terms of what you like to read.

3. It gives me confidence to carry on writing.

4. It makes the book more visible to other readers by convincing the algorithm its worthy.

5. It makes us writers feel loved and I'd like to share that love with you.

FREE BOOK

Claim your free book when you join my Keep in Touch Group
via the website https://www.jacrawshaw.com/free-book

Discover Your Creative Passion
Join the Art Group Today